Their Noble Deceit

A Harwell Heirs Legacy Romance

Harwell Heirs Book 6

Regina Kammer

Viridium Press

Published by Regina Kammer and Viridium Press, Friday Harbor, Washington
ISBN-13: (ebook) 978-1-953496-04-1
ISBN-10: (ebook) 1-953496-04-0
ISBN-13: (paperback) 978-1-953496-05-8
ISBN-10: (paperback) 1-953496-05-9

The Harwell Heirs

Victorian aristocracy has very strict rules concerning marital connections and familial obligations. But the Harwell heirs—Helena, Sophia, and Arthur—discover love doesn't always follow the rules. Scandalous affairs force these scions of society to choose between duty and desire, deference and destiny.

Book 1: *The Pleasure Device*

Book 2: *Disobedience By Design*

Book 3: *Where Destiny Plays*

Harwell Heirs Legacy Romances

Travel beyond England's shores for these stories featuring beloved secondary characters from the first three books of the series. The Legacy novels delve into the romances of the friends, family, and intimates of the extended Harwell family.

Book 4: *A Delicate Seduction*

Book 5: *Discovering Her Delight*

Book 6: *Their Noble Deceit*

Dedication

All families have secrets. Some of them go to the grave.
To the keepers of such secrets.

CHAPTER ONE

Nice, France, July 1880

Percival Wood, the Marquess of Norrington, stretched along the sheets, nudging the man sleeping beside him. Bertram Atherley, Viscount Ravensburgh, responded with a snort before he rolled onto his back, exposing his gorgeous nudity in a beam of morning sunlight.

A balmy breeze through open windows set the sheer curtains swaying. The evening had been sultry, and the coolness of the new day was welcome, especially as the flush of sexual exhilaration still prickled across Percival's flesh. Their break-of-dawn lovemaking had been energetic, Bertram no longer tipsy from imbibing absinthe the night before.

Percival snuggled against a feather pillow and gazed at his lover. Bertram's body was pure masculine perfection, from the chiseled chest, down the ridges of his abdomen to the sensual curve of the muscles at his hips. Fine brown hair furred his torso, the trail narrowing along his belly until it curled thickly at his glorious groin, where wiry strands wreathed a manhood slaked from earlier sucking.

Percival slid his hand down his own stomach to play with his now semi-hard cock. He wouldn't get any harder if he didn't piss soon. But Bertram was so peaceful, his respiration deep and even, it would be a shame to disturb their bed and wake him.

Beyond the fluttering curtains, rays of early morning sun glittered on the Mediterranean. The rumbling of rolling wooden cartwheels over cobblestones filtered up from below. The baker delivering their favorite pastries, perhaps. Another perfect day in a beautiful part of the world.

Such a shame everything would soon be at an end.

Bertram stirred with a low growl, opening his eyes before blinking at the ceiling.

"Good morning, Bertie."

Bertram chuckled. "You already said that, when was it? About two hours ago?"

"Well, I'm saying it again, because every morning I awaken with you is a good morning."

That inspired a grin.

Percival rose reluctantly from their seductive bed and shuffled across the Chinese carpet to empty the contents of his bladder into the white porcelain chamber pot. The weight of Bertram's stare lay heavy across his back.

"What's wrong, Percy, darling?"

Percival gave his prick a shake. "What do you mean?"

"There's an uncharacteristic touch of wistfulness in your voice."

Bollocks. Bertram knew him too well. "It's Father." Percival padded across the carpet and slipped back into bed.

Bertram wrapped an arm around his shoulder and drew Percival to him. "What about the duke?"

"A letter arrived yesterday."

"And you didn't tell me?" Bertram's tone rang sarcastically.

"We were having too much fun."

Bertram laughed. "Yes, yes, we were." He kissed Percival's head. "It's not horrible news, I hope." His words fanned hot against Percival's neck.

"Just that he wants me back home, because, well, you know why."

"Ah." Bertram danced the fingers of his left hand down Percival's torso, the gold ring on his pinkie glinting in a sunbeam. "I suppose that means Italy is off."

"Unfortunately." Percival eased his left hand out from between their bodies and grasped Bertram's fingers. He loved to admire their matching rings. He had them made during their holiday in Nice the previous year to commemorate their commitment.

"How long can you delay?"

"Given that my father thinks the French are uncivilized barbarians and that we'll probably be traveling by open cart, I say we have a few days before we need to catch the train."

"As if Armand would ever deign to travel by open cart." Bertram chuckled.

Percival joined him in his mirth. His trusty valet would scold anyone who attempted to offer anything but a well-appointed carriage. His amusement swiftly turned to resignation. "You don't have to return with me. You can explore Italy as you like."

"'As I like' would be with my lover and best friend. Not alone."

A luscious warmth bathed Percival at the expression of the sentiment. He pressed against Bertram's chest and inhaled sweat and spirits—a reminder of last night. "I don't want this to end."

Bertram held him tighter. "It doesn't have to. We'll find a way to be together."

"Bertie, I cannot fathom how a man can be married to a woman and carry on with another man. Surely a woman would discover his secret life. If there was no affection between husband

and wife—if there was animosity—a man such as I could be exposed, arrested…" He gulped air. "Imprisoned for life."

"Don't say that."

"All right. At the very least, subjected to blackmail."

Bertram sputtered an oath through his teeth. "Do you know who the woman in question is?"

"There is no woman. Not as of yet. As far as I know, there is only the idea of a wife, not one woman in particular. But we have been gone from England for a month, and it is the height of the Season…"

"Anything could have happened."

"Precisely."

Bertram traced two fingers up Percival's spine. "What about Penny?"

"Penny? Penelope Hardcastle?" Percival lifted his head to throw Bertram a quizzical glare. "Marry Penelope?"

"She knows…about us. Doesn't seem to mind. And we get along." Bertram nibbled on his lower lip a moment. "I mean you and she get along. I suppose it is of no consequence whether she and I get along."

"It is very much of consequence whether or not my future wife is friendly with my lo—" Percival checked himself. He'd have to get used to using a new epithet. "Is friendly with the man I am to blithely refer to as my best friend." He grumbled. "Damn this bloody marriage business."

"Well, Penny seems perfect."

"Except…what is her position in the aristocracy?" Percival nuzzled against Bertram again. "She's not Lady Something. She's merely Miss Hardcastle."

"She could be a viscount's daughter. Or some other type of daughter that isn't called 'lady'."

"She's never mentioned any of that."

Bertram sighed. "True."

"However, she does seem to know everyone."

"Because she's slept with most of them."

Percival laughed. "Don't let her catch you saying that."

"It's true and she knows it. She takes pride in it." Bertram grinned. "You know she slept with Nicky," he said as if divulging a secret.

"Your cousin?" Percival exclaimed. "Who on earth told you that?"

"Nicholas himself. It was before he was engaged, or even made earl." Bertram chuckled. "And if you married Penelope, she'd be ogling every man but you."

Percival sobered. "Bertie, do you think you could sleep with a woman?"

"You mean Penelope?"

"No. I mean any woman. Womankind, as it were."

Bertram let out a long exhalation. "Oh, I don't know. I suppose I haven't given it much thought, really."

Percival groaned. "Unfortunately, I am no longer able to postpone such thoughts. Marriage. To a woman." *Damn and blast.* "And then the expectation to produce children, especially a male heir…" He did not finish. It was all too positively vexing.

"Ah. I don't have the same pressures as you, Percy, love. And I don't think sexual congress with a woman would be such a terrible thing."

Percival sighed heavily. "That's the problem, though, isn't it?"

"Pardon?"

"The idea of touching a woman's body is thoroughly reprehensible to me. I don't think I could do it even for queen and country."

"Hmm." Bertram embraced Percival more tightly. "What if the woman were your very good friend for whom you already feel affection?"

A frosty frisson rippled across Percival's scalp. "You mean Penelope?"

"Yes."

Percival groaned. "Ugh. For the sake of the dukedom of Amesbury, I would have to try, I suppose." He squeezed his eyes shut in a vain attempt at blocking out such a prospect. "Good God, the very thought shrinks my stones."

Bertram pulled Percival more closely against him, the heat of his body warming the chill creeping across Percival's skin. "Let's talk to Penny. She may have some link to the aristocracy. If it's not as high a rank as your father would prefer, you can try to convince him you two are in love."

"Like by kissing her?" Percival shuddered.

"I've seen you dance with her. You can put your bloody arm around her for appearance's sake."

Percival chuckled. "All right. I suppose I can. In front of my parents." Why the hell couldn't he simply marry his Bertie? They understood each other, they got along, and they loved each other as much as any man might love a woman.

"Good." Bertram unwrapped his arm and slid down the mattress until he was poised over Percival's prick, his breath hot and humid. "Now that we've got that out of the way, I'd like to continue some of our adventures from earlier this morning."

Percival sighed as the wet heat of his lover's mouth enveloped his cock.

Davenham residence, Mayfair, London, that same July morning

A SHAFT OF LIGHT across her lids jostled Penelope Hardcastle awake.

Morning. Already?

Upon opening her eyes, the strange surroundings were momentarily unsettling until realization sunk in.

She'd fallen asleep in one of Lord and Lady Davenham's guest bedrooms after their festive and raucous affair the night before. Her muscles ached from huddling in an overstuffed and overly large slipper chair, but she shouldn't move until she knew her situation. She peeked around the side of the chair. The mustachioed gentleman from the night before was sprawled across the bed on his stomach, his head turned in her direction, the rhythm of his snores an indication of the depth of his slumber.

Which meant she'd still have to be quiet as she left but could avoid the awkward post-coital politeness.

Penelope unfolded her legs and silently stretched to relieve the stiffness. How did she end up on the chair? Right. Mustache fell asleep as soon as he had spent his seed, and she, wanting to feel a touch of romance, had left him to stand before the window and gaze at the moonlight.

She got up with a quiet sigh and went to that same window, the view of the back garden obscured by the foliage of a plane tree. Much further beyond loomed London, that wondrous yet lonely city. A city filled with people wanting, craving, hoping, and not always attaining.

Last night's encounter had been pleasurable, to be sure. His thick cock had filled her, but only after she had angled her hips had he rubbed that bliss-inducing spot inside. Mustache had known nothing of how to truly thrill a woman, to bring her to a rapturous peak. He had been solely focused on his own reward. Their whole affair had been—what was that quote Ravensburgh had used recently?—solitary, poor, nasty, brutish, and short.

Something had very definitely been missing from the encounter. She pursed her lips. Possibly that same something was missing altogether from every encounter she'd had of late. What it was precisely was difficult to pin down.

Penelope returned to sit on the slipper chair and put on her shoes. Very few of her conquests had understood a woman's pleasure. Those that had, stood out as stellar examples of lovers. Ravensburgh's cousin Nicholas Atherley was one such man. But he was married now—with a newborn—and desperately in love with his wife.

Besides, Nicholas was an earl. What did Penelope have to offer such a man? Nobles wanted to marry other nobles to acquire land and solidify ties amongst themselves.

And who was she? She was a mere gentleman's daughter, her sole connection to the aristocracy the man who raised her as his ward.

Penelope settled her frothy hair ornament on her head, then grabbed her gloves and her wrap. She tiptoed to the door and carefully turned the knob. Before exiting, she glanced back at Mustache to make sure he still slept as soundly as when he had rolled off her earlier that morning.

Yes, he was dead to the world at that moment. As dead as he was to a woman's needs and desires. One day she would find an attentive lover who wanted their mutual satisfaction to be the center of their universe.

One day.

CHAPTER TWO

Hertfordshire, England

Bertram stared out the rail car window at the green countryside passing by with a bit of a blur. While he and Percival had set up house together in London, he would always consider Hertfordshire—and especially the town of St. Albans—home.

The country was where he was born. Where the estate for the Atherley family and the Earl of St. Albans was located. Where cousin Nicholas, the current earl, had recently settled with his wife Helena and their newborn son. Where Mama dwelt at Ravensburgh Cottage, the family abode where Percival and Bertram's precious French bulldog currently resided while the two were on the continent.

Upon arrival in London, Armand had disembarked and journeyed to their home on Wilton Crescent with most of their baggage. Percival and Bertram had continued on to Euston Station, catching the train to St. Albans to pick up their beloved Orsa.

Spending time with Mama and visiting his old garden would also be a treat.

"I can't wait to see Orsa. She's such a dear sweet pup."

A grin spread across Bertram's face. Once they'd adopted a puppy, Percival had become something of a fussy parent. "I'm certain Orsa will be overjoyed to see you. Although she will be sad to leave her friends."

"Friends? Did the Viscountess Ravensburgh acquire another dog since our absence?"

"Nothing like that. Mama is devoted to her Winifred, despite Blenheim spaniels being a handful. But I can tell from Mama's letters that she has developed quite a fondness for Orsa. And, apparently, Wini is equally smitten. Wini and Orsa have become inseparable."

Percival slid his hand in Bertram's and squeezed. "Like we are."

The grin grew impossibly wider.

"I do need this holiday from our holiday before I see my father." Percival rested his head against Bertram's shoulder.

"You're certain he's in London?"

"I can't imagine why he wouldn't be. He's got Parliament, and the Season continues to plod along. He has no idea we've chosen to make this detour."

"Good. We can spend a bit more time together before our lives change irrevocably."

Percival sighed. "Let's not talk about it. I want to enjoy these last days together before my marital doom."

Bertram squeezed Percival's hand. They remained close, connected, contented, until farmland faded and the smokestacks of industry appeared. They were seated quite apart from each other as the train pulled into St. Albans.

They disembarked under the canopy of the station, and, as their carpet bags were unloaded from the rail car, stood casually chatting on the concrete platform. When in company, the two had learned to act as men who were purely friends, not lovers.

Such a deception would never occur to newlyweds who were man and woman.

A burly man approached from the railway building, his expression dour with a touch of hostility, focusing his attention on Percival as if Bertram did not exist.

"Welcome home, my lord," the man said as he removed his hat and bowed his head.

Percival froze with wide eyes at the address to his person. "Thank you, Bates." He flicked a panicked gaze at Bertram.

Bates was the Duke of Amesbury's coachman. Bertram had never seen him up close before, never not sitting high on the driver's bench. Beyond Bates, near the waiting room, two other vaguely familiar and equally well-built men loafed against the soot-stained and faded yellow brick of the station building.

Something was wrong. No one knew they were to arrive at St. Albans station. No one was supposed to be there to greet them.

Seemingly Percival had the very same thought. "Bates, how did you know I would be here?"

The man did not look at Percival, but instead kept his head bowed. "Yes, my lord."

Bertram chilled at the very odd response.

With an aristocratic shrug, Percival marched toward the station, waving to Bertram to join him.

But he couldn't. The other two men approached swiftly, blocking him, grabbing his arms, pulling him across the platform away from the station and his Percy. His struggles were only met with increasingly tightening grips, and the alarmed stares of disembarking passengers.

Percival turned, his expression livid when he saw the scene. "What are you doing? This man is my guest." He gestured at Bertram.

Bates seized the gesturing arm. "I think not, my lord."

Percival tried futilely to push Bates off. Another burly manservant, his scowl verging on belligerent, grabbed Percy's other arm.

Bertram simmered with rage, too aware of his impotence in the matter as his own arms were now being twisted behind his back.

"I want an explanation now, Bates."

Percival's plea fell on inattentive ears.

What the devil was going on? Why were he and Percival being forcibly separated? Did the Duke of Amesbury harbor such contempt for their connection that he needed to keep them apart?

Frozen in disbelief, Bertram watched as Percival was manhandled off the platform and into the station, his baggage retrieved by a somber servant.

His beloved now out of sight, Bertram closed his eyes against the heartache, fighting tears of anger. The grip loosened a bit but remained strong enough to prevent him from going after his lover. Or anywhere.

Wood Hall, Hertfordshire

As THE COACH CRUNCHED down the gravel drive, Percival fumed, the lurching rhythm only increasing his aggravation. The yellowing stone façade of Wood Hall came into view, sparking even more outrage. He turned from the sight, slumping in his seat to stare blankly at the tufted leather canopy.

The emptiness of the interior reminded him he was alone. He should not be alone. His Bertie should be with him. He *needed* Bertie to be with him.

The horses slowed, then stopped. Percival wiped the tears pooling in his eyes, tears of discontent, disbelief, or despondency, he did not know.

A footman opened the door and unfolded the step. Percival remained seated.

Father's secretary, Wilson, appeared at the doorway, shuffling his feet on the gravel. "I think His Grace should explain, my lord," he said quietly.

Damn Father. Damn the dukedom. Damn the whole fucking aristocracy.

He calmed himself. The secretary was not to blame. No need to subject him to any animosity. "Thank you, Wilson," Percival said cordially. He descended from the carriage and stormed into the house.

"The study, my lord," Wilson called after him.

Percival stomped into the preposterously masculine study, the smell of book leather, whiskey, and cigars tightening the muscles behind his eyes. Father sat at his imposing oak desk, waiting, his expression wooden.

"Welcome home, Norrington," he said steadily.

"How the hell did you know?"

Father winced at the profanity. "Your manservant told my men where you had gone. I received a telegram."

"Your men? You had spies in London?" *Jesus Christ.* "What did you do to Armand?"

"Your valet is unscathed."

"You threatened him."

"I did not."

Percival seethed at the deflection. "Your men, then."

Father huffed a sigh. "I assure you, they left him unharmed."

Percival held his ground, teetering on the thick edge of the Persian rug. "What the hell just happened?"

Father stared emotionless. No smug smirk, no gleam of triumph, all signs he'd not really wanted to be so rough.

"Where did you take Viscount Ravensburgh?"

"He was driven across town and put on the Midland Railway direct to St. Pancras Station. No need to change trains like your journey here." Father's voice was impassive. "I've instructed that he be watched until he is well on his way to London."

"Bollocks," Percival muttered. "What the hell for?"

"I do not want the two of you fraternizing anymore."

"Fraternizing? Is that what you've decided to call it?" Percival stared at Father. "What, may I ask, is really going on, Your Grace?"

"You are twenty-two years of age, my lord marquess. It is time you marry."

Fucking hell. "Marry? Really?"

"Yes, really. And before you ask, yes, marry a woman."

Percival scoffed. "Most men in my position are allowed time to sow their wild oats." He eyed Father. "Many men amongst the aristocracy do not marry until they are well into their thirties. Tell me, Father, how old were you when you married?"

"That is not for discussion at the moment," Father growled. "You have sown your wild oats. First with Jack. Then with God only knows who at Oxford. And now with Ravensburgh."

Jack was Jonathan Atherley, the eldest son of the late Earl of St. Albans, and Bertram's cousin. Excessively handsome and charismatic, Jack had too easily seduced a young and naive Percival. Jack's cruelty had culminated in a violent outburst, with Jack's mother an unfortunate casualty. Father had quickly sequestered Percival, packing him off to Oxford, far away from the villain.

There had been no one since the devil but the savior. Percival had been abstemious during his years at Oxford. It was Bertram who had shown him what love truly was. "No, Father, you are wrong. I've settled upon Bertram. He is not some experience of youth to become a quick memory."

"Damn it!" Father slapped both palms on his desk. His chair wobbled as he pushed it back to stand. "Percival Wood, you are the heir to the dukedom of Amesbury. You need to marry. A lover and a dog are not a family."

Jesus. Percival shut his eyes to staunch tears of anger. "They very much are."

"No, they are not."

"And a wife I do not love and who does not love me constitutes a family?"

A flush of red colored Father's visage as he narrowed his eyes. "Your friend Ravensburgh is distracting you from your duty."

"Bertram is not a distraction, Father. He is..." How to describe their utterly perfect bond? That they were made for each other? Father would never understand such a connection. He and Mother barely talked, never showed affection. "He is my best friend and confidante."

Father sighed heavily. "I do not want my son—my heir—gallivanting around Europe like a bloody Roman soldier on campaign."

"What? We went to France—"

"And last year it was Italy. Norrington, you need to start taking responsibility. You need to start acting like you are the heir to a dukedom established almost two centuries ago, instead of the reckless scion of some drunken earl who made a mockery of the aristocracy."

That was a dig at Jack, at the Earl of St. Albans, at the whole Atherley family of which Bertram was a part. "I comport myself discreetly, Father. There is not a shred of scandal."

"You mean to say, not anymore."

"Society has forgotten Jack, Your Grace. He's dead. The new earl is a fine upstanding man."

A grunt was Father's response.

Percival pursed his lips. "I cannot give him up. I need Bertram in my life."

Father looked askance, his jaw tensing. After a moment, he exhaled loudly. "I am merely asking you to marry, Norrington."

Interesting. Was Father suggesting that if he married, he could have his Bertie back?

"Then you are not asking me to end my friendship with Bertram?"

"No," Father said with a huff of resignation.

"All right. I'll marry."

Father's eyes slivered once again as he scrutinized Percival. "Good. Your mother and I have narrowed down a list of girls."

Christ. A whole list? "Oh?"

"You will accompany us when we return to London in a few days to finish out the Season." Father thinned his lips. "If we have to, after the Season, your mother and I will throw a hunting ball and introduce you to more candidates."

That sounded dreadfully horrid. And possibly dangerous if the woman in question could not accept his way of life. "Father, you should know I have become familiar with a young lady."

Father's countenance changed dramatically, almost brightening. "Oh? And who are her parents?"

Of course, the ever important question of heritage. "I'll make inquiries. I've met her at several social events. She's very well connected. Knows positively everyone."

The harshness of Father's face eased somewhat. "I suggest you make your inquiries today. We will leave for London in a few days."

Percival smiled and said a quiet prayer that Penelope Hardcastle was the daughter of somebody.

Phillips residence, Belgravia, London

BOLLOCKS, bollocks, bollocks.

In cousin Nicholas's guest bedroom, Bertram slammed his fist against the mattress, rage from what had transpired that afternoon still roiling his gut, keeping him from much-needed sleep.

Amesbury's men had remained on the platform to keep watch until Percival was taken away, presumably to Wood Hall. Once Percival was gone, Bertram had been driven in an unmarked carriage up Holywell Hill to the Midlands railway station. There he and his appointed ruffians had waited until the next train to London had arrived. Once the train had pulled in, the thugs promptly shoved Bertram and his luggage onto a railway car, then proceeded to join him. He had at least one bully leering at him all the way to Kentish Town.

Of course, once in London, he could have taken the next train back to St. Albans. Except such a notion seemed somewhat dangerous given the lengths the duke had gone to separate him from Percival.

From *his* Percy.

Jesus. Bertram hit the mattress once again wishing it were not ticking and horsehair under his fist, but flesh and bone.

Upon arrival in London, he had pondered where to go. Surely not to the home he and Percival shared not as mere housemates—the façade they had to project—but as a devoted couple. He could not ignore the possibility that more ruffians would be lurking around the entrance to keep him at bay.

So, he'd knocked on Nicholas's door, or rather, the door to the opulent house of Nicky's in-laws where Nicky and his wife had a suite of rooms. Nicky took him in readily, and listened to Bertram's complaints over a late supper, afterward leaving him to retire in the guest room.

Retire alone to ponder whatever the hell his Percy was doing at that moment.

Probably shedding the tears that Bertram himself could not release.

Instead, Bertram was of a mind to frig himself in a desperate attempt to forget his plight. Or perhaps to remember and reconnect with what the two of them had.

Bertram wrapped his hand around his burgeoning erection, his cock's awakening the usual response to thoughts of his lover.

The two worked best when the surprise of adventure was upon them. Or when they were comfortably settled somewhere without a care in the world. Or anything in between, really.

They were, simply, perfect together.

Bertram grinned as he slid the circlet of thumb and index finger down his shaft.

Like the other night when they'd purchased a bottle of absinthe from the man behind the bar in Nice. It was less than half full and they paid far too much money for it, but what did it matter? The barmaid had insisted they drink it diluted with water and sweetened with a little sugar. They'd paid her for turning a blind eye while they took familiarities with each other.

Familiarities that had continued, absinthe and water bottles in hand, to the bedroom of their rented villa several blocks away. Percival had relented in the cool of the night air, had spread his legs wide against the linen sheets while Bertram had slathered his almost painful erection with olive oil. Percival's arsehole had been tight but accommodating, the marquess puffing his acquiescence in rhythm to Bertram's thrusts, then saying nothing when Bertram had expired in a drunken heap at his side, the act unconsummated.

Of course, several hours later they had continued their exertions with more success, Bertram bursting with need, Percival pumping his own cock to match Bertram's sensual beat, the two reaching climax mere moments apart—

Bertram gripped his cock under the covers, letting his emission soil the sheets of the guest bed.

He gazed at the ceiling, the flame of the lamp on the bedside table dancing shadows across the plaster.

A tear ran down his right temple, then another on the left, both droplets coursing along his cheekbones.

He'd already written Percy. There'd been no response. He'd send word to Mama about their plight and ask her to let him know if she discovered any news.

Tomorrow morning, Nicky would be there at the breakfast table. He was always a sensible listener, always offered reasoned explanations and advice. His former life as a family doctor had helped him hone those skills.

And right now, Bertram needed someone who could offer some sage advice, who could help him figure out what the hell had just happened with Percival.

And how to get him back.

CHAPTER THREE

Stratton House, Mayfair, London

The clang of the letterbox at the front door roused Penelope from the lulling contemplativeness of measured stitches with needle and thread.

"Penny, be a good girl," Lady Gertrude Brazington said. "I'll put the kettle on while you fetch the post."

Every occasion was an opportunity for tea according to Gertrude. Just as Penelope lost herself in the act of sewing, Gertrude lost herself in the ritual of tea-making.

There was really nothing odd about it. The older woman once considered entering the convent where she would have endured numerous rituals. Luckily her brother, the Earl of Stratton, convinced her otherwise. Gertrude's absence would have left Penelope alone.

After her parents had died, Penelope was raised by Stratton and Gertrude as their ward. They were the only parents she ever really knew. If Gertrude had left for the nunnery, then, after Stratton had died, Penelope would have been entirely on her own.

That was a possibility she did not want to entertain. Solitude frightened her.

She retrieved the post from the entryway and sifted through the envelopes. She put Gertrude's on a small silver tray, then ensconced herself on the window seat in the parlor with her own correspondence.

An invitation. And another. Luckily, she always got several of those during the Season. Gertrude hated social events, but Penelope relished society's entertainments. One envelope in particular was intriguing. Definitely not an invitation, but a thick epistle. She rarely got those.

"Anything of interest?" Gertrude asked as she put down the tray. She poured a cup for Penelope and handed it to her.

"Would you like to go to a ball?"

"Oh, heavens, no."

Penelope laughed as Gertrude settled in with her own cup and letters.

They always had such convivial exchanges over the post, and then each was in her own little universe for a spell.

She sipped her tea from the gilded porcelain cup, a reminder of her tenuous hold on the aristocracy, then opened the cream-colored envelope, glancing at the signature.

The note was from the Marquess of Norrington.

Curiously, she'd received a note from Viscount Ravensburgh the day before. While she delighted in receiving postcards relaying news of their continental adventures, Ravensburgh's missive detailed a rather distressing episode of his separation from Norrington upon their return to England. Desperation and grief imbued the words on the stationery. Her heart bled for him, for the both of them.

She'd wanted to go to him, console him. But he was staying with his cousin Nicholas and his wife, Helena. Knocking on their door would most certainly have been awkward given Penelope's furtive fling with Nicholas over a year ago, before he'd become engaged to Helena. If having an unrelated bachelor sleep at her house could have been in any way deemed proper, Penelope would have insisted Ravensburgh stay with her.

And now, here in her hand, was a note from Norrington. What turmoil would be revealed in its pages?

Despair darkened every sentence. He, too, missed his lover. He was seemingly imprisoned at his family estate, but was to depart for London soon, to finish out the Season.

He reminded her of the last time they'd seen each other—at Lord and Lady Hawkhurst's ball at the beginning of June, before he and Ravensburgh had left for France. She smiled. There had been a young man that night awfully enamored of her until he saw a vision of loveliness dressed in pink, a girl much closer to his own age. Penelope herself had eyes on the Earl of Petersham, but realized the futility once he was dancing in the arms of a woman he clearly desired.

Norrington wondered if Penelope was planning on attending Lord and Lady Fretherne's gala. If so, he needed to talk to her regarding a matter of some urgency. If she did not have an invitation, he would be able to secure one for her. But she should only write back if she needed the invitation. She should not correspond otherwise.

How very odd. Clearly, some scheme was afoot.

Penelope shuffled through the afternoon's post. A thrill shot through her once she found the required embossed invitation.

She'd gladly talk to Norrington at the Fretherne ball. She'd do anything for such a wonderful pair who were meant to be together.

Phillips residence, Belgravia, London

THE LONDON HOME of Nicholas's in-laws, Mr. and Mrs. Phillips, was uncluttered and modern, a far cry from Bertram and

Percival's traditional yet rather opulent residence filled with *objets d'art* from their continental travels.

Across from Bertram in the morning room, Nicholas read a medical journal with genuine interest. "I like to keep abreast of current treatments and theories," he'd explained as he stretched on the sofa. "It relieves the boredom of Parliament."

Bertram had laughed at that. "I'm glad I'm not a peer of the realm. I'm sure Percy will be just as bored when he joins the House of Lords."

The cousins' comfortable silence had afforded Bertram the opportunity to gawk at the stylish furnishings and fittings. The chair he sat in matched the sofa on which Nicholas lay, the natural cherry wood joined at right angles, the tapestry cushions medieval in style. In comparison, the dark, curvilinear furniture covered in velvet strewn haphazardly around his London abode seemed stodgy and old-fashioned.

"I suppose this is what an interior looks like with a woman's touch," Bertram said.

Nicholas grinned over his reading material. "If that woman is Sophia Phillips and has heaps of her husband's money to spend, then, yes, this is what such an interior looks like."

Bertram met Nicholas's gaze. "I'm worried, Nicky."

Nicholas put down his journal. "About?"

"I've written Percy, at both Wood Hall and our London address. I've not heard a word of response. It's been two days." He rested his head on the back of the chair and stared blankly at the wooden beams overhead. "He's keeping us apart, and I don't know why."

"He?"

"The Duke of Amesbury."

"Ah."

Bertram lifted his head. "Nicky, I need to get a letter to Percy, and I need your help."

Nicholas sat up. "Yes, of course. I'll do whatever I can."

"I was thinking, I mean, I wonder…" Bertram sighed. "I don't think the duke would burn a letter from the Earl of St. Albans, do you?"

Nicholas chuckled grimly. "No, perhaps not. However, such a missive would not be above suspicion. I am not merely your cousin. It was my late brother who played a villainous role in Percival's past. Amesbury will most definitely be skeptical of any communication coming from me. He might choose to read it first. Or destroy it without even opening it."

"Bollocks." Nicholas was correct, of course. Nicky's brother Jack had been Percy's first lover—and almost his last, given Jack's violent tendencies.

"I can offer a slightly better solution," said Nicholas. "Helena's uncle, the Earl of Petersham, will, I am certain, be amenable to assisting you. Although he is related to you by marriage…"

Bertram quickly determined the connection. "Right. My cousin's wife's uncle."

Nicholas lifted a brow. "It's a little removed, don't you think? It's doubtful Amesbury would throw such a missive away."

"But why on earth would Petersham communicate with Percival?"

Nicholas pursed his lips in thought. "Ah-ha." He held up his index finger. "Parliament."

"Parliament? Percival's not in Parliament."

"Neither is Petersham—yet. He's been tasked by his father with learning the ways of governing as he has been avoiding his duties of late." Nicholas smiled. "Didn't you just mention how Percival will find Parliament boring?"

Bertram considered this. "And maybe Petersham's offering to help Percival learn governance?" He shook his head. "Sounds a little far-fetched."

Nicholas shrugged. "Then somewhere at the end of the letter Petersham can mention you in a cloak-and-dagger sort of way."

"'*St. Albans and Ravensburgh dined with me the other evening. The handsome cousins are coping with the stresses of their day-to-day lives'*," Bertram said in an overly aristocratic accent.

"Or words to that effect," Nicholas said with a chuckle. "Like you, Uncle Arthur is quite literary. You two can thrash out a turn of phrase that is both eloquent and clandestine."

The door to the morning room opened and Mrs. Phillips entered. About forty years of age, she remained a stunning beauty. She had, once or twice, even been mistaken as the sister of Nicholas's wife Helena rather than her mother.

"Good morning, gentlemen."

Nicholas straightened from his lounging position. Bertram stood and nodded his greeting.

She waved him back to sitting. "Have you no tea?" She scurried over to the bell pull and gave it a tug before setting a smile upon Bertram. "It is such a pleasure having you stay with us, Bertram. How is the pirate story faring?"

"Pirate *hunter* story," Nicholas corrected.

Bertram chuckled. "The final installment of 'The Adventures of Paolo the Pirate Hunter' will be published next month in *The Boy's Own Magazine*. A volume with all the stories will be published at some point, as well."

"How marvelous." Mrs. Phillips beamed. She turned at a light rapping on the door. A servant with a silver salver. "Ah, the post has just arrived." She thumbed through the missives, then glanced up. "A letter for the viscount."

The envelope was thick and addressed to *Viscount Ravensburgh in care of the Earl of St. Albans*. The familiar masculine script sent a wave of relief to wash over him. "Percy."

Nicholas looked up from his own passel of post. "Percival? He's written?"

Bertram frantically opened and read, summarizing out loud. "Percy apologizes that he's not been able to send a thing until now… Any post coming in or going out is reviewed by the duke… He assumes I've been trying to reach him, but he's not received any letters and believes his father is burning anything addressed to him. He's in London now. At the Wood family home—not ours. A maid is helping him send letters. He ascertained my whereabouts by writing to both Armand at our house, and 'Nicky's butler Mason in Hertfordshire'." Tears stung Bertram eyes as he read the next paragraph. "He says, 'Father is trying to keep us apart'."

Mrs. Phillips hid her distress behind her hand. A quiet knock on the door distracted her with the arrival of the tea tray. She took the tray herself and quickly dismissed the servant.

"To what end?" asked Nicholas.

"Because our relationship is 'corrupt'. And 'the Marquess of Norrington is required to take a wife'." Bertram sighed heavily. "He says he will be attending the Fretherne ball on Saturday night."

"That's one of the final events of the Season," Mrs. Phillips said as she handed him a cup of tea.

Bertram gulped the hot liquid. "Are you going?" he asked her.

"I assume we all are. I think all of London society will be there. Although Helena might not be of a mind to. You know, with the baby." She smiled sweetly.

"Yes, of course." Bertram had a new cousin, and the St. Albans earldom had a new heir. "Nicky, can you get me an invitation?"

"Probably." Nicholas checked the stack of invitations on the mantel. "Here." He handed Bertram a card with embossed lettering. "You take it, in case Amesbury tries to get you thrown out. Say you're my guest."

"But what if Helena decides she wants to go?" Bertram asked, knowing his cousin's wife loved such events.

"She'll attend with me and my husband," said Mrs. Phillips.

"Thank you." He turned a smile to her. That this beautiful woman was a grandmother was unbelievable. "You say all of London will be there?"

"Yes. All those who usually attend such events."

Which meant Penelope would be there. He had to somehow convince Penelope and Percival to appear as a young infatuated couple, a couple intent on marrying.

It was the only way to get his Percy back.

CHAPTER FOUR

Fretherne residence, Mayfair, London

Lady Viola Pemberton unfurled her fan perhaps with a bit too much unrestrained annoyance. She really shouldn't draw attention to herself, because then the guests at Lord and Lady Fretherne's glorious gala would surely know she was there in the ballroom. Perhaps if she tucked herself behind a column while hiding behind the fan she would be quite forgotten, thereby proving to Papa that she was not marriage market material.

Papa had grown tired of her avoidance of matrimony and had finally put his foot down. He had insisted she, at the very least, try to find a young man under whose roof she could spend the rest of her life rather than burdening her poor father. "Burden" and "poor" were not so far off from their reality, despite Papa being the Earl of Rochdale. He had paid a goodly sum to relieve the debts of her horrid and prodigious brother, Edwin, Viscount Warland, the ungrateful heir to the earldom.

Had she been the heir, she most certainly would not have squandered her inheritance by the ripe old age of twenty-six.

So here she was at a ball, a type of social occasion she detested—and one Edwin had refused to attend until Papa had convinced him his presence was needed to protect Viola's virtue. The Fretherne event was most likely the very last one of the Season, and her very last chance to find that rare man who didn't need his wife to necessarily love him. She had danced with a handful of young gentlemen, making sure to choose the ones with a feminine edge to their faces and mode of dress. She quickly discovered that meant they were either very young or overly influenced in fashion by their mothers and sisters. Too bad. She had hoped to find a man as anxious as she was to get the dreaded marriage business settled so she could move on to solidifying special friendships with members of her own sex.

Papa had said he had a candidate in mind, a marquess she'd never heard of, but the man had yet to make his appearance. Perhaps he wasn't coming. Perhaps he found a young bride at one of last week's society events.

Out of the corner of her eye, Viola spied her brother imbibing champagne. Why wasn't the burden on him to find some pretty, rich, innocent young lady? Because, he'd asserted, men of his age didn't settle down. Men needed to live life to the fullest and gain worldly experience—all of which apparently cost a pretty penny— before claiming a bride and heading off into the next adventure—

Marriage.

Like Lord and Lady Davenham? Or Lord and Lady Fretherne? Both of the ladies in question, previously known in society as the Roxton twins, were rather dull, probably because they were so very young and innocent of the world around them. They had recently been married off to "respectable" gentlemen of the aristocracy who were at least thirty or forty years their senior. The twins would start having babies soon and probably be rather content with that because they didn't know there was more to be had from life.

But Viola had tasted a bit of life during her time at the finishing school in Switzerland with her roommate, then with another girl during the summer after school had ended.

What she really craved was to find a patroness, a woman who, like herself, preferred the company of women. They could live as companions, which was a very polite and respectable way for women to live indeed.

Damn Edwin for putting her in this loathsome situation.

At least he had the right idea drinking champagne. Or lemonade for that matter. Something cool against the heat of the crowd.

Viola exited the ballroom to find the refreshment room. Perhaps on the other side of the foyer. It couldn't possibly be up the grand staircase, but there was clearly some attraction in an upper story, since a handful of guests were quietly padding up the treads.

The ladies' retiring room was on the first floor. She could definitely hide there.

Papa was nowhere to be seen. Probably gambling in some drawing room.

Viola climbed the stairs and turned down the corridor toward the retiring room. A man and a woman continued up the staircase.

Hmm. What was on the second floor?

Bedrooms?

Ah, yes. Bedrooms.

Viola waited a beat, then continued up the stairs. Then another flight. The bedrooms, it seemed, were on the third floor.

The couple entered a room, the click of a lock signaling their intention.

Not interested in listening in, Viola moved further down the corridor, finding an unlocked door and slipping inside. The room was dark, lit only by moonlight through the window. A dresser held some interesting accoutrements next to a hairbrush and comb. Silken cords and bands. For the hair?

Or some erotic act?

With a silent chuckle, Viola took off her shoes and sat on the bed. Perhaps she should also remove her dress? It would be far more comfortable. Sleeping through the rest of the ball was all the activity she wanted that night.

PENELOPE TRIED NOT TO SLOUCH against the wall in the Fretherne ballroom, but her spirits, along with her body, kept sagging. Ravensburgh was nowhere to be seen, nor Norrington for that matter. She had arrived a bit early with hopeful expectations. Too hopeful. She had pined for their company while they'd been in France. The Season had been dreary without them.

She perked up a bit when an elegant and remarkably attractive middle-aged woman wearing a dress ripped from the pages of the latest fashion magazine came into view. Well, if Lady Foxley-Graham was in attendance, then surely her close confidant Nicholas—or, rather, the Earl of St. Albans—and his retinue, possibly including Ravensburgh, would not be far behind.

Penelope quickly surveyed the crowd, her gaze darting with determination, catching a familiar glimpse, then doubling back to make sure it really was *him*. A flush shimmied down her spine, straightening it. Ravensburgh was ever so dashing in his evening attire with a decadently embroidered waistcoat. If only she were a man and could win his heart—

She stilled at the preposterous notion. But that's what it was, wasn't it? She loved both Norrington and Ravensburgh dearly, they were her very good and true friends. But recently she'd felt a little stirring when in Ravensburgh's presence. She'd eventually have to smother the futile crush, but right now she felt overly giddy and, as she hadn't seen him for weeks, her enthusiastic welcome would not be deemed out of the ordinary.

She hurried to him, slipping through the crowded ballroom as politely and unobtrusively as she could, unable to suppress the smile that spread across her face as she drew nearer to him.

"Pen—Miss Hardcastle!" Ravensburgh glowed when he saw her, making him even more handsome. As if that were possible.

"My lord," Penelope greeted with restraint.

He grasped her hands. "Darling, what a sight you are for a bedraggled man." He looped her arm through his.

"Have you seen Norrington?" she murmured.

"No. Not yet." He looked around. "I don't know if I can maintain my composure if I see him." He sighed heavily. "I'm terrifically overwrought."

She patted his hand as she took in his perfect face. "I'm here for you. As a friend."

His smile sent a sparkle of kindness to his eyes before he returned his attention to survey the ballroom. Suddenly he tensed, gripping her arm against his torso. She followed his gaze.

Norrington was spectacular in his perfectly polished apparel, the rich blue of his waistcoat a magnificent counterpoint to his striking blond hair. He smiled thinly at those he passed as he strolled with purpose through the ballroom. He offered a nod or a brief word to guests as needed, and when not engaged, glanced around as if searching for something. Because, of course, he was searching for something. Or, rather, someone.

He stilled the moment he met Ravensburgh's gaze. For one fleeting moment, his staid expression registered elated relief. Ravensburgh sucked air through his teeth.

"Penny, keep watch, please. I need to see him." There was desperation in his tone. "But I'm afraid of who might prevent us."

Arm in arm, they strolled carefully through the crowd, Penelope trying to be aware of anyone who might be taking notice of their progression.

Before long, the two men were face to face, maintaining façades of cool collectedness despite a twitch in Ravensburgh's temple and a tiny crease between Norrington's eyes.

"Good evening, Ravensburgh." Norrington's greeting held a slight tremor.

"My lord Norrington, a pleasure." Ravensburgh huffed a little too quickly, as if he had already danced several waltzes. "Are you well?"

"I am, thank you. Although I could have used a change of scenery these past few days."

A plaintive sigh escaped Ravensburgh's throat.

"Miss Hardcastle, a pleasure to see you here tonight." Norrington bowed his head.

"Good evening, my lord," she said dutifully. She espied the Duke of Amesbury not far away. She gave Ravensburgh's arm a warning squeeze.

"I adore these affairs," said Norrington, subverting his sarcasm with a smile. "The miasma of cologne and sweat"—he inhaled—"with a subtle hint of candle wax. It borders on orgiastic." He said the last in an undertone.

Ravensburgh glanced up at the chandelier ablaze in the center of the ballroom. "One would think Lord Fretherne would have converted to gaslight by now."

"Gaslight isn't as invigorating to the senses, Ravensburgh." Norrington looked askance to both sides. "And I think you know what I mean by invigorating."

Ravensburgh chuckled. "I'm not daft," he said in *sotto voce*.

"And I don't want to continue to suffer in my condition," Norrington said in a near-whisper. "We must do something very soon."

"We can't you know," Ravensburgh responded equally quietly. "Two men in a room alone. We need at least one woman, although two would be best."

Norrington sighed heavily.

Penelope was the obvious choice, as she was already sandwiched between the two men. She wouldn't mind being in a room alone with them. But reality crashed down when she slid her gaze to Ravensburgh and found Ravensburgh gazing lovingly at Norrington.

She'd just be an awkward third in a bedroom.

Ravensburgh lifted a brow. "Miss Hardcastle is in want of dance partners tonight, my lord. Can she count on you to oblige her?"

Norrington pursed his lips before he surreptitiously glanced side to side. "I would be honored, Miss Hardcastle." He took her hand and kissed the air above it.

Her heart fluttered at the gallant action.

"My lord," Ravensburgh said, "perhaps a cigar after your third dance of the evening? I will take my leave and await you."

A look tinged with wanting passed between the two men, lingering for a beat too long before Ravensburgh walked away.

The Duke of Amesbury glared at Ravensburgh before glowering at Norrington.

"Percival," Penelope murmured.

The use of his Christian name roused the marquess to their present circumstance.

"Ask me to dance. Ask me before anyone makes a scene."

"What?" Norrington whispered before noticing the duke. "Yes, of course." He shook his head. "Miss Hardcastle," he said loud enough for those nearby to hear, "will you do me the honor?"

She did do, and felt terrifically refreshed by the waltz. Norrington was a fine dancer, commanding her quite astutely.

Was he like this with Ravensburgh in bed? Did Ravensburgh love being commanded in his arms?

She quashed the thought as her arousal became evident when her thighs skimmed together on the upbeat of the waltz.

When the dance ended, Norrington looped her arm around his and escorted her off the floor. Penelope searched for Ravensburgh's beaming face, her spirits once again slumping when he was nowhere to be found. Her melancholia was overshadowed by Norrington pulling her toward the foyer and the grand staircase.

"Where are we going?" she asked in a low voice.

"You and I are about to have a tryst, Miss Hardcastle. In a third-floor bedroom."

* * * * *

Percival's heart raced as he practically dragged Penelope up the stairs, hoping he had understood Bertram's cipher of an invitation to find him. Once on the third floor, he knocked on every closed door—two quick raps and one slow—then waited only a second before moving to the next door.

The third door in the corridor cracked open following the slow rap. He slipped inside, hauling a surprised Penelope after him, and locked the door.

Bertram stood in the shadows. Desire pumped through Percival's veins, setting his heart to pounding, his cock to thicken. He released Penelope and strode to his lover.

As they fell into each other's arms Bertram let out a choking sob.

"Darling, darling," Percival murmured. "Don't, don't." He smoothed his hands on either side of Bertram's head, holding him steady. "We have only a moment." He smashed his mouth on Bertram's parted lips.

Every pore flared with excitement, encompassing his body in shivering heat. Bertram opened under him, sucking in his tongue, enveloping his torso with strong arms. *Heavens above*, he'd missed this. It had been barely a week, but he'd missed their unbridled physicality, as well as their emotional connection. How in bloody hell was he supposed to give all that up?

He leaned his forehead against Bertram's.

His lover emitted a whimper. "How are you, Percy, love? I've been frantic with worry."

"I know. I mean, so have I." He pecked the tip of Bertram's nose. "While a captive at my father's house, I had to endure the instruction of a dancing master, and peruse the lineage of five young women."

Bertram pouted. "Is that all?"

Percival chuckled and moved to the bed. He sat and patted the mattress next to him in invitation. Bertram took his place at his side. Percival wrapped an arm around his shoulders.

"And thus begins my descent into the wretchedness that is the marriage market." Percival squeezed his eyes to bank back tears.

"What about Penelope?"

Damnation. In the heat of the moment, he'd forgotten they were not alone. "Christ, Penny. I apologize." He patted the mattress on his other side.

Penelope came forward from the shadows. She climbed onto the mattress, and he draped his other arm around her shoulders. She sank into his embrace.

"How is this going to work?" he asked.

"Penny, we don't rightfully know your parentage," began Bertram. "Can we add you to the list of Percy's prospects?"

"Oh. Well," she said slowly, "I doubt I'm qualified to be a future duke's wife. You see, my only connection to the aristocracy is being the Earl of Stratton's ward."

"Stratton." Percival tried to dredge up something about the man. "I don't think I know him." Or had even heard of him.

"He's been dead for ten years now. I live with his sister, Gertrude. She never married. She wanted to be a nun at one time."

Percival chilled. "Good lord, you're not Roman Catholic, are you?"

Penelope laughed. "No, no. And neither is Gertrude. Nor is she very religious. I believe that was one of the problems she encountered at the nunnery."

Bertram chuckled.

"Ugh," Percival groaned. "I don't know how we're going to make this work. Have you been presented to the queen?"

"I was a debutante, yes. Several years ago."

"Why have you never married?" Bertram went straight to the point, didn't he?

She nestled into the crook of Percival's arm, almost tickling him. "I've never been in love. As the mere ward of an earl, I am allowed the luxury of remaining an unmarried woman as I choose." She gaze up at him. "Unlike you, I don't have to marry. And, as Gertrude and I have a very comfortable income, I am not compelled to."

"What legacy do you have? Land? What would I acquire with such a union?"

"Gertrude and I are allowed to live in the house in London. There's a new earl. As the previous earl, my guardian, died without a direct heir, the new Earl of Stratton is a cousin. He despises London, so rarely visits unless he has to. Usually only for Parliament."

"Bollocks," Percival muttered. "Father will not agree to this by any stretch of the imagination."

Bertram cleared his throat. "What if Penelope becomes with child?"

Penelope tensed at his side.

He glanced at Bertram. "What do you mean, Bertie?"

"If she's carrying your child—your heir—won't she have to marry you?"

Percival chuckled darkly. "As my father knows such a thing will be a rare occurrence, he might very well bend to the notion." But the mirth drained suddenly.

Could he perform the act necessary to get Penelope with child? The thought sickened him a little. Not that he didn't adore Penelope, but that he might have to touch her in such an unnatural way…

But she of all women would understand his reticence and accept that the task was an unwelcome necessity. She would acquiesce to whatever he needed to perform the deed to completion. Even if it meant Bertram had to be in the bed with them.

"I need to think about this," he said. "You understand, Penny?"

She gave him a wan smile.

Percival stood. "I've tarried too long. My absence from the dance floor will be noticed. I'm certain I have some, if not all, of those five prospective young women waiting for me in the ballroom."

He pulled Bertram off the bed and into his arms. "Kiss me. Kiss me like you'll never see me again."

"Oh, darling." Bertram cupped his cheek, the gentle caress soothing.

Bertram tenderly touched his lips to his, tempting him with pecks and nibbles. His tongue flicked tantalizingly across the seam of Percival's mouth, setting his heart to pounding once again.

"I never want to be parted from you," Bertram murmured against his lips.

Percival reveled in his lover's attentions. "Nor I from you."

Bertram delved in as Percival closed his eyes, his mind and body focused on their intimate joining. No one, absolutely no one, could inspire him as his Bertie could. He thrust his tongue in Bertram's hungry mouth, crushing himself against his hard chest, their hearts beating in unison. Bertram's cock would be as engorged as his own.

Percival broke away, panting. "I need to leave now before I do something very ungentlemanly." He brushed down his jacket and trousers and smoothed his palms over his hair.

He left, the pounding of his heart matching the rhythm of the sorrow pulsing behind his eyes.

From her spot on the mattress, Penelope tried to calm the thumping in her chest. Here she was in a guest bedroom alone with Ravensburgh, the evidence of his desire for his lover almost at eye level.

And herself terribly aroused by the spectacle of two exceedingly handsome men kissing. Their sensuality had left her flustered in such a new way.

She had never before seen the two of them kiss, well, not on the lips, and definitely never so passionately. It was quite possibly one of the most invigorating experiences of her life.

Ravensburgh turned to her, his expression droopy, beleaguered. He clearly needed her to be a friend right now, so she should stop thinking about him as the lover he just proved he could be.

She went to him and wrapped her arms around his waist, pressing her cheek against his chest. He hugged her close, her head rising and falling with his uneven breaths. The warming scent of his cologne swirled in her senses.

They stood embracing for a minute, maybe two, Ravensburgh's arms continuing to hold her, his hands flexing at her waist.

She pulled away, he not letting her go at first. "My lord—"

"Bertram. Please call me by my Christian name."

They *were* in somewhat of an intimate pose, and familiarities were warranted. "Bertram, we should not stay here too long." She gazed up at him.

He was so handsome, his cheekbones carved to perfection, his lips plump and full below his straight nose, his eyes so soulful.

"No," he murmured. "We should not."

Was his luscious mouth moving closer to hers? She swallowed in disbelief. Yes, Ravensburgh—Bertram was angling over her, his face right above hers, and if she lifted herself even slightly on tiptoe their lips would meet—

No. This couldn't be right. Bertram was hurting and she was being selfish.

Penelope extracted herself from his embrace. She sucked in a tremulous inhale as he stared at her in surprise.

She quickly exited the bedroom and hurried down the corridor to the right, away from the ballroom.

* * * * *

BERTRAM STOOD STOCK STILL in the middle of one of Lord Fretherne's guest bedrooms.

Stunned. Utterly stunned.

What the hell had just happened?

Perhaps it had been the emotion of seeing his Percy. Raw energy still pumping through him.

He had kissed his Percy, so he wanted to kiss his Penny. That was all. There was nothing wrong with kissing friends.

Except Percival was far more than just a friend. And the way he wanted to kiss Penelope, well, that would not have been friendly in the slightest. More verging on seductive.

And it was wrong to seduce one's friends, right?

Of course it was. If they were truly *just friends*.

But what if they were something more?

Bloody hell. Bertram spanned his hand across his forehead to rub his temples with thumb and middle finger. Penelope had fled from his embrace like she'd been burned.

He did not regret what he had done. Well, he did in that he should have kissed Penelope, should have let her know he needed her.

That he wanted her.

What?

How odd that he'd never realized until that moment how he felt about her.

And how odd that it seemed the most natural thing in the world to want to love a man and a woman at the same time.

CHAPTER FIVE

Penelope ducked inside the first yielding bedroom door and turned the key behind her. She couldn't go back to the ballroom. Not yet. She needed a moment to collect herself. To think about how she should act around Ravensburgh—Bertram—what she should say to him, if anything at all.

A moment to assuage the desire that welled within. The desire for him.

The room was dimly lit by the gray glow of the moon, and just beyond, the city gaslights through the window. She grabbed a side chair and moved it to face the view outside, then sat.

She pulled up her skirts and petticoats, bunching them as best she could around her hips. She loosened the split in her drawers and slipped her hand between her legs. As she'd surmised, she was swollen and wet from being in Bertram's arms. She drew a finger through the sticky arousal, but the expected pleasure did not come. No. Thoughts of what Bertram had tried to do plagued her, even though the almost kiss had clearly been of his own volition.

Penelope would be devastated if she were the person who came between the perfectly matched marquess and viscount. Ever since meeting the pair, then discovering their secret, she had been protective of their love, of who they were. They deserved happiness just as much as a man and woman. More so even, as many marriages these days were arranged affairs, and Norrington and Bertram were actually in love.

The prospect of Norrington marrying a woman out of necessity brought home how imperfect the established relations between man and woman could be. That only such relationships were sanctioned was utterly unfair.

Penelope sighed. The stale air of the bedroom still held the sweat and exertions of couples who had come before. And a faint hint of a delicate perfume—

She tensed with awareness. That was not a fragrance that lingered from some previous liaison. It was a fragrance that continued to linger because the wearer was still in the room.

"Who's there?" Her plaintive voice broke the stillness.

Rustling came from behind. She froze as a chill crept up her neck. Very slowly she removed her hand from between her legs and began to put her skirts to right.

The person behind the chair grabbed her hand. "Shh. Don't move." The alto pitch of the genial voice suggested either a woman or a young man. "I want to give you pleasure."

Penelope swallowed. The delicate scent affirmed a woman.

"Will you allow me this indulgence?"

From a woman?

If Norrington and Bertram could be together, then why not two women?

Penelope had never considered such a notion. And yet, that was why she was in the guest bedroom to begin with, wasn't it? She had planned for self-pleasuring, but...

Surely a woman would understand what another woman desired.

"I...I will allow it," she said.

"Sit back. Close your eyes."

Once she did so a silken band was placed across her face as a blindfold.

"I need to assure discretion and secrecy. You do understand?"

Penelope nodded.

The band was tied by nimble fingers, the same fingers that pushed her skirts back up to her waist, then urged her knees apart. The sticky-moist sound of parting sex seemed overly loud in the silent room.

The woman knelt between Penelope's legs, the heat of her body warming the triangle of space. She slid her hands along Penelope's calves, under her knees, squeezing when she reached the fleshy part of her upper thighs, then deftly opened the split in the drawers and tickled her skin as she began to explore.

Her fingers were warm and smooth, not calloused and pawing like a man's. Penelope smiled. It was a rare man who would touch her in this fashion to begin with. But this woman understood how to touch, where to touch, and that such touches were pleasurable.

Penelope drew in a long inhalation and slumped in the chair.

Hot breath against her pubic curls roused her. She opened her eyes behind the blindfold. The flick of a tongue against her sex elicited an astonished gasp.

The woman teased with the velvety tip, tasting the swollen labia shielding the blossoming pearl now beginning to fret for want of satisfaction. Penelope held onto the seat of the chair as she tilted her hips, hoping to give her nighttime lover more access.

The woman's quiet laugh fanned hot against her thighs. She kissed Penelope on her inner thigh, licking the tender flesh. She was taunting her, keeping her at bay, making Penelope wonder if the stranger had any desire to complete the act she'd started.

The press of a mouth against her sex surprised her. The thrust of a tongue into her depths utterly shocked her. Her rasp eased into a moan as she welcomed the invasion, the woman alternating laps to her slit with thrusts inside her flexing passage.

Penelope released her hold on the chair and dared touch the woman before her. Her hair, bare of any ornament, was piled on her head. Better not pull, as a hairdresser would be difficult to find after their encounter.

She fondled the woman's ears, adorned with drop earrings, the cut gems cool to the touch. Diamonds? Or another precious stone. So, this was a woman who could afford such baubles, or had a paramour who could.

Penelope continued her exploration as her lover continued her lascivious attentions.

A neck, sleek and slender, not too long, not too short, adorned by a necklace with stones as cool to the touch as the earrings. Further down were shoulders, completely bare and wonderfully soft. Penelope smoothed her hands over the curve of the shoulders until she found the fine cambric of the shift.

Which meant the woman had divested herself of her ball gown.

The familiar warmth that presaged the climb to the peak of ecstasy radiated through her belly. The woman's attentions were steady and slow, focusing on Penelope's pleasure, so unlike her anonymous sexual encounters with men.

This woman…who was she? What did she look like? Penelope let her imagination run free. Her dress must be an exquisite gown of pure white silk to complement her ivory skin and contrast with her raven-black hair. Diamond earrings and a matching necklace decorated her and reflected the knowing twinkle in her dark eyes. Her lips were red and plumped from pleasuring women so expertly.

Her beauty meant every man desired her. But Penelope had her at this moment, only Penelope, and this woman wanted Penelope, not those groveling men.

Perhaps she did not want a man at all.

The climb to ecstasy commenced, Penelope fighting to stay with the moment before release, but wanting more, wanting the woman to continue to suck and nip and lick forever… forever…

then reaching the crest, pausing to feel, to breathe, to relax against the building tension, unable to maintain—

Exploding with rapture as the woman lapped up her orgasm, drinking her in as if Penelope were the elixir of life.

Penelope exhaled heavily, exhausted, only then feeling the cramp of her fingers gripping the seat of her chair.

A waft of air indicated the woman had stood and moved away. More rustling. Was she putting on her white dress? Smoothing her black hair back into place? Penelope was free to take off the blindfold, to see her seducer, but something— appreciation for the pleasure and a desire to maintain the secrecy?—compelled her not to move.

Behind her the lock turned, then the door clicked shut. Penelope removed the silken blindfold, surprised to see it was not black as imagined, but an icy pink. Or so it seemed in the pale moonlight.

She tucked the blindfold into her bodice, then stood to tug her drawers back into place and adjust her skirts. She drew in a deep inhalation, letting it slide out slowly along with any lingering worries. She'd rejoin the crush of the ballroom now with a composure she wouldn't have felt had she simply indulged in solo pleasure.

CHAPTER SIX

Viola stood on the bottom step of the Earl of Fretherne's grand staircase and heaved a sigh. Exhilaration coursed through her. She was quite refreshed after her adventure upstairs in a guest bedroom, an erotic tang lingering on her tongue. Seduction was so easy when one's quest wanted to be seduced. Besides having blond hair and a low-cut décolleté, who the woman was, she had no idea. A sensual woman from her willingness and her floral perfume. If she were to ever meet her, she would have to thank her for a pleasant diversion from the hell that was proving to be her life that evening.

If she could only be with such a woman, her life would be quite settled. Well, if such a woman had an income to maintain the two of them. Not in a lavish lifestyle, just a meaningful one.

Unfortunately, Viola was a woman who wanted to be with women in a society that expected her to be with men. Or, rather, one man. One man who would "take care" of her. As if any man could understand her needs.

She squared her shoulders. Papa would find her and remind her of her duties any moment now.

Viola challenged herself to endure one more dance before she would find and engage female company in discussing something of interest. She was not of a mind to listen to men talking about which carriage was swifter than another, or how they excelled at one sport or another, or how clever they were with their recent investments.

Poetry or gardening. Or even gossip and fashion. Anything that did not seem to be of interest to men.

THE COOL EVENING AIR on the Fretherne's flagstone terrace refreshed Percival. He was utterly exhausted from dancing. Well, not from the act of dancing, but from having to maintain a semblance of politeness and interest in topics of conversation of absolutely no concern. Good lord, who really cared who was engaged to whom? Or whether a certain type of dress underpinning was so old-fashioned?

Really all he wanted to do was lie in Bertram's arms staring up at the night sky in Nice. Anywhere in France, really. Or Italy. In bloody England, for Christ's sake. It barely mattered where.

And where was the deuced viscount anyway? He'd left him in a third-floor bedroom with Penelope, who was also nowhere to be seen. Perhaps the two had taken advantage of their unexpected private situation—

Percival stilled. And what if they had? Did he care? That he really didn't was not so surprising, was it? They were each of them dear to him in different ways. Penelope was fabulous company and Bertie was his lover and most intimate friend.

Besides, Bertram would be expected to spend time with whatever woman was chosen to be Lady Norrington. Why wouldn't Penelope and Bertram take the opportunity to form a deeper connection?

Bertram had once intimated that he was not repulsed by the idea of a woman gratifying him in a sensual way. He and Penelope certainly got on quite well and were often rather affectionate with each other. Penelope had a certain smile she reserved only for Bertram; a fawning beam tinged with longing. She probably had no idea Percival had noticed.

He shook his head. Well, if the two happened to explore something, so be it. Right now, he needed to rejoin the fray and pretend he wanted to be with a woman.

Stepping inside from the terrace, why, lo and behold, he spied Bertram looking like a lost puppy. Percival caught Bertram's eye and elicited a grin. Bertram went to him.

"I've been looking for you, Percy. I didn't expect you to be outside, though. Have you been through all of your women already?"

Percival chuckled. "Well, I have danced with four of the five women Father picked out for me. I suppose I should find dear Mother so she can arrange the final pairing. A Lady Violetta Pemberley or some such." He studied Bertram. "Where is Penelope?"

"I haven't a clue. She, er, left, you know, the room soon after you did. And I departed the moment an older chap wandered in. That was awkward. But I don't think he saw me."

"Ah. Perhaps Penelope wandered in after that chap."

Bertram shook his head. "God, I hope not. She's got far better taste than that. Trust me."

Percival sighed. "Well, shall we try to find my mother or Penelope?"

"Let's go look for our Miss Hardcastle. Your mother will invariably find us."

"WHY LADY VIOLA, what a splendid surprise to see you."

Viola turned at the sound of the familiar voice. Lady Foxley-Graham was exceptionally ravishing in her lavender gown with plum overskirts. Of course she was. The lady would be breathtaking in sackcloth caked in mud and leaves and wrapped with twine. She was, frankly, that gorgeous.

"Yes, it is true, my lady. I have deigned to attend a ball." She sighed. "Papa said I should make an appearance before the Season ended."

Lady Foxley-Graham laughed.

A vision of loveliness stood at the lady's side. Auburn hair framed a glowing face with plump pink cheeks, eyes the color of moss, and rosy lips wanting kissing. The young woman smiled politely.

"Lady Viola, do you know the Countess of St. Albans?"

Countess? She was so young. Viola shuddered to think of the decrepit fossil she must be married to. "I have not had the pleasure." She nodded. "Countess."

"Helena," Lady Foxley-Graham said to the young woman, "this is Lady Viola Pemberton, daughter of the Earl of Rochdale."

"Pleased to make your acquaintance, Lady Viola." The countess had a melodic quality to her voice.

"How fares your garden, Lady Viola?" asked Lady Foxley-Graham.

"Very well, thank you." Although she had to forgo the elaborate iron-and-glass house she had wanted due to Papa's reduced circumstances.

"Oh, you keep a garden," said the countess with enthusiasm. "Did you know Lavinia has a rose named after her?"

Viola smiled. "I did. And I take great care in keeping my *Rosa Lavinia* bush alive."

Lady Foxley-Graham nodded in gratitude. "Lady St. Albans has new knowledge of keeping things alive."

The countess let out a clipped guffaw before covering her mouth with her fan. "My husband and I have just had our first child. A son."

"I offer my congratulations," Viola said politely.

"Now, Lady Viola, what's this I hear about you needing to find a husband?"

Viola sighed. "Yes, 'tis true. And me in my twenty-third year."

"Oh?" Lady St. Albans raised a brow as if keenly interested. "Have you not been engaged before? What sort of husband are you looking for? I suppose one who enjoys gardens would be fitting."

Viola stared at the countess in surprise. "The Countess of Banbury usually asks those sorts of questions, my lady. Are you, perhaps, her protégé in the business of matchmaking?"

Lady St. Albans blushed. "I do apologize. I suppose when one is so in love and newly wed one hopes the same for everyone." The blush deepened. "I supposed I am inspired to make matches and the hoped-for progeny so our little Robert has someone to marry in thirty years."

"Well, my lady, when one reaches one's twenty-third year one realizes she can quite possibly do without a husband."

"But, I suppose, Rochdale feels otherwise," remarked Lady Foxley-Graham. She gazed out among the crowd fringing the ballroom floor as if she might find an exemplary suitor.

"Yes, an unmarried daughter can be a burden." Viola followed her gaze and was immediately distracted by quite possibly the most beautiful woman in the world walking in their direction.

Heat flushed Viola's skin from her cheeks to her toes, bouncing back to coil in her sex.

It was she. Unmistakably. The blond woman from the third floor. The woman who had let herself be seduced. Her dress was a pretty shade of peach rather than the gray the shadows of the bedroom had led her to believe.

The beautiful woman approached, her perfume filling Viola's senses, dizzying her into a sensual dream. "Lady Foxley-Graham. Lady St. Albans." She nodded to both then offered a polite smile to Viola.

"Miss Hardcastle," said Lady Foxley-Graham. She glanced at Viola. "Have you two met? Miss Penelope Hardcastle, may I introduce Lady Viola Pemberton."

The lovely Miss Hardcastle nodded in her direction. "My lady."

"Miss Hardcastle, pleased to make your acquaintance." Viola hoped she did not appear overly eager.

Lady Foxley-Graham flicked her fan with a snap. "Miss Hardcastle, you look invigorated."

Of course she did. She'd had an orgasm not half an hour ago.

"The ballroom is quite warm, my lady, and I am so fond of dancing."

"As am I." Lady Foxley-Graham placed a hand on Lady St. Albans's shoulder. "I see your husband, Helena, with the Earl of Petersham. I will take my leave and attempt to convince one of them to dance." She sauntered away with a swish of her backside.

Miss Hardcastle sighed as she watched Lady Foxley-Graham join the men. "Such a handsome family you have, countess."

"Thank you, Miss Hardcastle."

Viola glanced over at the men Lady Foxley-Graham conversed with. "Which is your husband, countess?"

"Nicholas is on the left. The Earl of Petersham is my uncle."

Well, that was a relief. Her Nicholas looked to be of an appropriate age. Viola hated when women as beautiful as the countess were forced to marry men old enough to be their fathers. Or older.

"And both are very fine gentlemen," added Miss Hardcastle.

Viola turned to her, perusing the young woman's ensemble as a clandestine way to take in her beauty. "Such an enchanting dress. A delicious cut of the neckline." Dangerously low for such a well-attended event. "Is the style continental?"

Miss Hardcastle blushed and giggled. "Oh, no. My guardian, Lady Gertrude, creates many of my gowns."

Lady Gertrude knew how to show off a bosom, that was certain.

"You say you love to dance, Miss Hardcastle?"

"Very much so."

Viola dared to be bold. "If you and I could dance together with the crowd, what kind of dancer would you be? One who lets herself be mastered? Or one who would like to do a bit of leading?"

Another blush crept across Miss Hardcastle's cheeks. "What a curious question." She pursed her pink lips, apparently cogitating the notion. "I do like to be commanded. I feel there is a sort of freedom in letting a man take control—"

"Or in my case, a woman."

"Yes, of course."

"Control feeling like freedom? Isn't that contradictory, Miss Hardcastle?" asked Lady St. Albans.

"It does sound as such, does it not? But I suppose I mean how one is able to forget one's cares when in a partner's arms. Let the man—or the woman," she nodded to Viola, "have the responsibility of not colliding into another couple."

Viola and the countess laughed.

"Penny!"

Miss Hardcastle beamed as two exquisitely coiffed and dressed young men approached. She clasped their hands. "Norrington, Ravensburgh, come meet my new friend."

Friend? Were they already friends? *Good Lord*, she hoped so.

"I'll make the introductions, Miss Hardcastle," said the countess with a wink. "I should take responsibility for my family members." She nodded to Viola. "Lady Viola Pemberton, may I introduce my husband's cousin Bertram Atherley, the Viscount Ravensburgh, and my husband's boyhood playfellow—and Bertie's dearest friend—Percival Wood, the Marquess of Norrington."

Both men bowed slightly and muttered the required pleasantries.

Viola examined the blond man. "You're the Marquess of Norrington? I do believe I'm supposed to dance with you." *Or marry you. Ugh.*

"Oh?" He seemed surprised, relieved, and horrified all at once. "Oh. Yes, of course. Lady Viola Pemberton. Sorry. I had quite misremembered your name."

Viscount Ravensburgh flattened a palm over his mouth to cover a smile. Such an inelegant method of shielding one's emotions compared to a lady's fan.

Norrington maintained his composure. "You are the Earl of Rochdale's daughter, are you not?" A touch of horror returned to his countenance. "Viscount Warland's sister?"

Of course he knew that meant she was a penniless spinster in desperate need of a rich husband. "I am." She nodded. "And I am honored to have a duke's son on my dance card."

"Yes, sorry." Norrington glanced down at his feet. "Thank you."

"Let's not be so glum, Percy," Lady St. Albans said. "It is a ball, after all, and the last one of the Season."

"Norrington and Ravensburgh have recently returned from the south of France." Miss Hardcastle's lively voice immediately lightened the mood.

"Sounds wonderful," said Viola. "Did you visit any gardens while you were there?" she dared ask. Any why not? Better to direct the conversation away from carriages as quickly as possible.

"Oh, there are marvelous gardens," said Ravensburgh.

"Yes," added Norrington, his face brightening. "There are entire gardens filled with exotic cacti and succulents—"

"One walks along these chipped granite paths—"

"The reflection is so bright, one's face can become brown simply by looking down."

Ravensburgh chuckled. "I don't know which I prefer, the gardens of France or the gardens of Italy. What do you say, Percy?"

"Italy I should think, Bertie."

Viola stared disbelieving, trying to temper the grin that threatened to break out. The two were awfully endearing in their enthusiasm and their ability to finish each other's sentence. Why it was like observing an old married couple—

She stifled a croak of realization.

Norrington. Right. Viola had learned all about the men her father had picked out for her. Percival Wood, the Marquess of Norrington, was heir to the Duke of Amesbury. Surprisingly, he looked to be Viola's age, possibly younger. Why a man in his position was in search of a wife at such a young age was intriguing. Most men with dukedoms to inherit had to make their mark in society, learn the ways of the nobility they would one day be masters of, understand the operation of the vast tracts of land associated with their title, even have a scandalous affair or two, leaving half a dozen broken-hearted misses on the dance floor. Most heirs to dukedoms didn't marry until they were thirty or beyond.

Unless the duke was ill and dying. No. She'd have heard such a thing from Papa. What else would compel a young aristocrat to marry so young?

Oh goodness. Was Norrington being forced to find a wife because of his "unnatural" attachment to the Viscount Ravensburgh? Didn't Lady St. Albans describe Ravensburgh as Norrington's "dearest" friend?

Which would make Norrington an ideal husband. He could do whatever he damn well pleased with Ravensburgh. And she would have appreciative visitors to her garden.

Lady St. Albans slipped an arm through Norrington's. "Percy, dear, there's a waltz about to begin. Shouldn't you ask Lady Viola to dance?"

Norrington flitted a glance at Ravensburgh, an action so subtle one would have had to have been looking for it. Which Viola was.

The marquess's expression eased into a smile. "Lady Viola, would you do me the honor?" He untwined himself from the countess and held out his arm.

Viola touched his elbow. "It would be my pleasure, my lord marquess."

"Penny—Miss Hardcastle, we haven't had our dance yet."

Ravensburgh's mellow baritone drew Viola and Norrington's attention simultaneously.

"Are you asking me, Lord Ravensburgh?"

The interaction amongst the friends was genuinely heartwarming. The pet names, the familiarity, all were enviable. Relationships that developed over time, like a family's ought.

But Miss Hardcastle wasn't family, nor anyone's "dearest friend". What was her relationship to the men? Was she using the viscount and the marquess as a shield to her own secret desires?

Viola would just have to explore that notion and find out.

But first she needed to convince Norrington she was the perfect wife for a man in his predicament.

PERCIVAL ESCORTED LADY VIOLA to the dance floor, picking up the rhythm to merge into the maelstrom of couples. He surprised himself with his deftness in melding with the crowd, but his partner proved to be very nimble as well.

Dancing with Lady Viola reminded him of the one aspect of balls he enjoyed. And watching Bertram turning Penelope in his arms reminded him how fine a dancer the viscount was. If he and Bertie could dance together, who would lead whom? Would they take turns, as they did in the bedroom, with being the seducer and the seduced?

He chuckled.

"What do you find so amusing, my lord marquess?"

He caught Lady Viola's brown eyes and flushed. "Pardon. I was thinking I don't dance enough. But I cannot imagine dancing alone at home."

"Or in a French garden with Viscount Ravensburgh?"

Bollocks. He flushed hotter than a Mediterranean summer. Had they somehow been indiscreet?

He laughed it off and concentrated on dodging waltzing couples.

"Tell me how you met Ravensburgh. It seems you are both connected to the Countess of St. Albans's family?"

He'd practiced what to say when questions such as this came up. "As a boy, I used to spend time on the estate of the Earl of St. Albans. I found more adventure there than my family estate nearby. I grew up with Nicholas—who is Helena's husband—and occasionally Bertram would join us. Then a tragedy struck the St. Albanses." He always glossed over the part about Jack. "By that time, I was no longer a boy"—he was most definitely made a man by then— "so I stopped visiting, I suppose."

"But you maintained your friendship with Viscount Ravensburgh?"

"Er, yes, and Nicky, I mean Nicholas, who's now the Earl of St. Albans, as well."

"Ah."

Percival looked wistfully at Bertram. Bertie had saved him, saved his soul, taught him how to trust again, how to live again, how to love again.

Bertram caught his eye across the ballroom and for one moment it was as if they two were dancing together. Until another couple obscured his view. He sighed.

"It must be grand having longtime family and friends."

Lady Viola's remark brought him firmly into the present. Luckily without a misstep.

"Yes, I admit it is." Family and friends who were there for him when he needed them. "Do you not have close friends and relations?"

The moment he posed the question—really out of something to move the conversation along politely—he realized she quite possibly did not. Her infamous brother probably reined in her freedom.

Her cheeks colored. "Recent events in my family have kept me close to home, my lord."

So they both had secrets to suppress from society at large.

The music ended. *Good lord*, what to do next? Women expected conversation, maybe refreshments, right? He just wanted to be with Bertie.

Percival searched for Penelope and Bertram. He saw them leave for the terrace through the ballroom's French doors. It would be awkward to suggest they follow. Lady Viola would probably expect him to woo her in the moonlight, and Percival would not only be tremendously distracted he'd have no idea what to say to a woman.

Lady Viola wrapped her arm around his. "Shall we take a turn on the terrace, my lord? It might be good to get some air." She whipped out her fan as if in emphasis.

"Yes, Lady Viola, let's." He led her to the terrace where they were not the only ones seeking respite from the stuffy and fragrant ballroom.

The lady took control, directing him to the balustrade rimming the flagstones. She unhooked her arm and placed her hands on the railing, drawing in a long inhalation.

"Ah, the night air has a clean crispness to it, does it not?"

It did, he had to admit.

"I thank you for taking the time to dance with me, my lord. I can report back to my father that I did my duty. And, I suppose, you can report back to yours that you did the same."

Percival sighed. "Amesbury will ask which of the five young women I preferred."

"Five?" She laughed. "I was given the same number of beaux." She shook her head. "This marriage business is so tiring, is it not? If only young people could simply be with the person who incited fervor in their hearts and minds."

And loins. "If only." *Damn.* Did he just say something to make him sound like a cad? "I mean, not that you are not a fetching woman, Lady Viola."

"Thank you." She smiled. "But I am not the one who inspires romantic feelings within. Nor are you the one for me." She gazed out at the garden dimly lit with festive lamps. "Is that Viscount Ravensburgh with Miss Hardcastle?" She turned a smile to him. "Shall we follow?"

She angled toward him so closely he almost flinched. But propriety checked him. He did not want to cause a scene nor draw attention.

Her lips were at his ear. "I think we both would prefer to be with the one we most desire."

A prickle of panic slithered up his backbone. "How do you mean?" He kept his voice low.

Her lips stayed close, now almost tickling his ear. "You and Ravensburgh," she said quietly. "And me and Miss Hardcastle."

"Pen—" He stopped. He turned his head so abruptly she drew in a sharp breath, letting it fan against his mouth upon her exhale.

Good lord. Did Penelope fancy women? She was rather liberal in her physical favors, but she had never confessed to a predilection for women. Perhaps it was a new letch?

He stared at Lady Viola, their noses so close so as to be almost touching. "You and Miss Hardcastle? Do you know each other well?"

"No," she confessed, her body too close to his, feigning the expected intimacy of a besotted couple on the terrace. "I met her tonight. I am quite smitten. I would like to be her special friend."

Percival chilled. Why the devil was Lady Viola saying this to him? Although, if she wanted to be with Penelope, then perhaps she understood his relationship with Bertie? But how had she figured it out? *Fucking hell,* something he'd done had made it obvious. He closed his eyes, trying to shut out the reality of it all. He'd go to jail, be subjected to hard labor, dishonor his family name. But, God forbid, any of that should happen to his Bertie.

"My lord, I fear I have upset you. Please let me explain." She once again slid her arm through his. "Let us remove ourselves from this crowd."

He let her lead him into the garden, beyond the lamps, to a quiet corner. Thoughts of Bertie plagued him. Where was he? Would this be their final goodbye? He wasn't sure he could live without him.

Lady Viola steered him to the trunk of a tree, urging him against the bark, then looking side to side and even up at the branches.

"My lord," she said above a whisper, "I understand your desires because mine are the same."

"How do you mean?"

"I prefer the company of my own sex."

Now it was Percival's turn to look side to side and up the tree. He shouldn't admit to anything. "What makes you think such a thing?"

"Don't worry. Your secret is safe with me. I only came to the conclusion because I am wholeheartedly sympathetic to the feeling."

He still would not admit. Not until he got to know her better.

"I am in a far more secure position, I know," she said. "It is not criminal for women to form such friendships. You, however, are in a precarious situation, facing imprisonment and disgrace if you are charged and found guilty of an immoral, unnatural relationship." She slid her hands along the lapels of his jacket. "Trust me when I say I do not care what sort of relationship you have with Viscount Ravensburgh. And, if I am correct in my assessment, then I suspect you will not have a problem with the types of relationships I have. To further put your mind at ease with regard to Miss Hardcastle, she has already allowed me some liberties with her person not even an hour ago. She did not know it was me, of course, but she did know it was a woman. She accepted my attentions willingly. I intend to pursue my heart's desire."

Percival was stunned into immobility.

"Now, shall we go find your Ravensburgh and my Miss Hardcastle somewhere in this dark garden?"

Good God. Did he just find the most perfect candidate for a wife? "Yes, Lady Viola, let us pursue our hearts' desires."

Percival took her hand and went in the direction where last he saw his Bertie.

CHAPTER SEVEN

Bertram was having an emotional crisis in the middle of a blasted ball. He loved Percival, really he did. And he wanted to spend the rest of his life with him.

But Penelope was doing something completely unexpected to his sensibilities. And his cock.

First, they'd almost shared a kiss, then he'd become aroused while they'd danced, and now, as they strolled through the Fretherne's dimly lit garden, one whiff of her perfume was driving him mad with lust.

He had to tell her, he had to. Then he had to tell Percival. Or maybe tell him first? He and Percy had built a relationship on communication and trust. Such a level of intimacy was essential for all men who loved men. Their very lives were at stake.

What the hell would Percy say? He'd be upset. But he himself had to marry. Perhaps he'd begin to understand women a bit more? And how such a relationship could be beneficial?

"Bertie, slow down," Penelope complained. "You're practically dragging me. Where are we going anyway?"

Here was perfect, wherever here was. "Here." He moved her into the shadows beyond the party lamps. He took both her hands and stared at her face, letting his eyes slowly adjust in the dark.

She gazed up at him with a crinkle on her forehead, perhaps trying to see him in the dark.

"You've got something to say, don't you?"

She read him like a book. "Penny, I remember as my friendship grew with Percy, there was a very strong attraction. I knew immediately that I wanted to be with him in a way beyond mere friendship."

"I know the story. And I know you two are brave for pursuing your special friendship."

"Yes, well, I mean, I'd been with men before." He kept his words low, "So that part of the attraction was not surprising. It was more the desire to be with Percy in particular. That part was unexpected."

He drew in a long inhalation. God, how was he going to say it? "Then tonight, there was a moment that was equally surprising for me. But it was the opposite of what surprised me about Percy. Suddenly a particular attraction was surprising."

"A particular attraction?" Her voice was meek.

"For a woman." There he'd said it. Well, maybe only part of it.

"You're attracted to a woman?" She croaked a mewl. "I suppose that must feel strange for you. Is she particularly, um, mannish?"

He chuckled. "Oh, goodness, no. Far, far, far from being anything like a man." He squeezed her hands. "When we were upstairs, after Percy had left, and I was filled with emotion, you consoled me. Suddenly I was filled with, not appreciation for your sympathy, I mean I was, but more than that, I...I desired you."

Penelope emitted a gulping sound.

"We almost kissed, but we didn't. Then afterward, I realized I wanted to kiss you. I've never kissed a woman before. I've never felt the desire to kiss a woman before. But now I do. I mean, I want to kiss *you*, not just any woman. Maybe no other woman in the world. Just you, Penelope Hardcastle."

A little whimper escaped her throat. Was she upset? Surprised?

"Penny, say something."

She sucked in a breath, a squeak punctuating the end. "Bertie, I've had a case on you for a long while now. I knew it was wrong, so I kept it in check."

"It's not wrong—"

"No, listen. It's wrong to have such feelings for someone who's one's friend, someone one wants to keep as a friend forever. I'd hoped that the feeling would eventually fade away and that I would get to the point where I only felt friendship for you." She sighed. "But now you've said you feel desire for me, I don't think I can hide my own feelings any longer."

"What should we do?"

"Maybe we could kiss? See how that feels?"

His heartbeat picked up its pace to an alarming rate, rushing blood to his cock. The same sensation he'd had when he'd first wanted to kiss Percy.

He bent down and grazed his lips against hers. She was astoundingly soft, supple. This close, her perfume swirled in his nostrils, heightening every sense. He tasted her, dipping his tongue hesitantly into her mouth. She opened and let him slowly tangle with her, the act taking on a lewd quality, suggesting how a man might explore a woman, arousing him even more.

He parted from her, pressing his forehead against hers. "I see now how the feminine is so different from the masculine."

"And how is that?"

"You're so smooth. Men are rough and calloused, even on their lips. Definitely what's missing is that hint of whiskers."

She giggled. "Did you like it?"

"I did. But I already like you, so I think that helps."

"Maybe," she said dreamily. "What if I told you a secret? A secret about kisses?"

"Oh? Please. Do tell."

She huddled against his chest, and he wrapped his arms around her. "Earlier tonight, when I left you alone in the bedroom, I was so riled up I went into another bedroom. Someone was already there."

He chilled. Already jealous? He had no right to be. "Oh?"

"But it's not what you think." She tensed, then hugged him tighter. "It was a woman."

"Oh." Relief and curiosity burbled within.

"She seduced me. I cannot explain to you what she did, as I don't know if you would understand. But she pleasured me in such a way that a man rarely has. I guess because she is a woman she understands what another woman wants."

"But men and women have been paired for all of time. Surely a man can know what a woman wants?"

She chortled. "A good man knows what to do and an even better man does it."

He wanted to be that better man.

"So, you see, perhaps a person can change, or, rather, perhaps a person can expand their horizons. I mean, just because a woman pleasured me so incredibly doesn't mean I want to give up men. I guess maybe I want to explore women now." She lifted her head to look at him in the dark. "But it's difficult, isn't it? I mean how on earth do you possibly even start that conversation? It's one thing to be in a third-floor bedroom willing and ready for some sort of sexual encounter. But it's certainly another thing to be at an event, or at a café, or a park, or anywhere, and find someone of like mind."

"It certainly is. I am quite lucky to have discovered men of my ilk at university. I suppose that's how I learned to read the signs."

"Signs? I wonder if women have such signs."

"I would imagine they do."

She snuggled against him. "Bertie, what do we do now? I mean you and I for each other?"

"I don't know. I need to tell Percy I kissed you."

"I wonder if he's decided to marry any of the young women he danced with tonight?"

"As do I." And whether or not Penelope was still a contender in the marriage game.

Because if Percival didn't decide to marry Penelope, he would ask her. He wanted her in his life.

Even if she wanted to explore her new fascination with women.

A FAINT TRACE OF THE PERFUME of the woman from the third-floor bedroom drifted on the night air to liven Viola's senses.

"I do believe I've found your Ravensburgh and my Miss Hardcastle, my lord."

She tugged Norrington along the darkened path until they drew closer to a couple shielded by the shadow of a tree. A rustle of silk and a click of a heel against rock sharpened her attention.

"Norrington?" The voice was Viscount Ravensburgh's. Possibly he sensed the marquess's distinctive cologne heated from his exertions on the ballroom floor.

"We've found you," announced Viola.

"Lady Viola," said the viscount. "Are you still with Norrington after the dance? I had no idea he was so compelling a partner."

Norrington chuckled. Viola squelched a knowing grin.

"And now that my eyes have adjusted to this darkness," she said, "I see you are with Miss Hardcastle. I suppose this means everyone was enthralled by their dance partners so much as to take private walks in the moonlight."

An awkward silence ensued. Of course each of them was with the wrong partner, and quite possibly had been lamenting that very fact to the one they were with.

"Ravensburgh and I always have so much to gossip about," said Miss Hardcastle. "And we didn't want to drag Norrington away from his duties in finding a wife."

Norrington groaned. "Please. I would much rather gossip."

Viola precipitated Ravensburgh's chuckle by a split second.

"Lady Viola was helping me narrow down the choices for who was to be my marchioness," Norrington said. "And I've been helping her narrow down her choices for husband."

"Oh." Had Ravensburgh croaked this? Or Miss Hardcastle?

"'Tis true," said Viola. "I am to be married to a chosen stranger in much the same way as Lord Norrington."

"It's a horrid business," Ravensburgh muttered. "And one I am glad to not have to be part of."

Viola was a bit surprised. "You don't need to marry?"

Ravensburgh chuckled darkly. "My father is deceased, and our title is new. I do not feel the burdensome weight of tradition and expectation as do you."

If she and Norrington were to wed, the marquess's burden would be greatly lessened.

"Well," began Viola, "I am so glad we've found each other to say our greetings once again. Unfortunately, I must take my leave." Such began the lie. Really a trivial fib to extricate herself from the trio of intimates. "My father needs his rest due to a recent illness."

"Oh, I am so sorry to hear, my lady," said Miss Hardcastle exuding genuine sympathy.

"He is practically recovered. Just needs a bit of care for a while." Viola inhaled courage. "I would like to continue our connection, Miss Hardcastle, if I may be so bold as to ask."

There was a sliver of a beat before Miss Hardcastle responded. "I would very much enjoy that, Lady Viola."

Viola fished in her reticule for a calling card. She handed it to Miss Hardcastle. "My card. Please do call on me if you are nearby or send me a note if you would like to spend an afternoon together. Perhaps a walk through Kensington Gardens?"

"I'd love a walk through the park, Lady Viola. And I am, of late, quite free."

Viola smiled in the dark, hoping Miss Hardcastle could see or sense the emotion. "Then I bid ado to you all." She curtsied. "My lords, Miss Hardcastle, it has been a pleasure."

Pleasure. Indeed, that evening had had its share of them. As she walked away, she chuckled at her own joke. Now to find Father somewhere in a cigar smoke-choked gambling room. She couldn't wait to tell him she had found a husband.

And not reveal she had also found a lover.

Not bad for one night.

Wilton Crescent, Belgravia, London

PERCIVAL STOOD PASSIVELY as Armand removed diamond studs from his shirt front and gold links from his cuffs. As the valet placed each in the dish on the dressing table, the ping of metal against porcelain was the only sound in the otherwise silent bedroom.

The bedroom in the London house Percival shared with Bertram.

Being home—*their* home—was tremendously comforting.

"That will be all, Armand. Please see if the viscount is ready." Percival slipped off his braces and pulled the hem of his shirt from the waistband of his trousers.

"Very good, my lord." Armand bowed and departed through the adjoining doors between Percival and Bertram's bedrooms. Father had agreed that once Percival had met with the five candidates for the position of Lady Norrington, he could resume residing in his own town-house and not have to live at the

Amesbury mansion in Mayfair where the details of his life would be scrutinized excessively.

Thank God. He was desperate for Bertram's touch, desperate to be reminded their commitment to each other remained strong no matter what the future held for him.

The future… a *wife*…

Bollocks.

How the hell would he be able to keep Bertram in his life once he was married? Lady Viola surely wouldn't care if Percival's lover lived with them as some sort of lodger. But to the outside world, it would be quite peculiar. He and Bertram would no longer appear to be two bachelors sharing rooms until marriage, because one of them would be married.

Percival sunk onto the day-bed, dazed, numb. He hadn't thought it all through. The requirement to marry had been so sudden, so all-consuming of his days of late. He wanted to get the blasted business settled and go on with his life.

Except his life would irrevocably change after his wedding day.

He toed off his shoes and pulled off his socks. He couldn't live without Bertie, couldn't give him up because of some absurd expectations of the accursed peerage.

A yip presaged Orsa's animated entrance.

"Oh, my funny girl." Percival scooped up his beloved dog and nuzzled his nose against the top of her head, the silkiness of her tawny fur calming.

"Why so glum?"

Bertram's alluring baritone soothed yet provoked. The hem of his dressing gown skimmed his slippers as he sauntered into the bedroom.

Percival's shoulders knotted. He had to tell him.

Except as Bertram approached the day-bed, the split at the skirt of the dressing gown flapped to reveal bare legs. Which meant Bertram was thoroughly nude underneath.

He'd tell him later. First, he needed to be with his Bertie.

"Tired, I suppose," Percival said with a long exhalation as he put Orsa down. "The endless dancing and mindless chitchat. It's all rather vexing, really."

Orsa ran to her bed and, after three turns, settled down.

Bertram sat at Percival's side and took his hand. "I know the last week must have been difficult for you. I was frantic with worry. I'm glad we're together at last, Percy, my love." He kissed the center of Percival's palm. "I've missed you so."

The intimacy shot an intoxicating ripple of jubilation from Percival's hand to his heart, transforming into a tendril of lust that stretched to curl at his crotch. He reached for Bertram, cupping his cheeks, and pulled him to his mouth. He feasted on him, contentment spreading over every inch of his body while desire flared.

Bertram wrapped his arms around Percival's waist, his hands spanning his back, holding on as Percival pushed him to lie on the day-bed, his thighs straddling Bertram's hips. Percival broke from the kiss to nibble his neck while he unbuttoned the dressing gown. As expected, Bertram was nude underneath. He slid his hands across the lusciously masculine chest.

"God, I've burned for you." Percival bent over to kiss the flesh from nipple to nipple, twirling his tongue around each dark areola, his fingers digging into the corded muscles of his hips.

"That tickles." Bertram chuckled, and flinched before emitting a husky moan.

No woman could compare to Bertram. The female body was not perfect as was the male form. How the hell was he going to live a lie?

He needed to be taken in the most masculine way possible. Something a woman could never do.

"Darling, Bertie, I need you…" His mouth went dry, he swallowed. "I need you to have me…love me in a way only a man can love another man."

Bertram stroked his hair as he searched his face. "Percy, something's wrong, isn't it?"

He closed his eyes to dam the tears that threatened. "Please, let's savor this moment we have together."

"Yes, love, of course." He tugged playfully at Percival's shirt and slid his warm hands underneath the fine linen. He smiled and raised a brow. "What would you like me to do?"

Percival kissed his smile. "I need you to fuck me. Hard."

Bertram paled briefly, then blushed with a sly grin. "Don't you think it should be the other way around?"

"How do you mean?"

"If I fuck you, then you would be in the…how shall I put this? In the receptive role."

Percival blinked. "Oh, I see. Like a woman might be."

"Well, like a conventional woman might be." Bertram chuckled.

He was correct, really. Percival, as much as it went against his usual *modus operandi*, should act the sexual aggressor.

The viscount unplucked the buttons of Percival's trousers and drawers. "Although, I suppose, I could offer some encouragement."

Percival stood. Holding Bertram's gaze, he stripped off his shirt. Bertram slid out of his dressing gown. He licked his lips as Percival stepped out of his trousers and drawers, revealing his semi-aroused state.

Standing naked as he was should make him feel powerful and potent. He drew in courage, then went to the dressing table, grabbing a pot of cold cream and a towel. He placed both on the floor to the left of the day-bed.

All right. He was going to do this and do it properly.

Percival's heart thrummed as he knelt on the edge of the day-bed. He moved forward as if to grab Bertram's eager erection, instead grabbing his ankles and spreading open his legs.

"My lord viscount, how shall I take you? From the front or from behind?" Excited anticipation pulsed along Percival's cock. Both positions had their merits.

"Which is uniquely male, my lord marquess?"

"Ah." Percival let go of Bertram's legs and grabbed him around the waist, wrestling him until he landed on his hands and knees.

Percival dipped his tongue in the cleft of Bertram's buttocks, eliciting a twitch and a sigh. He wrapped his hand around Bertram's cock and slowly stroked as he continued to taunt the puckered hole of his arse.

Bertram groaned his approbation, thrusting out his buttocks to give better access.

"So eager, my lord." Percival chuckled, then fanned hot puffs on the flexing hole.

He bent down and picked up the cold cream. Bertram's body tensed as the lid scraped against the jar.

Percival smeared a dollop of the cold, wet cream where his tongue had just dallied, then gently worked the cream inside with two fingers, kissing the cheeks of his lover's buttocks as he delved further.

Bertram sighed.

"That's right, my lord, relax for me." Percival primed his cock with the remaining cream on his hand. "You know what I'm going to do to you."

Saying those words aloud empowered him. He positioned himself at the tight hole, then forged ahead. Percival's overwhelming sensual relief was met with a jolt and a yelp from his lover. Bertram sucked in air, then exhaled slowly, as if to calm himself. Percival continued slowly, occasionally pausing to give Bertram a moment to absorb the agony and accept it as pleasure.

Once fully embedded, a long rumbling growl emanated from his chest in chorus with a sputtered oath from his lover. He held himself in that position for a moment, his stones grazing Bertram's, before he began the glorious slide out.

On the return plunge, he grabbed Bertram's cock and pumped lazily, unevenly, distracted by his own sensual indulgence, his skin flushing as pleasure uncoiled, tingling the tips of his fingers and toes. This was what he craved, this quintessentially male connection.

He wrapped an arm around Bertram's waist and leaned over to press his chest to the curving spine beneath him. He panted ragged breaths as the beat of his heart kept pace with Bertram's. Together they sought physical release, together it would bring them joy. Together…

But not forever.

He tried to hang on to the utter happiness he felt at that very moment, to not let what lay in the future mar the euphoria of sexual connection and emotional gratification.

Percival gripped Bertram's cock harder and pumped faster as he slammed into his depths, squeezing his eyes shut against the emotional torments fringing the pleasure. Bertram was breathing hard, his torso bending and tensing under Percival's arm, all signs he was on the edge. Percival clung to his orgasm, not wanting to let go until Bertram could join him.

With a roar Bertram came, jetting his come onto the dressing gown draped over the day-bed. Percival slammed in one more time and let himself go, sagging against Bertram's back, clinging to him for purchase.

"Did that help take away your gloomy spirits?" Bertram's query held a playful tone. He gave a roguish shove backwards.

Percival chuckled. "Yes." He pulled free from their connection and stood up, grabbing the towel to wipe away the evidence of their love-making.

Bertram took the proffered towel to clean himself, then stretched his fatigued hands and wrists. He gestured to the bed. "Shall we?"

He'd missed sleeping with him. "Oh, absolutely."

Bertram climbed into bed, and Percival snuffed out the lamps before joining him. They slid side-by-side naturally, Bertram spooning, surrounding him, holding him securely.

He had to tell him. Bertram deserved to know. "Bertie," he said quietly, "I've chosen Lady Viola to be my wife."

Bertram stilled. "Oh? And not Penelope?"

"I cannot. I love Penny dearly." Percival sighed. "But trying to convince my father to accept her would be tiresome and aggravating. Father was adamant I choose from the five he and Mother had selected based upon what they said was weeks of research and investigation into a whole slew of women and their families. There would be a similar investigation into Penelope's background. Besides her lack of aristocratic blood, they would possibly discover her surfeit of lovers."

"Possibly." Bertram snorted. "Are all your potential brides virgins?"

"I don't know. I assume so." What a profoundly horrid thought to be the man who would deflower a virgin and not only not love her, but never want to perform the act again. "Bollocks."

Bertram lifted his head. "Percy?"

Tears smarted at the corners of his eyes. "I just want to be with you. Why can't I be with you?" How was he going to be able to be with his Bertie?

"And I want to be with you. It may take some time, some clever scheme, but we'll figure out a way to be together."

CHAPTER EIGHT

Amesbury House, Mayfair, London, the next day

Percival fumed as he paced the carpet outside the door to Father's study. Some urgent business had come up, a crisis that deserved more consideration than the pressing matter of the marriage of the duke's heir. The annoyance of the delay only heightened the irritating notion that the son of a duke had to make an appointment to see his own damn father.

The door to the study cracked opened, and Father's personal secretary, Wilson, poked his head out. "My lord marquess, His Grace will see you now."

Percival entered, the air in the room filled with frustration. Father sat behind his desk, his elbows on the polished mahogany, cradling his head in his hands.

"Your Grace, if this is an inconvenient time, I can return."

Father lifted his head. "Norrington," he began with a stale smile. "No, please, stay." He waved an envelope at the secretary. "You may go."

Wilson took the envelope, then bowed and exited, closing the door behind him.

Father inhaled deeply. "I always have time for my son." He chuckled uncharacteristically. "My son who will one day inherit all of this." He gestured at the piles of paper surrounding him. He leaned back and indicated the chair on the other side of the desk. "Please sit and tell me what this is about."

Percival sat, suddenly unsure what to do with his hands. He folded them in his lap. "Your Grace," he began.

Father shot him a beleaguered look. Perhaps he was tired of being a duke at that moment.

Percival cleared the frog in his throat. "Father, I have made my choice of wife."

"Already?" Father placed his palms on the desk and raised his brows as if incredulous.

"Yes."

He shook his head. "You had five dances with five women last night and you've made a choice?"

For a man for whom there was not much of a choice it was not a difficult decision. But what to say to one's father? "Yes."

Father sighed. "All right. But before you tell me who it is, I need to know one thing: Is she threatening to blackmail you?"

Good God. "Blackmail?" Should he even dignify that with a response? "Why would one of the women *you* selected blackmail me?"

"You are a duke's son, and you…" Father pursed his lips. "Well, you have a certain past."

And a robust present and future. Percival shook off his initial indignation. "No, the woman in question is not blackmailing me. She was, of all five, the only one I formed any sort of intellectual connection with. If I have to be married, then I would prefer it be to a woman who can hold my interest over dinner and, at the very least, be a friend to me." And a woman who understood his desire for Bertram.

"Fair enough, Norrington," Father grumbled. "Who is she?"

"Lady Viola Pemberton."

Father remained pensive for a moment. "Ah, the one with the greatest economic need to marry." Father eyed him. "She's truly not blackmailing you?"

Percival tamped down his anger. "Lady Viola is a very sweet young woman. And Mother will be pleased that I have chosen one so beautiful."

Father snorted.

"If you had scruples about her because of her 'economic need' why did you select her for me to begin with?"

"There is a sentimental connection your mother favored. Lady Viola's father—Rochdale—and I shared a room at Oxford." Father huffed. "Well, if there is nothing nefarious to worry about, then we'll move forward. Your mother will most likely want to hold a ball in your honor."

Christ above, not another ball. "I will do as you require."

"Good." Father eyed him again. "It was too easy."

"Beg pardon?"

"Your choice. I expected unnecessary quibbling and delays."

Percival sighed. "The deed had to be done eventually, Father. And, as you know, I have no need to woo a potential wife. I simply needed to pick from what was offered."

"Yes. I know all too well." Father smirked. "When you leave, send Wilson back in. I'll have to arrange meetings with the Earl of Rochdale and our respective solicitors."

Percival hesitated. "Shall I tell Mother?"

"Oh, please do. She will be so very happy for you."

By which he probably meant she would be greatly relieved.

Percival stood and left. The life he had been living was about to end. It suddenly felt all too real.

* * * * *

South Kensington, London, a few days later

PENELOPE TOOK A BITE of a dainty sandwich, trying to contain her giddiness that Lady Viola was her guest. Norrington had implied Lady Viola was perhaps not as wealthy as the daughter of an earl ought to be. So, when Lady Viola had sent a note suggesting a walk, Penelope responded with an invitation to stand treat for the lady at the South Kensington Museum Refreshment Room. The lady did not balk.

Lady Viola proved to be quite an agreeable and entertaining tea companion. And she and Penelope were more alike than one might think a daughter of a gentleman and a daughter of an earl would be. Lady Viola talked of making do with very little, of sewing her own clothes at times, and, because of that, diligently keeping up with fashion so no one would suspect her diminished circumstances.

The blue dress Lady Viola wore that afternoon was exquisite and set off the rich dark brown of her hair and eyes quite well.

Lady Viola placed her cup on its saucer and examined the tray of food. "The Marquess of Norrington and Viscount Ravensburgh are very close friends of yours, are they not?" She swallowed a crustless cucumber sandwich in one bite.

"Yes. We write when they are abroad and visit when they are in town. We're going to the ballet tomorrow night."

"Do you have many other friends? Other women friends?" Lady Viola had moved on from the sandwiches to the fancifully decorated cakes.

"Well, if my invitations are an indication, I have plenty of friends during the Season. I have accompanied Gertrude to her votes for women meetings. I've met a lot of women there."

Lady Viola smiled. A tiny crumb clung to the corner of her mouth. Penelope giggled.

"What's so funny?"

Penelope glanced around before licking the corner of her own mouth as a signal for Lady Viola to do the same with hers. The lady stared, puzzlement coloring her cheeks.

With another giggle, Penelope reached out and wiped the crumb from Lady Viola. The moment she did it, she realized she shouldn't have.

"Oh, my, that was boorish of me. I apologize." Penelope sought solace in taking a gulp of tea.

Now it was Lady Viola's turn to giggle. She raised her serviette to her lips. "It was a sweet gesture. I hope we can have the type of friendship where you feel you may do such things."

A flush crept up Penelope's cheeks. "I would very much like that." She really would.

When the teapot was empty and the sandwiches and cakes devoured, Penelope feared their afternoon was at an end.

"Shall we take a walk through Kensington Gardens?" Lady Viola suggested.

"Oh, yes. That sounds divine."

They sauntered down Exhibition Road arm-in-arm. To want to be so close, so intimate with a woman that the rest of the world slipped away seemed like such a natural thing to do.

"Let's turn here," said Lady Viola. "The path will take us to the Italian Gardens."

"A display of water will be restorative in this heat." Penelope unfurled her parasol. "You have a garden of your own, do you not?"

Lady Viola smiled shyly. "I do. It is a marvelous feeling to plant a seed, then see it sprout, and eventually to see it bloom and bear fruit. Or a flower as it were."

"What do you grow?" Penelope had never considered such a thing. What did one grow but roses? Perhaps violets?

"We have a very small back garden. I grow peas, lettuce, carrots. Some herbs. Strawberries in pots. Colorful flowers like violets." She offered a shy smile. "I've set up some discarded windows as a tiny glass house at the back fence where I can start some seedlings when the weather is still crisp."

"How very clever." They stopped before the Italian Gardens, a rectangular space divided into four quadrants of pools with fountains, the whole display limned by classical sculpture. "Is your back garden as big as this?"

"Our plot is long, not square like this. And very small." She indicated a bench. "Shall we sit?"

"Yes."

They sat on the bench, suddenly not quite sure what to do about their linked arms. Lady Viola unhitched their elbows, then took Penelope's hand.

"I've learned quite a bit about cultivating and nurturing since I've been gardening. Not all plants are strong enough to endure, and not all can handle a change of circumstance." She let Penelope's hand go with a squeeze and a shake. "Each plant is different. But more often, I've discovered incredible adaptability."

"What does that mean?"

"A seedling wants to grow. It wants to bear fruit. It will struggle against all odds." She gazed out at the late summer scene. "A plant has its determined nature. But sometimes, say under different circumstances, it is incredibly adaptable." She smiled at Penelope. "Like us people."

"Are we so adaptable?"

Lady Viola scrunched up her face. "Aren't we? Let's say you had expected to go to the museum's Refreshment Room and wanted chocolate cake. You had been hoping to have chocolate cake all morning. But they didn't have chocolate cake, they had made strawberry tarts instead." She looked deeply into Penelope's eyes. "Despite having wanted that cake, you have before you a delicious tart. What do you do?"

Penelope snorted a laugh. "I do like chocolate cake, yet I suppose if I could only have the strawberry tart, I would take that."

Lady Viola smiled. "Do you think it is the same for love?"

A flush crept up Penelope's neck. "Love?" What ever did she mean by that?

"I suppose I'm using the term loosely. What if you were offered a love affair with one lover and were very excited about the encounter, yet your lover could not appear and sent you another instead?"

"Sent me another lover?" Penelope laughed. "It would depend entirely on who it was."

Lady Viola leaned in closer. "If it were a woman?"

Penelope chilled. "A woman?"

"Yes, a woman as your lover."

She met Lady Viola's gaze. Did she know? How could she know? Only Bertram knew.

Lady Viola blushed then looked away. "I've been too bold."

"How do you mean?"

"I see the thought of a woman as your lover distresses you."

Penelope wrung her hands. "No, it does not distress me." That her secret was out distressed her.

"Then are you open to the possibility?"

Was Lady Viola flirting with her? Penelope had no idea how a woman might flirt with another woman. Lady Viola was very pretty, and something about her did attract. "I am quite open to new experiences. But how do you know I have not had a woman as my lover before?"

Lady Viola sucked in her lower lip then nibbled delicately, a crinkle forming between her brows. "I only know of the one."

Penelope's heart fell. "Did Bertram tell you?"

"The Viscount Ravensburgh?" Lady Viola gaped. "Oh. No." She lowered her voice. "It was I, Miss Hardcastle, in that third-floor bedroom at the Fretherne's ball."

A sudden dizziness descended. Lady Viola? Her lover that night? "How did you know?"

"How did I know what?"

"How did you know it was I on that chair, in that room?"

Lady Viola snickered. "Miss Hardcastle, you remember you were the one who was blindfolded. And there was enough moonlight to make out your features." She closed the sliver of space between them. "I could smell your perfume." Her lips grazed Penelope's cheek. "I still remember the way you taste."

Penelope's heart thudded as she tried to steady her breath. "You?" Her query fell hoarsely.

Lady Viola eyes widened as she knitted her brows. "Does this upset you?" Her voice dripped with frightened concern. "I don't want to upset you. I had hoped you might have enjoyed the encounter and would perhaps wish to continue." She shook her head. "Oh, I am a blackguard to have seduced you—"

"Shh, no, please listen." Penelope took her hand. "I was in the room to be seduced. It was wonderful. Such a nice change of pace to have been pleasured rather than being the one expected to give someone else pleasure." She drew in a breath. "Well, to give a man pleasure." Her eyes misted as she lifted Lady Viola's chin to look at her. Lady Viola's lashes were damp. "Don't cry."

"I'm overcome with emotion." She dabbed her eyes with a smile. "Shall we walk some more? I would like to spend time with you. Become better friends. I have another secret I am bursting to divulge."

What could be more astonishing than what Penelope had just heard? "All right."

Penelope stood, and Lady Viola followed suit. For a moment, a shy uncertainty made Penelope hesitate. Should they link arms as they had walking to the park? Would such a gesture announce to the world that they had been lovers?

Of course not. Everyone who saw them would think they were two friends in the park. Penelope linked her arm through Lady Viola's and led her back to the tree-lined path.

She gave Lady Viola's arm an affectionate squeeze. "So? What's your secret?"

"I am to be married to the Marquess of Norrington."

Penelope stopped abruptly. "Percival?" Her heart sunk. It was real. That Norrington was really getting married signaled the end to their close friendship. But that the bride was to be Lady Viola— "Do you fancy men as well as women?"

Lady Viola chuckled. "I most definitely do not. Only women."

"Oh."

"And I know about Lord Norrington's preference."

"Oh."

"I feel for this very reason we are a good match. And I am also quite pleased that a young lady I have set my sights on is his very good friend."

"Meaning me?"

"Yes, you, Miss Hardcastle."

"Please, do call me Penelope."

"As you wish. And I am Viola."

"Such an enchanting name. Like in Shakespeare's Twelfth Night." A play where the ship-wrecked heroine needed to dress as a man.

"Yes. I suppose my name is appropriate for me because of that." Viola laughed.

"I congratulate you on your impending nuptials, Viola."

So, Norrington was marrying one of like mind; an ally, so to speak, of his way of living. Would it make him happy? Probably. And that made Penelope happy.

CHAPTER NINE

Wood Hall, Hertfordshire, October 1880

Percival had never seen his ancestral home look so festive. Not even at Christmas time, although an early snowfall that year had made it seem they were in the very season. Garlands festooned windows, archways—really any and every dull space that invited decoration. Every guest was dressed to the nines, more so than during the Season.

Everything was exciting and perfect. The Duke of Amesbury was holding a ball to announce the engagement of his only son, the Marquess of Norrington, to Lady Viola Pemberton, the only daughter of the Earl of Rochdale.

The nuptial preparations were moving forward rapidly and easily. The settlement papers had been negotiated and signed by the relieved fathers. The poverty of the bride meant Lady Viola's request she have a proper wedding gown had to be honored. The best dressmaker had been hired and had already begun working on the dress. Percival considered it a wedding gift to have his bride dress as she had envisioned since girlhood.

Of course, she had, even as a young girl, imagined the preposterous notion of being married to another woman.

As he had imagined being married to a man.

He and Viola had fallen into quite an easy rhythm, each realizing how lucky they were to have brokered a marriage arrangement with someone who had no intention and no interest in sleeping with the other. Broken hearts, frustration, and misunderstandings would be avoided.

From his position on the fringes of the ballroom, Percival glanced at Viola. She raised a knowing brow, and a comforting reassurance washed over him. Theirs would be an unusual marriage, to be sure.

Absolutely everyone who was anyone was in attendance for the engagement ball. Percival's face ached from smiling out of politeness. Viola was remarkable in her ability to make pleasant chitchat with complete strangers, who, in time, would be annoying extended family.

A small orchestra stood at the ready to accompany the couple in their symbolic waltz. A nod from the duke sent the orchestra master scurrying into position. Percival took Viola by the hand and led her to the middle of the floor. As the orchestra commenced playing, they began their dance.

After a few measures, family dignitaries joined in. From the corner of his eye, Percival saw Mother dancing with the Earl of Rochdale. She was smiling cheerfully, probably because her recalcitrant son had finally deigned to be a respectable member of Society and take a wife.

The earl was smiling just as widely.

Apparently, the joyful emotion was infectious.

Genuine elation coursed through him as he turned a smile to his fiancée. She returned the expression with a touch of mystery. She seemed to be in love—or some such emotion women felt—with someone.

He grinned at her. He was in love as well. And he was determined to have his Bertie be a part of their marriage.

BERTRAM DRANK FREELY from the champagne that flowed at Percival's engagement party. Lady Viola seemed like a fine choice. The marquess had assured him the lady was quite disinterested in men.

Except the lady was smiling too broadly as she danced with his Percy.

Damn. Who was he to talk? He was half in love with their Penelope.

She stood at his side as they waited their turn to join the engaged couple on the dance floor. She grabbed his crystal coupe and handed it to a passing servant.

"Lord Ravensburgh, I need you to be able to waltz steadily," she chided. "But I fear you've had one too many glasses of champagne."

He'd probably had. "I'm celebrating, Miss Hardcastle."

"You're mourning, my lord."

Christ, she knew him too well. "I'll be fine to dance, Penny. And you know how to lead if I falter. You're quite good at that."

She chortled. "I've had experience with tipsy partners. Too many, really."

The music swelled in invitation for the rest of the party to join the couples on the dance floor.

He turned to her. "Will you do me the honor, Miss Hardcastle?"

Penelope took his hand and together they merged into the whirling vortex of dancers.

They moved as all couples attuned to their partners did: in perfect unison. His hand at her waist pressing and directing, she responding to his command, his view of her daringly low-cut neckline distracting, her perfume drifting up to tease his nostrils.

And for one moment—no, several actually—Bertram stopped looking at Percival and gazed into Penelope's blue eyes.

A blush colored her cheeks when she caught his gaze.

"Penny, a penny for your thoughts."

It was a silly joke, but a joke she laughed at nonetheless.

"I feel an intensity in your regard, my lord." She licked her lips. "It sends a thrill to my heart."

His own heart skipped a beat at her confession. Could he forget Percival for a moment while the marquess danced with his fiancée? With Penelope in his arms, he could.

The music came to its inevitable conclusion.

"Shall we say something to the happy couple?" Penelope asked eagerly.

The happy couple was suddenly deluged with other well-wishers.

"No. We'll have plenty of time later. In private." Bertram had a better idea. He leaned close to her ear. "I know this house," he said in *sotto voce*. "And I know where Percy's bedroom is. He won't be using it for a while."

Penelope flashed him the most astounding look of incredulity mixed with lust. "Oh. My lord. How intriguing."

"Would you like to accompany me on a little adventure, Miss Hardcastle?"

A flick of her fan covered her smile. "I would love to, my lord."

Bertram knew the way up the back stairs, through the servants' corridors. As boys, he and Percy had utilized the service access to his bedroom, thinking it quite daring at the time. In the last year, since they'd become lovers, Bertram had become quite adept at slipping back down the stairs unseen just before dawn after a night of passion.

The walk back to Ravensburgh Cottage wasn't far. It was frustrating that despite the two men sharing a home and bedroom in London, when they visited family in Hertfordshire, they were not allowed to share the same room.

Tonight, skulking around the Amesbury mansion should be a bit easier. While extra staff had been hired for the event, they were posted in the kitchen or in the public areas. Most likely there would not be staff in the family's bedroom wing until the party waned.

He took Penelope by the elbow and, as if dancing another sort of waltz, led her through the crowd of guests in the main gallery to a door tucked behind the grand staircase. There they padded quietly down a narrow corridor to a door behind which was a service staircase, the worn wooden treads attesting to centuries of use. He held a finger to his lips to indicate she should step lightly and carefully. She went first, he behind her as a gentleman ought in case she slipped or stumbled.

At the top of the stairs she turned to him and he nodded for her to continue up one more flight. Once upon the landing, Bertram slowly opened the door to the second floor, peering both ways before signaling Penelope to follow him. The carpet running down the center of the corridor muffled their footfalls as they glided along. Bertram examined the doors—some led to sitting rooms, some to bedrooms—finally seeing the indentation in the trim around one door. Percy had done that. He'd accidentally banged a heavy bottle of champagne against the wood trim and had paid a footman a guinea to fix the chipped paint in the middle of the night.

Bertram opened the door, a little afraid of what he might find—or feel. The room thrummed with memories of him and Percy making love, still in that passion of initial exploration and infatuation.

Was that all over? He loved Percy desperately. Was *in love* with him.

God. When was the last time he'd actually said that out loud?

He quickly ushered Penelope inside and closed and locked the door behind him.

What was happening now had nothing to do with him and Percival. No. It had everything to do with the dictates of the society in which they lived, the requirements of the aristocracy. Bertram was simply lucky he didn't have to bear the burden of being a duke.

Penelope emitted a breathy gasp.

The sound made him remember precisely why he was there: to seduce her. Or attempt to, at least.

"Such a masculine space," she observed in a whisper.

He looked at the furniture, the canopy of the bed angular not sensually curved, the upholstery and drapes bold stripes not fanciful *toile*. He'd never really noticed that such details signified masculinity, but a woman of fashion might.

"I suppose it is," he said quietly, letting her know they didn't have to whisper. Seduction was difficult at that level of volume.

She began to explore the room, brushing fingers across furniture, picking up objects. There was not much of Percy left. He had moved anything personal to their London house. Only historical objects remained, those which belonged to the dukedom and not any individual. The bedroom suddenly had the feel of another guest bedroom at a society event.

And Penelope was very much experienced with such venues.

He took her hand and led her to the bed. *Bollocks*. That was too obvious. Christ, what were they doing there anyway?

Bloody hell. He was ridiculously nervous. However, she didn't seem to be. She climbed up on the bed and sat in the middle, then pushed against the mattress with her hands and bounced a little.

She giggled. He clambered up next to her and tapped a finger to her lips.

That made her giggle more.

"Darling," he said. "Shh."

Penelope kissed his finger, then took his hand in hers. "Oh, Bertie, you're being too cautious. No one will be here for hours. We are utterly alone."

"I suppose. But the duke and duchess's bedrooms are only a few doors down."

"There's a party downstairs for their only son. They won't be retiring for quite some time."

Of course she was right. They were truly alone. Had he been looking for an excuse to not seduce her?

"Penny, I don't know how to do this."

She pressed her lips to the hollow of his palm, her breath warm, her kiss alluring. All sensation centered on that spot, then slowly spread out, somehow jumping from his hand directly to his crotch, instead of the long pathway up his arm and down his torso.

When she lifted her head, his palm was suddenly cold and bereft. She smiled at him. "I've imagined this moment for longer than you, Bertie. I've practiced it in my head. So, you need not be nervous since at least one of us knows what we are doing."

She sat on her knees and unbuttoned his jacket, then pulled it off, her movements as practiced as Armand's, and folded it carefully over the foot board. His waistcoat received the same treatment. She positioned herself once more before him, laying both her hands on his shoulders, then angled forward and skimmed her lips against his.

Desire for her flared, the same desire that had been sparked in the ballroom but had dissipated once the bald reality of seduction had come to the fore. He let her taste him, let her lead the way, let her ease him into the act. His body reacted as it would were she a man, his breath quickening, keeping pace with his heartbeat, each thump sending more blood to his prick.

He slid his hands up her arms, past the frill of her sleeves to her smooth, white shoulders, He traced the neckline across her back, hoping he might find the fastenings that could be opened for better access.

Access to what, he really wasn't quite certain. He'd imagined this moment as well. Apparently not very accurately.

She deepened the kiss, dipping her tongue inside him, so small, so easy to suck, so effortless to dominate with his larger mouth and need. Her body would be equally small against his and be swallowed by his embrace.

Hands on his chest, she pushed back, panting. "You're ravenous, Lord Ravensburgh." She giggled. "I need a breath."

"Of course, darling." He tucked a stray curl into her chignon. A curl that had fallen free during their waltz. If that were the result from only a dance, how disheveled would she be after making love?

"However do you maintain your freshness, Penny?" He kissed the pulse on her neck. "I want to spear my fingers through your hair and tear off your clothes." He flicked his tongue under her necklace and licked her skin under the jewels. "But eventually we must rejoin the party."

Her head fell back as she moaned, a sound so invigorating he had to restrain himself.

"If you were with a man," she said with a breathy cast to her voice, "what would you do?"

"Suck his cock. Or he'd suck mine. Whoever dropped to his knees first."

She giggled again. "But if he were sucking your cock, wouldn't you feel compelled to spear your fingers through his hair?"

"All he'd have to do is comb it back into place. Even with his fingers."

"Yes, I see. Men aren't as complicated as women are expected to be."

"We're rather boorish, especially when it comes to sex."

She met his gaze with a smile. "I know." She gave him a light shove. "Off. I want you standing."

Her command was exciting—and relieving, as he clearly had no idea how to seduce a woman.

He stood and waited as she climbed off the bed, then came toward him. She sucked in her lower lip as she tugged at the waistband of his trousers and worked on the buttons of his flies. Every flick of her fingers thrilled his cock, the anticipation of uncovering his eager member heightened by her perhaps deliberately slow-moving efforts.

His buttons undone, she moved her attention to his braces, unhooking them from his trousers at the front. He was entirely undone, yet his cock remained tucked inside his clothing.

She gripped his shirt and pulled him to her. She stood on tiptoe to rub her nose against his. "You're a virgin, aren't you?" Her tone conveyed a feminine sensuality he was unfamiliar with.

"I hardly think so."

"I mean with women."

"All right. I'll concede to that."

She licked her lips until they glistened in the pale moonlight. "When you fuck Percy, do you do it from behind? Or as a man might fuck a woman?"

Ah, now he could see how a conventional man would fall under her spell. She was unabashedly sexual. Such a refreshing attribute for a woman.

"We each do both."

Her eyes widened in surprise. "Oh." She placed her hands flat on his chest, her heat penetrating to his pounding heart. "Not the answer I was expecting."

"Which was?"

"I imagine you taking charge."

Was it an invitation? He wanted to, but how to proceed? Did he just—

Penelope was on her knees before him, taking his cock out from the unbuttoned flies, wrapping her warm, soft hand around him, taking the head into her mouth…

He jerked at the erotic touch, almost spending. He needed purchase. One hand gripped the bedpost, and he inched his legs wider apart.

Holy Christ. Penelope sucked with a vigor comparable to any man's but imbued with a delicacy a man would never consider. He swallowed oaths, so profoundly aware of her gender, not wanting to offend.

Then as suddenly as she had begun, she released him, letting his erection bounce free. She stood and kissed him, the taste of sex lingering on her lips, then pulled back. She lifted her skirts to fumble underneath. Her drawers dropped to the carpet. She picked them up and folded and draped them alongside his jacket.

She moved to the bed and beckoned him to stand behind her. "The best position for not mussing one's hair or dress is from behind." She bent over the mattress, lifted her skirts, and increased her wide stance.

Her buttocks were glorious, so…fleshy. Wide, and more voluminous than a man's. He rubbed his hands across the pale mounds, letting his fingers sink into the pliant plumpness.

"Do you know what to do?" she asked.

Did he? He thought so. "I…"

"Don't worry. I'll guide you." She wiggled her buttocks at him. "Aim just below where you might fuck Percy."

That was direct. And accurate. He grabbed his cock and slid it through the cleft of her bum, aiming lower than the puckered hole, exploring, prodding gently…

And finding a different sort of heaven.

So tender, so wet, so facile. He pushed further, Penelope's breathy moans encouraging. The passage was tight but slick and willing. He continued as long as his cock could go, pulsing with excitement as the passageway flexed and clenched around him.

He held himself there and let out a long exhale. He was inside his Penelope. The moment was everything and nothing like he thought it would be.

Slowly, he began the pull back, relishing every inch going out as much as he did going in. Penelope murmured exhortations, delighting in the act as much as he.

At least he hoped so. "Darling, are you all right?"

Muscles gripped his cock, sending a shiver of lust to spike his stones.

"I guess the answer is yes."

She giggled and rocked her hips in encouragement. "Just fuck me, Bertie."

He did so, increasing the pace of his movements, enthralled by the pulsating heat wrapping his every thrust. He gripped her hips, steadying her as he slammed harder, his rhythm frantic now, desperately needing to spend.

Desperately not wanting to.

The moment of orgiastic rapture came too quickly. He barely held back a growl as he pumped his seed, each jerk enervating. There had been no time to savor the rush, the explosion.

No time to consider that he had not taken precautions. He knew damn well how children were made.

"Penny?" He reached over to grab his jacket and fumbled for his handkerchief. He pulled out of her slowly, capturing his wet prick with the linen. "I apologize. I was incautious."

She straightened from her position bent over the bed, then grabbed her drawers and put them back on. "I'll be fine."

There was a melancholia to her tone. As if she had not found the act as satisfying as he. But her writhing and moans had implied otherwise.

He put an arm around her shoulders and steered her to the divan near the dressing table. He sat and scooted to lean against the back, then pulled her down to nestle between his legs.

She tensed for a moment before relaxing into him. His Penny was finally his.

PENELOPE LET OUT a long exhalation. "That was lovely, Bertie. I'm glad to have been the woman who introduced you to our way of having sex."

He hugged her close, his heat enveloping her. "But something was missing. I presume it was your pleasure." He kissed her hair. "I apologize for my inexperience and ignorance in how to please a woman."

At least he understood that. "It's rare for men to know how to do such a thing."

"I want to learn."

She twisted in his embrace and looked up at him. "And it's rare for men to want to learn." She nuzzled back against him. "I welcome the opportunity to teach you." Fleeting images of what his lessons might be like made her giggle.

He touched his lips to her temple. "Are we lovers, then?"

"I suppose we are. But what about Percy?"

"I don't know," he said with a sigh. "I mean, I love him, I want to be with him. I hope he is still able to be with me after this marriage business." Bertram shuddered.

Did marriage have to keep the two men apart? "Does Percy know you love him?"

"I'm certain he does."

"Have you said it?"

"Yes."

His answer held a trace of hesitancy. "When was the last time you told him you loved him?"

Underneath her, Bertram deflated. "I don't actually remember."

Penelope kissed his arm embracing her. "I implore you to tell him."

"I suppose there is some urgency now, isn't there? I only have three months before his wedding."

"I don't think his marriage to Viola will change how he feels about you."

"Viola? Not 'Lady Viola'?"

Was that too obvious? She should tell him, shouldn't she? "We've been spending time together. Taking walks. She's quite companionable."

"So why wouldn't this companionable young woman try to sway Percival's heart and mind?"

"Because she prefers the companionship of other women."

Bertram sat up. "In what sense do you mean?"

"In the physical sense."

"Oh." Bertram seemed to comprehend. "So, what Percival told me about her is true."

"What did he say?"

"That she was not interested in relations with men. That she understood his interests did not lie with women."

"Ah. But you're uncertain of her claims?"

Bertram huffed. "Admittedly, I do not know her. But she is from a family of compromised means and somehow worthy of Percival's hand. I don't know what to think, to be honest."

"Well, I can put your mind at rest regarding where her sensual interests lie, at least." Penelope faced him. "I had a most gratifying encounter with her at the Fretherne's ball. In a dark third-floor bedroom."

Bertram lifted an eyebrow. "The woman you told me about?"

"Yes." She turned away.

"You didn't know it was Viola?"

"I couldn't see her. I knew it was a woman, but she placed a blindfold over my eyes—"

"A blindfold?" Between their bodies Bertram's cock responded favorably to the notion.

"Yes." Penelope giggled at his reaction. "But *she* could see."

"And she pleasured you in a way most men never do."

"I told you that, didn't I?" Mortification rippled through her. "Perhaps it is more accurate to say most men I encounter do not pleasure women in such a way. There are a few gallant men out there."

Bertram chuckled. "My cousin Nicholas."

Penelope smiled. "Well, the Earl of St. Albans is one such man, yes." His wife was a lucky woman. "Viola knew it was me. And when we met face to face that night, I, of course, remained innocent of who she was."

"But she told you later?"

"Yes." Penelope snuggled into his embrace. "So now I have two lovers. I've never had so many lovers. I mean, lovers I want to continue to be with."

"The two of you have continued your affair?"

"Well, not exactly. We've spent time together. And there's been some kissing. That was delightful." Penelope sighed. She wanted to pursue more with Viola, but the engagement got in the way. "Now that she's to be a future duchess, she has so many obligations."

Bertram burrowed his nose into her hair. "Are we to remain lovers, you and I?"

"I would very much like that."

He kissed her temple, then her cheek. She turned around in his embrace and pressed her lips to his.

Lust seemed to overtake him. This time around he was not gentle with her. Instead, he devoured her like he might devour a man, thrusting his tongue as if he were thrusting in another part of her. He pawed a breast, massaging it roughly, a little ineptly.

She moaned under him, letting go, relinquishing herself to his virility.

So unlike kissing Viola.

She could definitely get used to the duality of lovers, the softness of a woman and the hardness of a man. She could be with both, could love both, could form a life with both.

And Bertram, with his exploration of her feminine form, was clearly discovering the notion of duality at that moment.

He broke free of the kiss to kneel before her. "Darling, Penelope, will you consent to be my wife?"

Silenced by incredulity, she sought air, disbelief and exhilaration smothering her. "Your wife?"

He grinned. "Yes. You and I together as husband and wife. Our lovers married. The four of us bonded."

It was daring, it was modern. But they were young and would be the vanguard of a new way of life.

Lucidity descended. This was real. "I would love to marry you, Bertie."

He embraced her with fervency, kissing her mouth, her cheeks.

"I'll talk to Percival. We don't want to intrude on their plans. Perhaps a very simple private affair for the two of us in one or two months' time. Before Percy and Lady Viola are married. Let them have all the fanfare."

"Yes. Yes. Whatever you wish."

In the meantime, there was so much to do. Life was taking quite the unexpected turn.

CHAPTER TEN

En route to Nice, France, January 1881

Viola stretched in a very unladylike fashion along the leather bench in the railway carriage, the *ca-chunk* of the train wheels lulling her into a state of pure relaxation. She rested her head in Penelope's lap and let the viscountess smooth her hair. Occasionally, Penelope dipped her head down to rub noses.

On the other side of the private car, her husband and the Viscount Ravensburgh talked and guffawed about something all the while touching casually, perhaps a bit erotically.

After their two weddings this was the first time the four of them had been together alone. The privacy of the first-class rail car meant they could be themselves for a moment.

Railway travel was wondrous in that one comprehended one was going somewhere rather than staying home not going anywhere, which had been Viola's life for too long. This current somewhere was Nice, France. The only other somewhere Viola had been was to finishing school in Switzerland.

And now she had done the precise deed which was the whole point of finishing school. She got married. To a duke's heir, no less. Just yesterday, in fact.

The wedding had been a pleasant affair, even with the snow and cold. Due to the reduced circumstances of the bride's father, the Earl of Rochdale, Viola's wedding was held at the Cathedral of St. Albans near the seat of the Dukes of Amesbury. Norrington had to live at Wood Hall, his ancestral home, for more than a fortnight to establish residency, pacifying the bishop and conforming to the requirements of the marriage license.

Despite Norrington's grumbling that he hadn't seen his true love Ravensburgh for far too long, the wedding had been a jovial and satisfying occasion. The wedding breakfast had been held at Wood Hall. Edwin had acted like the elder brother—and viscount—he was supposed to be. Papa had fawned over the Duchess of Amesbury, and she seemed to appreciate the attention. The Duke of Amesbury had given a toast, his well wishes for the bride and groom tinged with relief rather than triumph. Afterward, Viola and Penelope had taken a stroll on the grounds of the estate and shared a furtive kiss behind an ancient oak.

The two had spent a glorious couple of months preparing for their respective nuptials and deepening their friendship. During that time—with her wedding gown and trousseau plus traveling clothes all graciously paid for by the duke—Viola endured a lifetime of trips to the seamstress. Luckily, Penelope, and oftentimes her guardian Lady Gertrude, always accompanied her. Both women had knowledge not just of the latest French fashions but of what a lady of the *ton* might need and conferred with the *modiste* to garner the perfect attire. Plus, having Penelope by her side made every pin stick and corset tightening worthwhile.

Penelope herself was gathering the requisite wardrobe as she prepared to become the Viscountess Ravensburgh. The couple had decided to be married at the end of December in St. Albans, the bishop himself presiding. Compared to Viola's lavish wedding, the ceremony was simple yet elegant with an informal breakfast at the home of the Earl of St. Albans and his gorgeous wife.

And now that they were, the four of them, married, they were on their way to the south of France. The Duke of Amesbury had made all the arrangements: a house in Nice near the coast with exquisite gardens and servants aplenty to fulfill their every need. A perfect spot for a honeymoon.

Who was to honeymoon with whom would be intriguing. Viola and Penelope would spend time alone, she would make certain of that. From the viscount's glances at his bride, and Penelope's blushing at his attentions, the two were genuinely in love. And, of course, Ravensburgh and Norrington had a deep love for each other.

Unlike Viola and Norrington. She had been able to appear as the dazzled and awed bride at her own wedding because she truly was. She had always fantasized about an elaborate affair, a gorgeous wedding gown, and a journey to somewhere—anywhere far away from her brother. Norrington had certainly been a dashing groom and the consummate host.

Like any young newlywed couple, Viola and Norrington had been nervous. But unlike the typical newlywed couple, their nerves were not tinged with excited lust, but rather fear that they would have to go against their natures.

Because of progeny.

What would it be like for a man to be inside her? Viola had no desire to know and was not happy with the prospect of having to find out. The very idea revolted her.

And across the rail car, there was Norrington, caressing Ravensburgh, revealing a man who had no interest in bedding a woman.

She sighed. Her wedding night was not something she was looking forward to.

* * * * *

PENELOPE SLID DEEPER into the porcelain tub, the warm water embracing her like a lover's caring arms, soothing the queasiness that had started on the boat and had continued on the train.

From her vantage point, late afternoon sunlight spilled forth, drenching the bedroom in a golden glow so totally different than the bluish haze of England.

Magical. As was being a viscountess.

Ever since she was a little girl, Penelope had dreamed about her wedding night: the bridegroom handsome as could be, both of them nervous about their first time being alone and allowed to do as they pleased. She hadn't imagined the specifics, though: the who, where, and how. So being the wife of Bertram Atherley, Viscount Ravensburgh and spending the night in a sumptuous room in a villa in the south of France was wholly unexpected.

Bertie had been a gentleman, making sure she had everything she needed, including her lady's maid, a hot bath, champagne, and roses. Of course such gestures were probably subterfuge for his nerves. And everything he did was certainly a balm to hers after such an important journey and the first time Penelope had ever traveled abroad.

A light rapping resounded on the door. Probably her husband being a gentleman. She giggled. Her *husband*.

"Come."

Bertie strolled in with a bottle of champagne in one hand and two coupes in the other. His eyes widened at the sight of her. He blushed thoroughly before turning his back to the view.

He poured champagne into a coupe and handed it to her, his gaze averted.

She took the drink. "Have you never seen a woman before?"

He directed his attention to his own glass. "No."

Of course not. His one and only time with a woman had been with her while she'd been fully clothed. He'd proposed that night, but since then, propriety and circumstance had meant they'd not had occasion to be intimate beyond stolen cuddles and kisses. Not even after their wedding breakfast.

"Do you want to see me?"

"Very much so," he said, his back still to her.

"And I very much want to see you." She took a sip. "Are you a gentleman, Bertie?"

"What?" He turned, looking at her with incredulity. "You know I am."

"You can already see some of me obscured by the water. I want to see some of you." She sipped her champagne. "No. I take that back—"

His shoulders sagged.

"I want to see all of you. Right now."

He blanched as his forehead crinkled. Slowly, a blush crept over his cheeks. "I suppose I hadn't thought of that. You haven't seen me either." His brow furrowed. "But you have seen other men, right?"

"Yes." She eyed him. "Are you afraid I'll be comparing you with all the others?"

"Good lord, how many have there been?"

She laughed. "I'll never tell. Unless you tell me how many you've had."

He chuckled. "Touché."

"Have you ever compared Percy with another? Such as his form isn't as athletic, or his prick isn't as thick?"

"Heavens, no. Percy is perfect."

She smiled. "Of course he is. So why do you have scruples about my seeing you?"

"I do wonder how I will measure up in your estimation. I've no idea what a woman might think about a man. A man sees another and has a certain level of understanding about, well, aesthetic considerations." He glanced out the window and let out a long sigh. "Penny, I'm scared, I'm nervous. I love you. And I love a man. How are we going to make this work?"

"I don't know. But we'll find a way." She didn't want to talk about that right now. There would be discussions amongst the four of them soon enough. They hadn't even resolved their future living situation. "First, I need to see you naked."

He laughed, then gulped the rest of his champagne and put down the coupe.

His dressing gown was buttoned up from the waist all the way to the neck. He wore trousers, socks, and slippers. What else? Should she goad him by making a game of it?

Bertram began to pour another glass.

"Stop, Bertie."

He looked at her, the bottle in his hand. "Stop? Stop what."

"Fill your glass, but don't drink."

He filled his glass.

"Now fill mine."

He did as instructed, a dubious gleam in his eye.

"You may take a sip of champagne for every article of clothing you remove."

"Damn," he muttered. He put his coupe down on the dresser. "Anything in particular you want me to remove first?"

"Slippers and socks? That's four sips."

His mouth opened to speak.

"I'm not counting garters, darling."

He chuckled and sat down to remove his slippers and socks. His feet were not pasty pale like a typical English aristocrat's but retained the faded burnishing from his summertime adventures with Percival.

Did they sunbathe in the nude? A stimulating thought.

He took his four sips.

"Trousers."

He smirked, then turned so his back was to her. He fumbled under his dressing gown, probably unhooking his braces and unbuttoning the fly. He hunched over and stepped out of his trousers, then turned around with a flourish, his dressing gown billowing to show bared legs…

All the way up to his crotch; the glimpse she caught far too brief.

"You're not wearing drawers, my lord."

"I am not."

"Is this a regular occurrence?"

"It is, my lady, when in southern climes."

"How titillating." She sipped leisurely. "Your dressing-gown, Lord Ravensburgh, if you please."

He once again turned his back to her. The movement of his elbows indicated he was unbuttoning the robe very slowly. So slowly he began to hum a little tune.

"Is that Verdi, my lord?"

He chuckled but did not lift his head nor turn around. "Yes, my lady."

The Verdi progressed. Seemingly, his disrobing did not. Penelope dropped her head back on the rim of the tub. She slid her fingers along the champagne coupe, the coolness of the crystal discordant with the heat of the bath.

"Is this at all to your liking, my lady?"

She lifted her head. Before her, Bertie stood fabulously nude—well except for a set of braces still slung across his shoulders, the sight ridiculous in contrast to his supreme manliness.

He was sculpted to perfection, the curve of his pectorals, the straight line of his torso meeting the seductive curve of the muscles at his hips, angling toward his groin…

Good God. His groin. Dark brown hair curled and coiled around a cock jutting out prominently, below which hung a weighty sac between muscular thighs.

Penelope sat upright in the tub, jostling her champagne, trying desperately to calm herself. "I see you have one garment left, my lord. Have you had your sip from this last revelation?"

Bertie grabbed his limp braces and threw them to the floor before snatching his glass and downing the contents. He set the coupe on a side table with an exaggerated huff of satisfaction.

Penelope's heart picked up its pace.

He sauntered toward the tub, reaching her in two slow strides. He plucked the coupe from her hand and placed it next to his, then gripped the curved porcelain rim and bent over her. "Have you been satisfied, my lady? Or is there something lacking?"

She swallowed hard, her lungs heaving. "I am beginning to feel the inception of satisfaction, my lord."

With a grin he plunged his hand into the water. "My turn."

He grabbed everywhere, his fingers frenzied, unpracticed, unwittingly tickling her in the process.

And then he plunged both arms in, encircled her waist, and lifted her out of the bath, water sluicing down her body.

She stood before him, wet, naked, shivering, drips and droplets pooling at her feet. His gaze should have warmed her, but its intensity sent a chill through and through.

He grabbed a towel and dried her, his movements random, not wiping away every drop, his eyes not looking where the towel was placed, but elsewhere, at her breasts, her hips, her thighs, her mound.

His chest heaved at a rapid pace. "Penny, heavens above, you are a vision of loveliness." He fell to his knees. "I want to worship you." He embraced her around her legs.

Tears spiked the corners of her eyes. "Bertie, please. I am your wife. I should not be worshiped but joined with you."

He stood, traces of awe still limning his face. He lifted her in his arms, carrying her to the bed, where he turned back the covers and lay her down.

She tugged the sheet and counterpane over her still damp body, but he pulled them back.

"I want to see you. All of you."

His gaze darted about, his hands following the random pattern.

"You are so beautiful. I want to look at you, then touch everything."

She relaxed into the mattress and pillows, letting him have his fill of her, surreptitiously staring at his impeccably sculpted and honed body, touching him when she thought he might not notice.

He cupped her mound, licking his lips as he stared at his prize. "This is the locus of pleasure, is it not?"

She smiled at his innocent query. "One of them."

He maneuvered his body until he was between her legs, bending her knees and spreading them open, his face at the apex of her thighs.

A puff of hot air on her quim made her jerk up. Her husband placed his hands under her buttocks and steadied her.

Using his thumbs he parted her sex, licking his lips as he did so. She was incredibly wet for him.

Bertie stared at her plump sticky folds. She flexed. He gulped.

"I saw that." His voice was tinged with incredulity.

"You were meant to."

He fumbled, then seemed to comprehend the landscape before him. "Ah, here it is. The pearl of pleasure." He leaned in and flicked his tongue with startling precision.

She gasped. And as he continued sucking and licking, her gasp melted into a long slow moan.

Somehow this man who loved men had learned a woman's primal pleasure. He continued to bedevil her, adding his finger to the mix.

And then he pulled back to let his hand take control.

How he knew what to do, she didn't want to know, she just wanted to wallow in his attentions. He massaged her clit until he reached that point between too much and not enough.

She relented, letting her body sink into the mattress as her mind tried to make sense of the sensual onslaught. He slid up the mattress to lay beside her, his breath hot on her cheek, murmuring encouragements as he relentlessly pleasured her. She sucked in air, her mind chaotic, simultaneously letting go and wanting to seize the sensations, to keep them, treasure them, grappling to not let them slip from her grasp—

The inexorable explosion of pleasure was too brief. She'd wanted it to last forever, wanted Bertie's nude body against hers, his warm whispers on her cheek to last forever.

Instead, she would have to be satisfied with his slaking one moment of her lust.

She stared at the ceiling. "Oh my, Bertie. Wherever did you learn to do that?"

He skated a finger between her breasts. "My cousin is not only a doctor who can provide very accurate descriptions of body parts, he is, rumor has it, a fabulous lover and knows which of those body parts elicits pleasure."

She glared at him, mortified. "You talked to Nicholas about me?"

He grinned. "I asked him about women." He fondled a breast, flicking a finger across her puckered nipple. "I never mentioned your name. I only called you my bride. Of course he knew who I was talking about. Still, he kept the information very general."

She shook her head and laughed. "I will have to thank the earl one of these days."

"I think, perhaps, seeing your glowing smile while you cling to my arm at some society event will reflect your gratitude well enough."

She reached for him. "What about your pleasure, my husband?" The epithet still seemed peculiar to say.

Bertram rolled on top of her, urging her legs apart as he lay between them. His prick prodded her sodden cunt.

"What about my pleasure, Lady Ravensburgh?" He slid inside, his thickness filling her, spiraling her once more to the beginning of ecstasy.

He plowed ahead, slowly at first, too quickly picking up his pace as one excited about his first time. Because indeed it was his first time—with a naked woman, the woman who was now his wife.

He slammed inside her, lifting her off the mattress with every impelling thrust, his arms surrounding her in an exquisitely masculine embrace. He panted in rhythm to his frantic pace, filling her ear with the sounds of impending release.

She shattered in his arms, surrendering to his lust, letting him take control for the finish. He pounded into her one last time with a rumbling growl. He held himself aloft as he jerked his seed inside her, his face twisted in ecstasy.

Bertram balanced over her on trembling arms, his humid breath fanning across her face. "Penny, oh darling, that was amazing." His arms folded torpidly until he lay on top of her.

She stroked his hair, her heart and lungs recovering slowly from their exertion.

"It was, my love, it was." She kissed the top of his head. "Like how our marriage will be."

PERCIVAL LOOKED OUT the French doors of the master bedroom in the villa, the vista of a moonlit ocean romantic and compelling. Well, it would be if Bertram were his conquest for the night.

But no. A woman awaited him. His wife.

His hapless wife.

He opened the doors and strode onto the balcony, a cool breeze fluttering through his hair. He tugged on the collar of his dressing gown and closed his eyes, dreaming of Bertram's arms around his waist, of his lips tickling his nose, of the scent of his cologne suffusing him with sensual need.

A long inhalation returned his senses to the present, to the clean, crisp night air. Nice in January was not muggy like the summer. Neither was it snowy like England's current clime. Still, he'd be freezing if he weren't wearing his nightshirt and his robe. His new valet, Laurent, had insisted he be nude under his dressing gown to entice his bride. Armand would've never had suggested such a thing, which was probably the reason why Father had hired a new valet for his honeymoon.

Bloody Christ, he was on his honeymoon.

How in hell was he ever going to perform with a woman? The idea sickened him.

"My lord?"

Lady Viola's timid query came from the threshold.

And destiny crashed upon him like a ton of bricks.

"Yes?"

She slipped beside him, clutching her dressing gown, and stared at the moonlit view. "I know neither of us wants to," she said with a tremble in her voice, "but I think we should at least attempt to consummate this marriage. For purely legal reasons, if nothing else."

Yes. If there was no "consummation", there was no marriage. And, God forbid, there be no marriage. He couldn't go through another one.

Somewhere in the depths of his soul he found fortitude. He'd try. For the blasted dukedom, he'd try.

"How do you suggest we proceed, my lady?"

"Perhaps if we went inside and not shivered on this balcony?" Her arms were tightly crossed over her chest, her hands under her arms.

He chuckled. "I agree." He slid his arm around her shoulders and escorted her into the bedroom. He closed the French doors and drew the curtains across, not wanting anyone to be witness to what he had to endure.

She stood in the middle of the bedroom, her face twisted in, what? Concern? Fear? Sadness?

"Perhaps if we disrobed, we might find some aspect to excite the senses?" she suggested.

Christ. Viola was as nervous and as reticent as he.

He went to the edge of the bed. "Perhaps." He sat. "How shall we do this?"

She sat beside him and took his hand in hers. "I don't rightly know. I can take my clothes off first. Then you. Then we'll get into bed under the covers."

Her tone was so disconsolate, it moved him. "All right. If you want to go first, that would give me courage."

She stood and, keeping her back to him, slipped off her dressing gown and lifted the hem of her nightgown over her head. A moment later, she was nude. Her backside resembled the Greco-Roman statues he and Bertram had seen in the museums of Italy. She was not unpleasant to look at from an aesthetic aspect.

She turned around to face him. The statue analogy faded a bit as her breasts proved to be much larger than those of a Venus Pudica, and her hips perhaps not as wide. The hair covering her groin surprised him a little, but as it was a slightly masculine attribute, the effect was agreeable.

"Well?" she asked.

"You seem like a Greek sculpture come to life."

"Is that good?"

"I like Greek sculpture."

She smiled, then crossed her arms over her ample chest. "I suppose it's your turn?"

He rose and gestured for her to sit on the bed. She took her place in the middle of the mattress, crossing her legs under her. The crinkled tips of her breasts suggested she was chilled.

Percival stood where she had a moment before and unbuttoned his dressing robe, thinking about Bertram with every slip of a button through a buttonhole, his cock responding favorably to his thoughts. He slipped the garment off, then his nightshirt, tossing it onto the Persian rug to reveal all.

With a glance at Viola on the bed, his cock immediately went flaccid.

He felt exposed and embarrassed. The whole situation was not arousing in the slightest. It was demeaning and debasing. He suddenly realized Viola must have felt the same. God, to have put another person in this situation was despicable.

She affected a smile, perhaps trying to soothe his trepidation. Well, he could play this damn game if that's what it took.

He turned slowly to display himself in the round, cool air breezing across his cock and stones.

"So, how do I measure up?" He offered a thin smile.

Viola pursed her lips. "I'll admit there is a certain admirable quality to your physique," she said, "above the hips."

He laughed. What a way to start a marriage. Most likely if they'd been attracted to each other, they would not have seen the need to pose like this.

He climbed on the bed beside her. "Now what?"

"I suppose we get under the covers."

"All right."

After turning off the bedside lamps, they climbed under the covers and lay there, side by side, not touching, not wanting to touch.

His body was not responding in any sort of sensual way. He really wanted to go to sleep, but his brain was miserably agitated.

"Viola?"

"Yes?"

"Would you be upset if I went to sleep?"

She exhaled heavily, then giggled. "Not at all. I must admit I was not looking forward to the act."

"I don't think I could, er, 'perform', as it were."

"Nor could I."

Relief poured over him, so much so he reached for her, and pulled her to him. She resisted a moment, then her tension melted as she nestled in the crook of his arm. Her skin was cold. He embraced her more tightly.

"This whole business is frustrating," he said. "I wish"—it was preposterous—"Christ, I wish society could just accept that some of us do not want to be with a person of the opposite sex. It is as natural for me to want to be with Bertie as it was for the queen to want to be with Prince Albert."

She laid her hand over his heart. "I completely understand. I much prefer to be with my own sex. However, I have known it to be true that a person can love both sexes. Unfortunately, for our sakes, I do not share the sentiment. Although I do accept that Penelope wants to be with her husband."

Ah, yes. Bertram certainly was relishing his freedom to explore his fascination with Penelope. It rankled, but Percival clung to the hope that Bertram would choose him, should a choice have to be made.

He sighed. "So, what do we do now? I'm supposed to produce an heir. I mean, *we're* supposed to produce an heir. How the hell do two people in our position produce heirs?"

"Honestly? I have no idea."

Neither did he. Surely, he was not the first peer to not fancy women? There must have been others. What had they done? How could one perform one's duty if one were currently as flaccid as he, even while holding a naked woman in his arms?

How did a man become erect? Perhaps if he thought of Bertram? Or—dare he think it—if Bertram were with them in their bed? Bertram could suck him until he was on the verge of spending, and then he could deposit his emission inside his wife…

What a horrid, vile thought.

Especially since, as he'd heard, a woman might not get with child on the first go. *Jesus,* how many times would they have to perform such a bizarre threesome?

"What if Bertie could perform the deed?" *Bollocks.* Had he just said that out loud?

"Bertie?" Viola raised herself on an elbow. "Now you want me to sleep with Lord Ravensburgh?"

"No. Sorry, I simply meant that at least he could perform, whereas I cannot."

She let out a breath. "I suppose it is an idea to keep in mind. I'd want Penelope in the room with me, though."

Percival chuckled.

"What's so funny?"

"That is exactly what I was thinking. To have Bertie in the room with you and me, to help me perform. And then I thought, why not just have Bertie do it instead."

Viola got out of bed and put her nightgown back on. "Well, my lord, if I have to do my duty and carry a child, it is only fair that you do your duty as well."

"Do you not want children?" Percival put on his nightshirt and returned to bed.

"The idea has never been appealing to me." Viola climbed in beside him.

"Oh." She was right. If she had to carry the brat, then it was only fair the brat be his. "Damn, maybe this marriage wasn't the best idea."

She swatted his chest. "Now you tell me."

"Let's both think this through. At the very least we can keep up the semblance of a marriage for appearance's sake and sleep together from time to time, such as we are now."

"I suppose." She twisted in his arms to press her back to his chest, her feet tangling with his momentarily.

"Jesus! Are your feet always this cold?"

She laughed. "Oh, no. Sometimes they're colder."

He gave his wife a squeeze. Rumpled sheets would be the sign that they had slept together, and if any of the French servants were hired to spy on him, word would get back to Father that Lord Norrington had indeed slept with Lady Norrington. That should satisfy the duke.

Percival sighed inwardly as he made himself comfortable. To merely sleep. On his wedding night.

BERTRAM PUT DOWN his coffee cup and savored the cool morning air. The scent of sea and sand swam in his senses. The honeymoon villa was in a different part of Nice than their usual residence, and the view from the terrace outside the parlor was of the water rather than of the town. A lovely spot for breakfasting.

The door to the terrace flew open and Percival strode through, plunking himself down on the seat across the table. "My wedding night was a disaster. How was yours?"

Bertram eyed him. The marquess was dressed in his morning suit. He scowled as he poured his coffee, while behind him the gorgeous view of the Mediterranean went unappreciated.

"Well, given that I'm actually in love with my wife," Bertram dared, "I would imagine that my wedding night was a damn sight better than yours."

Percival glared at him. "Did you even think of me?"

"What? On my wedding night?" Bertram glared back, then grinned. "Yes, love. I did think of you." He thought of him too much.

"Humph." Percival returned to his coffee.

"What happened last night?" Bertram asked with genuine concern.

Percival shook his head. "I can't, Bertie. I just cannot have sexual relations with a woman." He slapped his hand on the table rattling the porcelain cups. "How the bloody hell am I supposed to produce an heir?"

It was clearly a rhetorical question, but Bertram was willing to give it serious consideration. "I don't know, Percy. But we'll come up with something." He should change the subject. "Why are you already dressed? Do you have an early appointment?"

"Larron thought it unseemly that I breakfast with you *en déshabillé*. Armand would have never said such a thing."

"No, he wouldn't." Clearly, since Armand acted as Bertram's honeymoon valet and Bertram was indeed in his dressing gown. "Who's 'Larron'?"

"*Un larron.* As in a thief. My pet name for my father's chosen valet Laurent as he deprives me of my liberty and privacy."

Bertram chuckled.

"When I said a dressing gown at breakfast was *de rigueur*, the disapproval on his face was quite apparent. Somehow, Laurent knows about you and me. And I'm pretty sure my father is using him to keep us apart."

"Blast," Bertram muttered.

"Do you know he was puttering about in the room when I awoke?" Percival's finger circled the rim of his coffee cup. "Armand simply knew when I needed him."

"Armand does have that knack."

"What if Viola and I were in the act, as it were, and he barged in?" Percival shook his head.

"So, Viola spent the night? In your bed?"

"For appearances' sake," Percival said quietly. "To make it seem as if we consummated the damn union."

Of course. "Interesting then that Laurent was there in the morning. As if spying on you two."

"I know. My thought exactly." Percival reached for a croissant. "Do you think he's sending reports to my father?"

"Hmm, possibly. He does have a strange accent when he speaks French, and not quite a French accent when he speaks English. As if he's lived in England for most of his life."

"Which means my father could have engaged him there."

"A disquieting thought."

Percival downed the contents of his cup, then poured himself another coffee. "Where is your comely bride, by the way?" he asked as he added milk.

"In bed waiting for your bride to join her, I should think." Penelope had been sleeping when he'd left her, and he'd seen Viola in the corridor before going down to breakfast.

"I miss you, you know." Percival finally turned his attention to the vista of blue sky and turquoise ocean, his placid countenance seething with some emotion underneath.

"I miss you too." Under the table, Bertram squeezed Percival's hand, his fingertips cold to the touch.

The marquess brightened at that and squeezed back. He smiled thinly. "What are our plans for today?"

"Our wives want to see Nice and visit the beach. Penelope has never felt sand between her toes."

"Never?"

"Never. And if one is to feel one's first sand between one's toes it ought to be Mediterranean sand."

"Oh, most assuredly." Percival sipped his coffee. "Even if it is winter."

"Percy," Bertram began tentatively, "what are your plans for today."

The glum countenance returned. "I don't know." He sighed. "I'm tired. I didn't get much sleep last night from all the stress." He shook his head. "Jesus, I couldn't get a stander because of stress, and now I'm tired because I couldn't sleep because of stress." He exhaled heavily. "Is this the life I have to look forward to?"

Bertram went to his lover, leaning over behind his wicker chair to envelop him in his arms. "You need something to take your mind off your worries," he murmured against his ear.

Percival stroked Bertram's arms under his sleeves. "I do. I really do." His tone lifted in pitch.

"Luckily I know a very good way to relieve stress." Bertram kissed his temple.

"Oh?"

"And I know a certain marquess who enjoys stress relief in Nice."

That drew a smile to Percival's lips. "I do."

Bertram pulled Percival's chair away from the table. He hovered over him, his hands on the chair back on either side of his shoulders. "Do you want a view of the coffee pot or the deep blue sea, my lord?"

A whimper fell from parted lips. "The sea, if you please."

"Right."

Bertram turned the chair around until the marquess was gazing at the view of the Mediterranean under the acute light of the winter sun. He tugged Percival's knees apart, then knelt before him, gliding his hands slowly up tensing thighs, squeezing the juncture at the hip, eliciting a twitch and a sigh.

The bulge at Percival's crotch strained his trousers. With languorous deliberation, Bertram plucked open the fly, anticipation intensifying in Percival's expression as each button slipped through its hole.

The purplish head of Percival's cock finally sprang forth, eager for satisfaction. It jerked toward Bertram's face.

He chuckled. "Patience, my lord."

A low rumble of an exasperated growl was the answer.

Bertram swirled his tongue over the bulbous crown before flicking along the seam on the underside, eliciting an ethereal groan. He licked the head until it glistened, then wrapped his lips around and slowly drew Percival's prick into his mouth.

Percival flinched. "Oh, God, yes."

Thoroughly wetting the shaft ensured the glide down and back was smooth. He loved tormenting his Percy this way, pressure with lips and tongue on the down stroke, easing a bit on the upstroke, every movement ponderously slow.

With both fists, Percival grabbed Bertram's hair. "Damn you, Bertie." The harsh tugs sent exquisitely erotic chills across his scalp.

The marquess always preferred a quick suck. But Bertram wanted to prolong the agony of frustration.

He picked up the pace a little, adding a scrape of his teeth on the upstroke. Percival sucked air through his clenched jaw, the sign he was on edge, wanting desperately to spend.

His hand wrapped around the thick lower shaft, Bertram increased his tempo, mouth and fist working in concert. Percival's thighs crushed Bertram's torso as he angled his hips upward. A glance at his lover revealed Percival no longer took in the view of the Mediterranean. Instead, his eyes were closed against the outside world, fingers still tangled in Bertram's hair, as his thigh muscles contracted and released.

Bertram slid his free hand inside Percival's trousers to hold his balls. As he sucked frantically, he squeezed the stones gently, satisfaction warming him as they tightened in his palm.

The marquess was almost there.

Now only using lips and tongue on the tip, Bertram gripped and stroked the shaft with vigor. A moment later, Percival jerked and tensed, hands steadying Bertram's head as he spewed his seed. Bertram sucked and swallowed every drop.

Slumped in his chair, Percival panted haltingly, his thigh muscles and his hold on Bertram's hair slowly loosening. Bertram sat back on his heels. He snatched a serviette from the table and wiped his mouth.

"Thank you, Bertie. That was magnificent."

"My pleasure."

Percival drew in air, his breath quavering and juddering as he sucked it into his lungs.

Something was wrong. Bertram raised himself on his knees.

Percival reached out to him. "I want to be with you, Bertie." Emotion twisted his face, his eyes bloodshot. "Why can't I just be with you? Why the hell do I have to go through this masquerade?"

With hands on either side of Percival's head, Bertram pulled their faces together until their noses touched. "Because the dukedom of Amesbury is a fine, long-standing title. You are a part of history."

"History. What is history to me? Does history respect men such as you and me?"

"You and I are not the first men of our kind and we will not be the last."

"Are you going to have children with Penelope?"

"I would like a son and a daughter. If it happens, it happens."

Percival stared at him. "Why don't you feel the weight of history?"

"Because my own title was given to my father posthumously for his heroism in the Crimean War. I respect my father's sacrifice and the queen's honor, but I was not brought up with aristocratic expectations. I inherited the title at a very young age and was the first to bear it. There is no weight of history behind the Viscountcy of Ravensburgh." He kissed Percy's nose. "You, however, were born into a two-hundred-year-old tradition."

Percival drew in a long inhalation, then let it out slowly. "Darling, will you help me?"

"Help you? Help you do what?"

"Create an heir."

"That's an odd request. What did you have in mind?"

Percival flushed. "I cannot perform with Viola. I need assistance. I thought, perhaps, if you could do something like what you just did, you know, getting me ready for the act, and then I could, er, penetrate my wife. Perhaps I could do it from behind while I look at you." He let his head fall back. "Bloody hell, I don't fucking know."

"That sounds intriguing. And what does Lady Norrington think of this?"

"She is amenable to creative ideas."

"Ah, well. Then perhaps she might also want Penelope in the room giving her pleasure."

Percival blanched. "Good lord. Will my heir be created from some perverse orgy?"

"Now won't that be fun?"

Percival laughed, a joyous melodic sound.

Bertram stood and returned to his chair. "And now, if you please, I would like to resume my breakfast."

CHAPTER ELEVEN

Penelope tried to open her eyes, but her lids felt as if lead weights were pulling them down. She'd been feeling very sluggish in the mornings of late, and this morning was no different, perhaps even worse. She felt as if she'd had too much to drink the night before. But she hadn't indulged to excess; well not with drink, only with Bertie.

So maybe that's why she felt so lethargic? Too much sex?

She rolled onto her back, hoping the new position would liven her a bit more.

"I'm glad to see you finally awake."

Penelope bolted upright. Viola sat on the divan near the balcony doors, a book in her lap, the sunlight streaming down upon her like an image of Danae being showered with the gold of Zeus.

Viola's eyes widened. The book slid to the floor with a thunk.

Only then was Penelope cognizant of her own nudity. She clutched the covers to her breasts.

A look of disappointment soured Viola's expression.

What was she doing? She wanted Viola. But she had never been nude in front of a woman before. Except her lady's maid, but that was different. So very different.

She relaxed her hold on the sheets. "Good morning."

"I didn't mean to startle you, Penny. I simply needed to see you after last night."

"Was it so very terrible?"

"It was nonexistent."

Penelope patted the space on the bed next to her. "Come." She scooted back to rest against a surfeit of pillows propped up on the headboard.

Viola strolled forward, the white silk dressing gown made for her wedding night hugging her curves perfectly.

She joined Penelope, slipping her legs under the covers, and melted against Penelope's shoulder, wrapping her arm around Penelope's waist.

Penelope kissed the top of her head and tried to remain nonchalant despite the warmth of Viola's touch on her bare skin. "Tell me what happened."

"I don't want to dampen what appears to have been a most agreeable night for you."

"Viola, you're hurting inside. Tell me."

"We couldn't do it. We literally could not do it. I remain a virgin, as, I suspect, does Percival. Well, in the conventional sense, at least. The marriage was not consummated. And we don't think it ever will be." She snuggled against Penelope's waist, under her breast. "Penny, I don't know how we're going to do the one thing that's required of us."

Penelope tried to understand. Like how there were some men she couldn't fathom bedding. "I'm so sorry, Viola. We'll find a way."

Viola kissed her stomach. Penelope flinched in surprise.

"Apologies." Viola pulled back. "I shouldn't have presumed. But you're so comforting." Her gaze fell to the sheets. "I feel so empty inside."

She looked so forlorn, so needy.

Penelope reached for her cheek, a blush blooming under her touch. She slid her fingers down Viola's neck to the buttons of her robe. One by one she unbuttoned the placket, revealing the diaphanous nightgown underneath.

She tugged the dressing gown off her shoulders, Viola helping to slip her arms through the sleeves. Before her was incredible beauty, Viola barely covered by thin silk cut and sewn to be as provocative as possible to a young groom on his wedding night.

But now Penelope had the benefit of the sight. She licked her lips.

"It's beautiful. Can we leave it on?"

Viola laughed. "It is fine, is it not? I'm glad there is someone to appreciate it."

Penelope brushed her lips against Viola's cheek, lightly pecking a trail to her mouth. She cupped a bountiful breast through the silk, the buoyant weight sending a thrill to her sex.

"Viola," she murmured in her ear, "I don't know what two women may do, besides what you did to me at the Fretherne's ball."

Viola fingered Penelope's nipple. "Well, being naked and fondling is one such activity."

She took Penelope in a kiss that burned with the passion of one desperate for intimacy. She pressed Penelope back to the mattress and rolled on top, thrusting her tongue into Penelope's mouth, the act bordering on the lewd.

"Do you know how to pleasure yourself, Penny?"

"I do." She found herself performing the act too often after unsatisfying liaisons.

Viola pulled up the skirt of her nightgown until it wrapped around her waist. "I have a special way we can pleasure each other. I would love it if you would help me, as my night was so disappointing."

"By all means."

Viola sat back and stretched out her legs. "You do the same."

Penelope sat up with her legs before her.

"So beautiful to see all of you, my love." Viola raked her gaze across Penelope's bared body, then maneuvered herself so her right thigh lay over Penelope's left thigh, her other thigh under Penelope's right.

The softness of thigh against thigh shot a bolt of lust to Penelope's core.

Viola scooted closer, then even closer, the hair covering her mons tickling the sensitive flesh of Penelope's inner thigh. Viola smiled as she inched forward until the lips of her sex were against Penelope's in a sort of kiss.

Penelope gasped and flushed at the new pleasure.

"Now rock your hips, like you are riding a male lover."

Wet sex met wet sex, the smacking sounds like lovers kissing, the sensation like a lover's mouth. Could both kisses happen at once?

Penelope grabbed Viola at the waist, holding her still as Viola ground against her. She wrapped a hand behind Viola's head and leaned in for a kiss.

Their bodies merged, tongues twining, as below their nether lips joined in sensual union. Viola adjusted herself, rocking against Penelope in a new way, shooting jolts of pleasure through her.

Viola pulled back from the kiss, breathless. "Can you pleasure me with your finger?"

Penelope pushed her hand between their joined bodies, sliding over her own clitoris with her middle finger. She bent her hand back to touch Viola, her fingers awkwardly fumbling.

"Your thumb. Use your thumb."

The angle was much better. She tweaked the flesh around the nub, eliciting jerks and mewls. She spread the sticky wetness over the nub and stroked delicately, evenly. Viola gaped as her eyes glazed over.

Penelope wanted more of her lover. She nudged her backward, keeping her connection with her hand, moving a little to the side so she could use all her fingers, bending her head over Viola to take a nipple in her mouth.

"Yes. Oh, Penny, yes," Viola rasped.

Keeping her thumb on Viola's clitoris, Penelope slid a finger, then two inside her sodden cunt. As she sucked the tender pink peaks of her bounteous breasts, she fucked her with her fingers, her touch no longer delicate on her clitoris but relentlessly rubbing.

Beneath her, Viola writhed and moaned, murmuring appreciation. Penelope was herself dripping wet, yearning for her own satisfaction. But Viola's needs were paramount.

Viola inhaled sharply as her hips lifted off the bed. "Yes," she cried. She choked out more moans before pulling away from Penelope's touch, Penelope following her.

"Penny," she croaked. "Penny, please."

Had she had her orgasm? Penelope was mortified that she had missed it. "Viola?" She sat back on her heels.

Viola stared up at her, flushed, a sheen of perspiration on her rosy cheeks. She reached up to stroke Penelope's face. "I know, it's different with a woman. You'll get used to it. You'll get to know and understand the signals." She smiled. "Oh, my Penny. Thank you."

Penelope sighed. "It was wonderful and new." A grin spread across her face. "And I want to do it again. Soon."

Viola laughed as she scrambled back to lean against the pillows. She smoothed the spot next to her. "Lie with me a moment. Before we go to breakfast."

"Yes." But an urgency cramped her bladder. "Excuse me." Penelope pulled out the commode from under the bed, and was about to open the lid. "You don't mind, do you?"

Viola grinned. "One of the pleasures of true intimacy is to be able to piddle in front of one another without qualms."

Penelope opened the lid, squatted, and relieved herself. She stood and turned to close the lid of the commode when a wave of nausea overtook her.

She vomited into the porcelain bowl.

Viola jumped off the bed and was at her side, holding her hair, a hand on her shoulder.

"Darling, Penelope. Are you ill?"

"I...I don't know." Penelope drew in deep breaths to calm her now shivering body.

Viola helped her back to bed, wrapping her in the blankets. She went to the pitcher and bowl on the dressing table and returned with a damp towel to wipe Penelope's face. "Was it so awful with me that it turned your stomach?" Worry twisted her face.

"No! Viola don't say that." Penelope sighed. She knew what it was but had been avoiding admitting it to herself. She should just voice what she thought was happening. "I haven't had my courses for two or three months." She gazed up at Viola. "I think I'm pregnant."

Viola flashed a quizzical look. "You and Ravensburgh? Before you married?"

"Yes."

"Does Lord Ravensburgh know?"

"I haven't told him yet since I wasn't sure. Do you think I ought? I mean," she said quietly, "do you think I really am with child?"

"I will admit I am not an expert, but I think the evidence points to such a happy conclusion." She took Penelope's hands in hers. "Tell him. Today. As soon as you can. Make him the happiest man on earth."

VIOLA NEEDED TO COLLECT herself before performing her part in the play that was her marriage. The day had been wonderful. She wasn't quite sure which had been better: Penelope pleasuring her or feeling warm sand between her toes while holding her lover's hand.

One more exhalation and she knew it was time. She dismissed Mathilde, the lady's maid hired by the duke, then slipped through the doors adjoining her and Percival's bedrooms and sauntered in slowly. Percival's valet Laurent was still undressing him from his dinner attire. Percival raised his brows as he flashed a knowing glance her way. They had decided that being seen by the servants together in an intimate setting would only strengthen their claim as a happy newly married couple.

She wore her white silk honeymoon dressing gown over her wedding nightgown to emphasize the importance of her attachment to Percival. She took her place on the bed, making herself comfortable against the headboard, and watched Laurent fuss over her husband.

Husband. It was still such an odd thing to say.

"Thank you, Laurent. That will be all." Percival waved the obsequious man away. When the valet was gone, Percival continued to fumble with his clothes.

"Would you like some assistance, my lord?" Viola asked from across the room.

He scowled. "No. I'm fine." He sat down on his slipper chair to awkwardly remove his shoes and socks.

She should broach the topic first. "Such a surprise about Penelope's condition, isn't it?"

The scowl lingered. "I suppose," he said with a grumble. "Or perhaps not. Bertram is smitten." He smirked. "And he's quite the bull in bed."

Ravensburgh had revealed the news over port in the drawing room that evening. Penelope had sat on the sofa, a smile stretching her face, her cheeks a pretty shade of pink.

"Do you think the duke will be angry?"

Percival turned to her, his braces hanging at his sides. "Angry? My father will be ecstatic that Bertram has found a woman to keep him preoccupied and keep his hands off me." He stripped off his shirt.

Viola snorted a laugh. "Ah, but Penelope's increasing condition might make the viscount want to seek out other opportunities for pleasure?"

Percival laughed. "Oh, Father is going to love you once he gets to know you better."

"How on earth does one even get to know a duke?"

He snorted. "I haven't the foggiest idea." With trousers off, he stood before her in the nude. His physique was quite pleasing— from anyone's perspective, really. Not enough to arouse the senses, but agreeable to look at, nevertheless. Like artwork in a museum, as he had said on their wedding night.

She unbuttoned her dressing robe. "Is the nightshirt no longer a fashion?" She slipped out of the robe and tossed it to the end of the bed.

"Well, since I don't have a spiffy silk gown such as yours, this will have to do." He stood before the bed, his hands on his hips, his cock swinging from a jounce of his hips. "Full nudity at bedtime as an antidote for sodomy."

God, how she hated the implication of that word. Acts that were unnatural and immoral. Well, she was very much natural, thank you very much.

She climbed under the covers, the sheets chilly. Percival turned off the bedside lamps, the dull glow of the moonlit sky their only light, and climbed in beside her.

In the dark, she reached for him, his flesh warm but his response frigid.

"I thought we might try to kiss, my lord. And see if it leads to anything."

He tensed and hesitated. "All right."

His hand slid across her shoulders, up her neck, to her cheek, as if he were determining where she was precisely in the bed next to him. He found her chin, her mouth. He traced her lips, then the skin around her lips.

"How very odd to not feel the abrasion of whiskers," he mused quietly.

"How very odd to feel whiskers abrading my smooth skin."

He chuckled. The heat of him signaled he was leaning toward her. She held steady in the dark, closing her eyes, waiting.

He crushed his lips against hers, hard and unmoving. No spark ignited. Nothing. She felt nothing.

His lips moved. Nothing turned to disgust.

She sputtered, spitting him away, recoiling back against the pillows.

A flush of abashment crept across her. "I apologize. I did not expect to feel such revulsion. You are a fine man, Percival. But, perhaps, not—"

"All right, all right. I understand. It's not pleasant for me either." He retreated to his side of the bed. "What the hell do we do now? Keep kissing until it just becomes something to do and let our bodies follow? Perhaps we should not bother with kissing and try…you know…the other bit."

She shuddered. "Not unless we have to." Perhaps it was time to bring up her brazen and audacious idea.

Viola had thought her idea too shocking at first. After more consideration, she'd wondered if she were the first bride in her position to think of such a thing.

"Percival," she began tentatively.

"Hmm?" Had he already begun dozing?

"What if we pretend Penelope's child is our own?"

He sat up, jostling the mattress. "What?"

"What if we ask Penelope to give us her child? We're all planning to live together anyway, so it's not like Penelope would be separated from her offspring. It would be more like she would give up any rights to name the child."

"Or have any say in where the child could go to school, or whom the child could marry."

Despite the darkness, Percival's gaze burned into her.

"I'm simply suggesting that we ask her. If she says yes, then we continue to stay abroad for six or seven months until she gives birth." She shifted against the pillows. "And when we return from the continent, we'll show the world the new heir to the dukedom of Amesbury."

A beat of silence persisted for too long. "Are you mad?"

"No, my lord, I am quite sane. I also know Penelope is young and fertile and can have another child after she gives us a son."

"Holy…" the expletive remained unfinished. He exhaled through his teeth with a slight whistling sound. He turned to her. "Have you discussed this with Penelope? Or Bertram?"

"No."

"No?" he barked. "Need I remind you it is their child?"

"You do not. I know that all too well." She was being foolish and selfish. "I guess I was thinking only of myself."

Percival plopped back against the mattress. "It is an intriguing plan." He folded his hands under his head. "We should discuss this as a foursome. I don't want any secrets among us."

"Of course. I didn't plan to kidnap their child."

"You just expected them to give it to you. For no reason."

Viola huffed. "For the reason that I love Penny and want to give their child the best life possible."

"Shouldn't we be asking the poor or our servants to give us a child, then? I suspect any child of Bertie's will already be given the best life possible."

"The poor? Our servants?" She huffed. "Are you going to boldly inquire about their courses and if they've shagged lately?"

Percival muttered an oath.

"At least Ravensburgh and Penny are already married, already pregnant. She's blond, he's dark-haired. You're blond and I'm dark-haired. Trust me, no one will suspect."

Silence descended. Not tense, merely quiet.

Finally, he grunted. "I suppose it would not hurt to ask."

Viola exhaled a sigh. "I'll ask tomorrow. But right now, I really want to sleep."

She'd wake refreshed, able to make the bitter proposition to her perpetually happy friend.

* * * * *

PERCIVAL PACED THE CARPET of the drawing room, watching his tea growing colder with each pass. He stopped before the polished side table and took a gulp from his porcelain cup. The brew was exquisite. Their villa cook had stocked up on a very fine Turkish tea.

"Darling husband, your frantic parading will surely frighten the Ravensburghs should they ever arrive."

He stopped and turned to Viola, the tension on his face melting as he saw the distress twisting hers.

"You're nervous as well." It was not a question, but an observation.

"Of course I'm bloody nervous—"

The shock of her swearing spiked his hair on end.

"I love Penelope, and I'm asking her to do a positively dastardly thing."

Good God. Dastardly? Were they both cowardly cads who would not fornicate because of mere squeamish qualms? Should he—they—just bloody step up and get it over with?

Of course they should. But only after they had asked Penelope for a very large favor. If she balked, then he and Viola would have to address those squeamish qualms.

Perhaps if they got sufficiently drunk…

The door to the drawing room creaked open, and the Ravensburghs entered.

Bertie was a sight for sore eyes. Dressed immaculately for a mere Thursday afternoon, his face flushed and grinning. He guided Penelope in, gazing down at her, she glancing and smiling and blushing up at him.

"So sorry we're late," he said as he turned his grin to Percival and Viola.

"Not a problem," Viola said. She tugged on the bell pull to request a fresh pot of tea.

Bertram led his wife to the sofa, helping her sit as if she were more than a few months pregnant. He took his place at her side and held her hand. He turned his attention to Percival.

"You said there was something we should discuss?"

Percival had fretted about how on earth to have a conversation with Bertram and Penelope. Were it six months ago, he would have asked them to meet him at a tea shop or his morning room and everything would be terribly casual.

But, *Jesus*, this was not six months ago. Every fucking thing had changed. Including whom each was fucking. Or not fucking.

He tried not to chuckle at his dark joke.

A quick knock on the door presaged a servant entering with the tea tray. Viola quickly dismissed the maid and poured tea for their guests, smiling wistfully at Penelope as she handed her a cup.

"Thank you for joining us," said Percival after a sip to ease his nerves. "First, we want to congratulate Viscount and Viscountess Ravensburgh on their happy news."

Bertram squeezed Penelope's hand as the couple gazed into each other's eyes.

Percival took another swallow of tea and a deep breath. He set his cup down. "We have a proposition"—no, that wasn't quite right, was it?—"a favor, rather, to ask the both of you."

Bertram placed his cup and saucer on the tea table and met his gaze. "By all means, Percival."

Another deep breath. "We would like to request you consider offering your child to us as our heir."

Silence sliced the room like a saber through paper. Bertram paled. The blood drained from Penelope's head and neck, rendering her a sickly shade of gray, her teacup rattling. Bertram took it from her before it could spill.

Viola ran to Penelope's side, kneeling before her, taking her hand, kissing her knuckles. "Darling, sweet Penelope. Is it such a shock?"

Penelope stared at her. "Shock? Of course it is. I was not expecting such a monstrous request." Her eyes glazed.

"But darling,"—Viola leaned in—"your son will be raised as a duke's heir and will inherit the dukedom of Amesbury. Surely that must be a wonderful notion."

"My son a duke." Penelope smiled, her eyes dreamy and pensive. Or perhaps confused and vacant.

"No." Bertram's curt reply was tinged with acrimony.

Percival met Bertram's pointed glare from across the room.

"Damn it, Percy. What the hell are you thinking?" He stood and paced the other side of the carpet. "My first child? I had never even considered I might be a father. I had thought I would be a life-long bachelor. But now this has happened,"—he gestured at Penelope's middle—"and my world has changed irrevocably. I will be a father, I'm thrilled to be a father, I want to be a father." He narrowed his eyes at Percival. "Don't you want to be a father?"

He wasn't sure he did. But he would have to be. "It's been a difficult few nights for us, Bertie," he admitted bleakly. "I guess I cannot expect you to understand, now that you're… you're…" He couldn't say it. Now that Bertie was no longer inverted. "We've made an effort, believe me." He glanced at Viola, pallid and teary-eyed at Penelope's side.

"I think I'm going to be sick." Penelope wiped away a tear before covering her mouth.

"Damn, damn, damn, damn, damn." Percival resumed pacing the carpet. He hit the air. "I apologize. It sounded like a good plan last night, after we tried…you know…in bed. I was being selfish." He pursed his lips. "I have a beautiful bride." He glanced at Viola. "I should accept my lot." He closed his eyes to bank the tears, but they fell anyway.

The room was painfully silent. Percival's head, however, pounded with overly loud self-berating.

"But then you wouldn't be true to yourself."

Bertram's calm words broke the silence.

"What?" Percival turned to his erstwhile lover.

"It is not natural for either you or Lady Norrington to be with a member of the opposite sex." Bertram sat and took Penelope's hand in his. "Penny and I feel differently. We can sleep with either gender. Well, I suppose, I couldn't imagine being with any other woman than Penelope. But that's neither here nor there. I guess what I am saying is that—" He choked with emotion and fell to his knees before Penelope. He wrapped her hands with his. "Darling, I love you. I love Percy—"

Percival's heart skipped a beat at the public affirmation.

"I know this is our first child. But I want our child to be raised by the four of us. If we all act as mothers and fathers, does it matter whose name the child holds? Which set of parents society believes the child has?"

Penelope blinked at him. She looked around at everyone in the room. "The four of us as parents?"

Viola got up from the floor and sat beside her on the sofa. "We'll raise it as our own. Two mothers."

Percival laughed. "God help us."

"Two fathers," said Bertram.

Penelope looked at Bertram and Viola, uncertainty clouding her visage. "But what if it's a girl?"

Percival closed his eyes. *Jesus.* He hadn't considered that. "Then you'll have to give us another child. As many as it takes until I have a son," he said.

Viola flashed him a perturbed look. Bertram fumed, keeping his apparent indignation in check.

Penelope rubbed at the deepening furrow above the bridge of her nose. "Am I, then, never to have a son for myself? For Bertie and I to love as our own?" Her voice cracked. "I might never have my own son for years." Tears flooded as she choked on her sobs.

Bertram wrapped his arms around her and offered murmured condolences.

Bollocks. This is not what Percival had intended. "Of course you may keep all your daughters." That did not come out right, did it? "Fuck," he said aloud.

Viola jumped up and went to him, her face stricken in anguish.

"Percival, I cannot have her in this state. She's wretched with grief. I need you to promise me you'll make an effort"—she gulped air—"that we'll both make an effort to have our own children."

"Damn it, Viola," he muttered. "You know neither of us can."

"I'm so in love with Penelope that I swear I will. I'll just give you my backside—"

He winced at that.

"And you can damn well pretend it's Ravensburgh you're fucking."

She did have a certain charm when she spoke with expletives. But would it be enough to turn him? "Damn." He spanned a thumb and index finger across his forehead and rubbed his temples.

"I can't stand this," sobbed Viola. "You are asking her to give up her child."

"Oh no." Percival held out his hand in defense. "Don't make me the villain. It was your idea, Viola, darling wife."

Penelope squeaked. "Is this true, Viola? It was your idea?"

Viola looked askance, lips twisted. "Yes," she said, finally looking at Penelope. "Yes, it was. It was my idea to have you give us your son, a bit of foolish rashness on my part, a protective measure. I should have realized what a horrific idea it was and how horrible it would make you feel, darling Penelope. I am so sorry. I would do anything to redeem myself."

"Including having my child?" Percival asked.

"No." Bertram broke in. "Percy, if it makes you happy, if we have a son, I would be honored for my son to share your title."

Percival met Bertram's emotion-laden gaze. *Christ*, he wanted to wrap his arms around him so badly.

"Or," Viola began, "if Viscount Ravensburgh and his wife would oblige for the viscount to be my bedmate, I would except. I would concede to have a child by him, as he does not find the notion of bedding a woman too repugnant."

"What?" both Percival and Bertram squawked.

Percival squeezed his eyes shut against the farce. They hadn't discussed the details of *that* particular point. It was wrong to spring it on poor Bertie all of a sudden. "No, no, Viola, darling," he said in an attempt to diffuse the situation, "I don't think any of us wants that."

Viola looked as if she was going to burst into tears. "I need a moment to think." She stared at Percival pleadingly. "May I have a moment?"

To think about bedding him? About possibly bedding Bertram? About whether Bertram and Penelope would consent to her bedding the viscount? Or whether they would consent to having their son be an heir to a dukedom?

Good God. There was far too much to think about.

"Yes," he said. "Please take as much time as you need."

Viola fled the drawing room.

CHAPTER TWELVE

Penelope rolled over in bed, extending her arm along the sheet beside her.

Empty.

Neither Bertie nor Viola was at her side that morning.

Well, she *had* slept late. Probably past breakfast.

She stretched, trying to ward off a wave of nausea, breathing deeply to calm her stomach. The queasiness subsided quickly, a hopeful harbinger that perhaps sickness every morning would soon be over. Some of Gertrude's friends with children had mentioned something like that.

Sunlight streamed through the partially open curtain shears, slanting over the floral motifs scattered across the Aubusson rug. Another fine day in paradise. Except that now it was a little less paradisiacal.

Yesterday, after the unsettling tea with Percival and Viola, the foursome had gone their separate ways. Penelope had felt betrayed, by everyone really. Bertie had held her hand as she'd cried in their bedroom. He'd apologized for his own behavior but could not account for the actions and thinking of their friends.

Later, after Penelope had cried herself out, she and Bertie had a simple supper at a restaurant with a view of the *Promenade des Anglais*. Conversation was mostly about the sites of Nice. After a few too many glasses of wine, they took a walk along the Promenade, arm in arm, in silence.

The quiet stroll had afforded Penelope an opportunity to think about Viola, how upset they both had been. She loved Viola, and her situation did warrant sympathy.

Two men had approached then, one gray haired, one Bertie's age. "Viscount Ravensburgh?" the gray-haired one had said with more than a touch of incredulity.

That had pulled Bertie out of his funk. He knew the men from his first journey to Nice. The middle-aged Earl of Berrick and his younger lover, Mr. François Bisset, seemed not merely incredulous that Bertie was in town during the winter, but that he was walking with a woman.

"My wife."

Lord Berrick had looked utterly shocked at the revelation. "We must have you over for tea," he'd said before the couple took their leave.

Then Bertie had explained that the two men were lovers. That France was more amenable to their kind of love than England, so they lived in France.

Suddenly, she truly understood that Bertie and Percival treasured their sojourns to France because of the freedom they felt. Men who loved men—and women who loved women—had to navigate a unique world.

That evening, Penelope had gained a deeper appreciation for what Percival was going through with the requirements of his marriage. And her heart broke for him.

She stared up at the ceiling, dark wood beams making a pattern of squares, each coffered space painted in intricate gold and blue curlicue decorations.

Her son a duke's heir? Her son a duke?

Penelope squelched a sob.

She could do it. She had to do it.

The door opened. "My lady?" Aline, the lady's maid the Duke of Amesbury had supplied her, strolled in.

Penelope quickly dabbed her eyes with the sheet.

"Oh, but you are still in bed."

"Yes, I am afraid I have overslept."

"Perhaps you are tired because *le vicomte a ronflé*...er, how do you say, he respired loudly last night."

That made her smile. Yes, Bertie did snore last night. Probably because of the wine—

Wait. How on earth did Aline know Bertie snored? Had she entered the room while they were sleeping? Perhaps the maid who lit the fires told her?

But why? Why would the servants talk about them in such detail? And why would Aline be so indiscreet?

"Will you take breakfast in bed, my lady?"

"No. Not this morning." Penelope pulled off the covers and sat on the edge of the mattress. "I would like to dress and have a simple breakfast of tea and toast on the terrace, please."

"Very good, my lady."

After that, she would smooth things over with Viola and face her fate as the mother of a duke.

IN THE LATE AFTERNOON quiet of the library, Viola stared at the half-filled page in her journal, emotions burbling through her at too rapid a pace for her to write them all down.

She and Penelope had spent much of the day together at a busy tree-lined park overlooking the Paillon river talking about their futures. And the future of their son.

The child would be *their* son, as Penelope had said she would only agree to giving up her son to Viola and Percival if she and Ravensburgh were fully involved in the child's upbringing.

"No nursemaids or nannies. We four should be enough to raise the child until we need a governess for his education. It will help us bond as a family."

Overwhelmed with gratitude and relief, Viola had merely nodded to everything Penelope had said. She'd agree to anything if it meant she and Percival did not have to be physically intimate.

Tears blurred her vision, and one dropped on the open page of her journal—where she had absentmindedly been drawing a portrait of her Penny.

She grinned. She used her handkerchief to blot the page.

A knock on the library door made her wipe her eyes as well. "Yes?"

Armand, Ravensburgh's valet, entered, his movements practically balletic. He came before her and bowed his head. "Good afternoon, Lady Norrington."

"Good afternoon, Armand. To what do I owe the pleasure of your company?"

He almost smiled. "Ah, I was looking for the Viscount Ravensburgh."

"I thought I saw him leave for a walk up the hill. But that was an hour or two ago." She gazed out the window at the fading afternoon sunlight. "I'm certain he will return soon."

"Of course. I only ventured into the library because reading is a pastime for *le vicomte*."

She offered a nod of understanding. At that moment, any other servant would have taken their leave. Armand did not look as if he was going to leave.

Something was wrong. Viola had no experience of how to face such a situation.

"Is your lady's maid satisfactory?"

Ah, but Armand had the proper skills to navigate the awkwardness. He got right to the point.

"Oh, my, no. Mathilde is terrible. She's never there when I want her, and yet she appears at the most inopportune moments." She tapped the cover of the journal. "I keep my journal in a locked box, and I am certain someone has tried to open it."

"Hmm. And Laurent, your husband's valet, is he adequate?"

"I suppose. He hangs about a bit too much. And when I go to my husband at night, he lingers. A valet should not ogle a wife in her honeymoon attire, should he?"

Armand steepled his hands and shook his head. A moment later, he nodded. He wandered over to the tea tray and fingered the silver teapot. "Shall I pour you a cup, my lady?"

"I can do—"

But he was already at her cup, pouring tea. Armand leaned in until he was close to her ear.

"I beg your pardon, my lady, but I must be candid. I fear the servants are not what they seem. I am concerned for your safety and that of my lord Norrington."

The gray-haired valet was something of a father figure to Percival. That he wanted to protect them was comforting.

That they needed protection was unnerving.

"Thank you, Armand. Is my husband aware of your concerns?"

"I am not certain. This is why I wanted to find Lord Ravensburgh. I am officially only acting as the viscount's valet during this *voyage*."

He placed the teapot back on the tray, then returned to her side. "That is an accomplished portrait of Lady Ravensburgh."

Viola flushed, her first reaction to cover the page of her journal.

"Did you know Lord Norrington has a talent for drawing? He is quite good."

"No, I did not know that."

"And Lord Ravensburgh is a writer." Armand pointed at the words on the page of her journal. "Like you."

She did not know that either.

Armand went to the door of the library and opened it. "I think the four of you will all get along very well."

Viola stared at the door as Armand exited.

BERTRAM FLATTENED HIS HANDS on the cool railing of the stone balustrade. Before him, lit up with a plethora of lamps, lay the manicured and terraced gardens that fronted the villa, the geometric order of the gardens at odds with the chaos of emotions churning inside.

Percival should have approached him first, alone, before he'd proclaimed his hare-brained scheme in front of Penelope. Yesterday, she'd had to retreat to the bedroom, tired from the stress of if all, confused about who was going to sleep with whom to create which children, and whether or not she was carrying her own child.

They'd had to separate themselves from Percival and Viola the rest of the blasted day and through the night. Only late that morning did Penelope finally settle her differences with Viola.

It was odd that Percival did not want to make love to his own wife. Well, perhaps not odd for Percival, but once Bertram had realized his desire for Penelope, the idea of being with a woman was not so strange. At least one very particular woman.

He'd found women beautiful before, on an aesthetic level. His cousin Nicholas's wife Helena was one such beauty. But no other woman had sparked a libidinous interest until Penelope. Something about her enthralled and attracted.

But Percival was wholly inverted, a man who loved only men, as Bertram had once thought himself to be.

And Lady Norrington—Viola—what of her? Bertram was not necessarily against the notion of sleeping with her until she was with child, but she also seemed to be much like Percival in her aversion of the opposite sex.

So, clearly there were men and women who only wanted to be with their own sex. How did such people procreate? And, if they did not, how did nature keep producing such people who only wanted to be with their own sex—and why?

He'd never before considered such notions. When he was younger, he knew he wanted to be with men, and once he had spent time with Percival, he realized he wanted to be with only one man. It seemed so natural. Not something to question.

Well, except that it was illegal. But so was a widower marrying his dead wife's sister. The law was not always reasonable, and often did not keep up with modern times.

Through all the recent changes of his heart, he never lost his desire for Percival. In fact, since he'd been apart from him just this one day, he craved him even more.

How odd it was that the heart and body were able to love and desire more than one person and more than one gender all at once.

The prickling sensation of a presence behind him disturbed his thoughts. Suddenly, the presence was at his side. Percival placed his hands on the balustrade, mimicking Bertram's pose. The marquess was as handsome as ever, a gentle breeze ruffling his blond hair, his dinner attire impeccable and hugging every taut muscle on his honed body.

Percival inhaled deeply. "My lord viscount, a penny for your thoughts, as mine are quite confused."

Relief oozed over Bertram. "As are mine, my lord marquess."

"Are we still friends?"

Bertram hid a smile. "Oh, very definitely so."

Percival sighed. "Thank God."

"Especially if I am to bed your wife."

Percival glared at him. "Darling, that was…a ridiculous notion."

"Lady Norrington is quite a luscious piece."

The glare turned into a scowl. "Don't you dare." Percival returned his attention to the gardens. "Viola and I are alike. Too alike, really."

"And that's why you two cannot perform with each other."

"Yes."

"And why you want to take my first child away from me."

Percival slapped his palm on the stone railing. "I swear to God I was not thinking clearly, Bertie."

"Percy," he said, drawing out the familiar name in an exaggerated way, "trust me, I understand. You voiced a rash thought brought on by revulsion at the prospect of sharing a woman's favors."

Percival glanced away. "You know me too well."

"I know you intimately. And I know your father is putting too much pressure on you."

Bertram approached his lover tentatively, the swell of emotion from missing him, from not being able to hold him in his arms, constricting his lungs. He placed a hand on Percival's shoulder and took his hand, a respectable and gentlemanly gesture should anyone be watching. "Penelope and Viola have already discussed the situation and have come to an agreement. But I need your guarantee that you mean what you say."

"About?"

"That we four will raise the child. I need your assurance that Penelope and I will be part of the raising of our own child, even if the boy thinks you and Lady Norrington are his parents."

"I truly mean that, Bertie," Percival said hoarsely. "The four of us…. What a curious idea, right? Perhaps when he's reached his majority, we'll tell him the truth?"

"Unless he despises the idea of being a duke."

Percival looked at him with incredulity. "And threaten his four parents with blackmail? Then we'll keep it to ourselves, won't we?"

Bertram smiled and looked deep into Percival's blue eyes. There was comfort there, history there, longing there.

Percival evaded his gaze. "There is another matter."

"Oh. What else?"

"What you said in the drawing room."

Bertram thought for a moment. He had said a lot of things. "What do you mean precisely? What was it I said?"

"That you loved me."

Bertram's heart clenched. "Of course I do."

"You've never confessed it in front of others." Percival gazed out on the manicured garden. "I suppose I was astonished. And thrilled."

Bertram's muscles strained from want of holding Percival in his arms, his lips quivered from want of kissing him senselessly, his cock stirred in his trousers, craving connection with the man he loved.

"It's true," he admitted. "I love you. And I will confess it to the heavens." He smiled. "That is why I am willing to go forward with this deception. I love you, and I want you to be in my life until death us do part."

"And I will love you for as long as we both shall live."

Tears blurred Bertram's vision, but not so much he could not see the tears beaded on Percival's lashes.

Bertram fought his body's impulse tugging him toward his lover. "Bloody hell, I want to kiss you."

Percival looked away. "Don't. Don't even think of trying. Please."

"Because of the servants?"

Eyes wide, Percival glanced around. "I'm certain my father has spies in this house. Not just Laurent," he said in a whisper.

"Armand is of the same mind," said Bertram. "He's certain the lady's maids are suspect."

"I've seen Laurent talking with some of the servants who seem to understand English a little too well. I've engaged a few in conversation and their French accents are not altogether authentic."

"Damn."

"That's why Viola comes to my bed every night. Not that you're not allowed in my bed. But I'm certain that if my wife does not warm my sheets enough on this honeymoon, I will get an earful when I return to Wood Hall."

Bertram offered a twisted smile. "So, I am allowed a night or two?"

Percival blushed. "I suppose." He smiled. "I hope." He sighed heavily. "But that brings up another issue. How are we to make it seem Viola is pregnant if she is not increasing?"

"Can she alter her clothing? Follow Penny's lead and make a pretense of it?"

"But then two pregnancies and only one child?"

"Right," Bertram sighed. "That is a problem."

"The lady's maids would know for certain. I don't know if Viola can hide her courses. If not, the maids will report back that the child is not Viola's." Percival huffed. "Damn. I should have thought this through."

Bertram blew out a breath through puckered lips. "Then we have to leave."

"Leave?" Percival croaked. "And go where?"

"I don't know. Italy?"

"Too obvious a destination, I should think."

Right. They'd spent time there two summers ago. Where else? And who could help them?

"Berrick," they said simultaneously. Their friend in Nice would understand their situation completely.

Percival laughed. "Can you get a message to the earl as soon as possible? Perhaps Armand can help?"

"I'll take care of it, love. Don't worry." Bertram squeezed Percival's hand. "Let's join our charming wives for dinner, shall we?"

CHAPTER THIRTEEN

Percival could not care less about the perfect view through Lord Berrick's sitting room windows. Sunshine glinting off palm trees lining the *Promenade des Anglais* was meaningless to him at that moment. Instead, he wanted to luxuriate in the feeling of utter insouciance he'd not felt since their arrival in Nice.

"My dear marquess, we can leave you to your reverie and discuss important matters elsewhere."

Basil Goring, the Earl of Berrick, was an exceptionally handsome man for one in his midlife, with the wit of a confident young man in his twenties. He did not stifle his amusement as he stood with crossed arms, leaning against the wall next to the perfect view.

Percival straightened in the easy chair. "I do apologize. There is a distinct lack of anxiety in your household that renders it particularly enchanting."

François Bisset, Berrick's lover, guffawed, then returned to fussing over the tea service.

The overly loud clink of a silver spoon against a porcelain teacup enlivened Percival to look up. Bertram narrowed his eyes in his direction.

Percival cleared his throat. "Thank you, Lord Berrick, for inviting us to tea—"

"Clearly as some sort of subterfuge," Berrick muttered. "I am surprised to see you in Nice as *hivernants* during January and not mere *étrangers* in July."

"Yes, well, indeed we appreciate your involvement in this subterfuge," said Bertram. "Lord Berrick, we need your help. We're in a peculiar situation and need not just material help, but ideas on how to escape."

"Escape?" Berrick and François exchanged glances.

And there was Bertram, clinging to his teacup in some sort of nod to aristocratic politeness, explaining the details of it all. How Percival could not create a child, and yet Penelope carried a child, but the wrong woman carried the child, and they needed to hide for six months so they could produce the child as Percival's.

"We suspect the staff are sending reports to the Duke of Amesbury," Bertram concluded.

"Where are your wives now?" asked Berrick. "Shouldn't they be part of this discussion?"

"They're walking on the *Promenade*," said Percival. "Pene— Lady Ravensburgh is inclined to the fresh air, given her condition."

"Even they have suspicions about the staff. As does Armand." Bertram nodded at Berrick. "You remember Armand Thibaut?"

"How could I forget," said Berrick with a smile. "An incomparable valet for the marquess."

"He is acting as my valet during this honeymoon, as the duke insisted Percival take on a man we've never seen before named Laurent."

Berrick raised an eyebrow at Bertram.

"Which is why we need to escape."

"Ah. I see." Berrick took his place on an embroidered love seat, his expression pensive until François brought him tea. All at once, his countenance brightened to a man in love.

François blushed and returned to the teapot.

Berrick's flush in response was fleeting.

That such an intimacy could be expressed openly was enviable. Percival slid a glance in Bertram's direction. The viscount caught his gaze and offered a heartfelt if weary smile.

"Well, I suppose this is a situation beyond having Lady Ravensburgh wear a wig and pretend to be Lady Norrington," said Berrick. "I cannot believe Neville would hire staff to spy on you." Incredulity dulled his tone.

Percival scowled. "My father has his reasons." He brightened. "You know all the servants in Nice and where they work, do you not?"

François chuckled. "He's right, Basil. You do."

"So," Percival began, "do you know anything about the servants at our villa?"

Berrick shook his head. "I confess I do not."

"I'm certain my father hired all of them in London to keep watch over me and Viola and to keep me and Bertie apart." Percival met Bertram's gaze. "Only at the last moment did Bertie have the idea to take Armand on as his valet."

"Please do have Armand communicate directly with me and François with names and any other information." Berrick sipped his tea. "What sort of chicanery were you imagining?"

Percival stood. "We need to leave Nice. We cannot pretend anymore." He massaged the pads of his fingers against his temples. "*I* cannot pretend anymore."

"All right," said Berrick as he put his teacup down. "Let's think about this. You cannot simply get on a train and leave because, presumably, you'll be followed. So, somehow, we need to make it seem natural that you are touring outside of Nice, but then you depart on a train or perhaps a boat to somewhere else. Have you thought about where?"

Another exchange of glances with Bertram. "No. Just not Italy. My father would think of that."

François held up his hand. "One moment."

He left the sitting room, and for a few minutes everyone turned their attention to their tea.

"Europe is at your command, my lord marquess." Francois carried in two large atlases, probably ill-used in the earl's library.

Maps. Percival loved maps. They held all manner of information. He jumped on the task of tearing through the volumes, consulting the indexes and tables of contents, searching for some kind of sign.

An atlas of ancient history gave him his answer. "Spain."

Bertram stared at him. "Spain?"

"*O lovely Spain, renowned, romantic land,*" muttered Berrick, quoting Byron.

Percival grinned at Bertram. "Remember when we traveled from Italy to Nice along the route the Visigoths took when they kidnapped the princess Galla Placidia?"

"Yes." Bertram laughed. "We took the train over the mountains when a boat would have been so much quicker."

"Well," Percival began with raised brows, "we'll continue to follow Galla Placidia's path to Spain. She ended up in Roman Barcino, which is now"—he consulted the legend—"Barcelona."

"Barcelona's a big city," said François.

"Darling," Bertram began. "Let's find some place quieter. Some place we can more easily keep track of the servants."

Servants. Right. "Do we need servants? We'll bring Armand. We can trust him. I'm certain Viola and Penelope can act as each other's lady's maids."

Berrick and François laughed.

"Who will cook your food?" asked Berrick.

"Go to the markets to buy your food?" added François.

Damn. "We'll rent a house with a local cook and whatever staff we need when we get there."

"Do you know any Spanish?" Berrick was full of questions it seemed.

"I do not," Percival admitted. "But Bertie knows a little Italian, and we both know French."

"Percy can rattle off Latin at the locals," said Bertram with a smirk as he set down his teacup.

"We'll manage." They'd have to, really.

Berrick chuckled with a shake of his head. "I'll send a note to Cora—you remember the Countess of Suffield? We'll arrange a dinner party where we can all mull over ideas."

The countess was another English exile living in Nice. While she and Berrick were friends of Father's, they both understood how the expectations of England's aristocracy could be burdensome.

"And if the two of you need a bit of privacy, for planning—" Berrick glanced between Percival and Bertram, his countenance sympathetic. "Or whatever really, François and I are happy to offer you our flat. As you know, Nice is known for providing respite to invalids." He offered a consoling expression. "Including invalids of the heart."

A pang of gratitude gripped Percival. "Thank you, my lord. That is very gracious of you." He glanced at a wide-eyed Bertram.

Berrick stood. "François, I think we need to confer with cook about today's shopping, *n'est-ce pas?*"

François took hold of the earl's hand. "*Oui*, Basil, we do."

Together they left the sitting room.

Percival met Bertram's stunned gaze. They were alone now. Alone in a place they both knew was a safe haven for their love.

In two strides, Bertram was in his arms, holding him tightly, his chest rising and falling with deep and measured breaths.

"Percy, I've missed you so."

Tears smarted in Percival's eyes. "I can't remember the last time I kissed you."

A grin spread across Bertram's face, his lashes also damp. "Here's a new memory."

He pressed his lips to Percival's, opening his mouth to slide in his tongue. Percival equaled the viscount's enthusiasm with his own sensual exploration.

Their longed-for reunion enlivened his heart and sensibilities.

Percival drew back a little. "I think we can do this. The four of us."

"With help from sympathetic friends."

"To whom I will be eternally grateful." The viscount's arms around him were comforting and intoxicating. "Kiss me again."

"With pleasure, my lord."

The DINING ROOM at the Countess of Suffield's mansion was beyond anything Viola could have imagined. Sumptuous green velvet draperies framed the view of the deep blue evening sky over the glittering sea. The heavily-gilded blue and white porcelain dishes were said to be from imperial Russia, the silk rugs from Ottoman Turkey. The silverware service was a century-old family heirloom.

The company around the dining room table was lively enough to take one's mind off the lavishness of the surroundings. The food was exquisitely prepared and wonderfully delicious. The service was impeccable. Yet despite all the trappings of high-born privilege, there was a distinct informality about the whole affair.

This informality extended to after dinner in Lady Suffield's drawing room where all gathered at once, and the men and women were never separated. Those who wanted to smoke cigars—Lord Berrick and Mr. Bisset—were asked to do so on the balcony and rejoin the group when they had finished.

Viola decided this was precisely how she would be handling future post-dinner activities as Lady Norrington. Whether or not the Duke and Duchess of Amesbury supported her in that decision was inconsequential.

The servants were not present in the drawing room, which encouraged unfettered conversation. Lady Suffield poured cognac and port according to her guests' wishes, choosing a tawny port for herself. The *grande dame* then took a seat in a wingback placed so she had a view of—or command of—the entire room.

"Now, gentlemen and ladies," she began with a toss of her gray coiffure. "Basil told me very little of your circumstance. Who are we saving? And why?"

On the love seat across from Viola, Bertram—their scheme had elevated their intimacy to the use of first names—cleared his throat and Penelope tittered nervously. Percival seemed unaware that anyone else was present as the drawing room was filled with classical antiquities. Lord Berrick and Mr. Bisset were still on the balcony.

Well, if no one was going to say anything… "I'm afraid, Lady Suffield, all four of us need a bit of saving."

Lady Suffield took a sip of port. "Go on. Tell me everything."

Viola fingered her port glass. "Lord Norrington and I are on our honeymoon—"

"I must say that part alone is astonishing." Lady Suffield glanced at Bertram.

"Well, Percival had to get married eventually. It was best he marry a woman who was like himself."

Lady Suffield raised a well-groomed eyebrow.

"You see," said Viola, "I, too, prefer my own sex. In fact, I am much enamored of a young lady—"

"Me," chimed Penelope. "The young lady is me."

Lady Suffield's brown eyes widened.

"And as Percival and I are finding it very difficult to…" *Good God*, how did one say it delicately? "Perform our marital duties, as it were, we are unable to provide the Duke of Amesbury with the one thing he hopes to get out of our union."

"A grandson and heir."

"Right."

Lady Suffield snorted. "Neville should be more patient."

"Pardon?"

"The duke himself did not marry until he was thirty-one. As I arranged the match, I remember it very well."

Arranged? Perhaps it was how marriages were done a generation ago. Except Mama and Papa were a love match. Or were they?

"Well," Viola said, "the duke may get his wish. You see, Penelope is with child."

"Congratulations, my dear," Lady Suffield exclaimed. She took a sip of port, then glanced around. "Oh, my goodness gracious, you mean to produce Lady Ravensburgh's child as your own?"

Lord Berrick and Mr. Bisset chose that moment to return to the drawing room.

"From the shocked and dour expressions, it seems Cora has just discovered the ruse." Lord Berrick oozed his lanky frame in a cozy club chair. Mr. Bisset took his place on the cushioned arm. "Lord Norrington, don't you think you should be a part of this conversation?"

Percival looked up from examining a Greek pot. He shook his head and took his place at Viola's side on the love seat across from where Bertram and Penelope sat.

The countess studied the foursome. "Just last summer, Norrington and Ravensburgh were here in Nice having *une liaison*, and now each of you is married? And the wives are having their own *aventure amoureuse*?"

Lord Berrick chuckled, the corners of his greenish eyes crinkling. "That is correct, Cora."

"Oh, what a tangled web we weave, *n'est-ce pas*?" Lady Suffield let out a heavy sigh. "Basil told me you are having problems with your servants in the house Neville leased for your honeymoon. You're certain they are spying on you?"

"Very certain, my lady," said Percival.

"I have confirmed all the suspicions with Armand," said Lord Berrick.

"Well, I suppose if I were a duke and unsure whether or not my son would sire my eventual heir, I might feel compelled to do the same." Lady Suffield stood. "The Amesbury dukedom has quite a long history." She went to the port decanter and poured herself another glass. She waved at the decanters before she returned to her seat. "Please, help yourselves."

Viola was so very tempted. Bertram availed himself of the cognac. Viola took the opportunity to sit by Penelope and squeeze her hand. Bertram was left to sit beside Percival. All at once, Percival's shoulders relaxed and he leaned a bit toward his lover.

That the countess was sympathetic to people such as they was a little bewildering. What had transpired in her past that made her readily accept people like she was, like Percival was, like the earl and Mr. Bisset were? Accept that some men and women, like Bertram and Penelope, had a predilection for either sex?

"Lady Norrington, what is your parentage?"

Viola was not expecting that question.

"Viola is the daughter of the Earl of Rochdale," said Percival gallantly. "Her father and my father shared a room at Oxford."

"Rochdale?" yelped Lord Berrick.

"You are Cedric and Violet's daughter?" said Lady Suffield. She briefly threw a glance in Percival's direction.

"You know my parents?" Viola squawked in surprise. She stared at the countess. "You knew my mother?"

Lady Suffield offered a serene smile. "I did. She was a kind-hearted, sweet woman."

She really was. But that's how children remember their parents, right?

"And I knew your father—and Norrington's father—at Oxford," said Lord Berrick. He glanced at the countess before returning his attention to Viola. "I never knew your mother. I was fraternizing with a different lot by the time your parents met."

"I only ask," the countess began, "because we'd want to know if your family would seek to pursue you if they heard you had suddenly left Nice."

"I don't think my father has the funds to search for me."

"I am aware of Rochdale's circumstances," Lady Suffield said with empathy. "That Basil and I know both your fathers does make it easier for us to continue with whatever fiction we all agree upon. Your families will trust us that we are telling the truth."

"Which might foster mistrust toward the servant-spies," offered Lord Berrick.

The countess smiled. "So, do you have any plan in mind?"

"I thought, perhaps, we could go to Spain," said Percival.

"In such a manner where we not only evade the servants, but don't even raise concerns," added Bertram.

"Spain?" Lady Suffield took a sip of port. "I had a lover once in Girona."

Viola flushed at the confession. But why shouldn't an older woman have fond memories of a love affair?

"And my maid Fidela is Spanish." Lady Suffield examined her audience. "I don't suppose any of you speaks Spanish?"

Lord Berrick chuckled.

"No, my lady," said Bertram.

"Well, Girona is just over the border, and most speak Catalan there anyway, so your French should be adequate." Lady Suffield stood and slowly paced the carpet, her abundant blue silk skirts undulating like waves. "I'll lend you Fidela. She'll be of great assistance. And your Armand will be indispensable. He is rather clever." She clapped her hands together. "Now, let us discuss how we might enact this plan."

CHAPTER FOURTEEN

Girona, Spain, February 1881

The late morning sun warmed Percival's cheeks as he tilted his chin to meet the rays. Beside him on the bench, Bertram's closeness lulled him further into torpidity. The hushed giggling of Penelope and Viola across the table lifted the corners of his mouth into a smile.

Contentment. Finally.

They sat outside a tavern in Girona, Spain, a town not too far from the border with France. The plan they had concocted with Lady Suffield, Berrick, and François, plus Armand and Fidela had worked as hoped. However, the execution had taken two weeks. Two very slow weeks.

"Something about you is so sublimely attractive, my lord," Bertram whispered in his ear. "A certain tranquility has descended. The crease between your brows has softened."

He *was* feeling something approaching serenity. And it had been well earned.

With nine of them in on the plot, there had to be quite a bit of strategic scheduling. Penelope and Viola began the ruse by visiting Lady Suffield with some regularity. The countess took them on little excursions around Nice and the environs, sometimes with Fidela in tow.

At the same time, Percival and Bertram commenced regular visits with Berrick and François. Percival loved hearing stories about Father from Berrick. They had been best friends at Harrow, but their friendship had mellowed when they'd entered Oxford.

"Was it because of who you are?" Percival had asked during a walk one day. "I mean because of, well, your persuasion?"

Berrick had grunted a chuckle at that. "Your father knew about my proclivities, even while we were at Harrow. I think we grew apart because I enjoyed all that life had to offer, while Neville began to feel the weight of his ducal responsibilities once at university. We drifted to different social circles."

"How well did you know Viola's father, the Earl of Rochdale?"

"Not very. He and your father were perfect roommates. They were both studious. I was, er, not so studious."

In the meantime, Armand had secretly brought some of Bertram's clothes over to Lady Suffield's house. He also covertly sabotaged some of Percival's wardrobe, loosening buttons and renting seams. Upon seeing a greatly annoyed Laurent carrying the clothes in the servants' hall, Armand had offered to take the clothes to the countess's house where they had an exquisite team of mending maids. Laurent had agreed to that readily, and thereafter brought all of Percival's mending to Armand.

After just over a week of these activities, Lady Suffield had invited Viola and Penelope for a holiday in Marseilles. The countess had also sent along lists to Mathilde and Aline about what to pack for their ladies, plus a note saying all would be taken care of so they need not come along. The maids' disappointment, astonishingly, did not lead to their harboring any suspicions.

The countess, Viola, Penelope, and Fidela went to Marseilles, taking with them luggage containing Percival and Bertram's clothing as well as their own. The wives sent postcards to their husbands, telling them the city was so remarkable they would be staying a little longer.

In actuality, Viola, Penelope, and Fidela had departed for Girona. Lady Suffield had stayed in Marseilles and sent along additional prepared postcards from Viola and Penelope to their husbands in Nice.

Meanwhile in Nice, Percival and Bertram had hosted a few dinners for Berrick and François. One night, while servants stood at attention in the dining room, Berrick proclaimed that since the wives were in Marseilles, the four of them should take a holiday of their own.

"Why don't we go to Cannes? Marseilles is such a big, busy city. Cannes is marvelously idyllic. It's something of a resort away from this resort we call home." Berrick had then reached out and grasped Francois's hand, the two exchanging expressions that conveyed the great love they had for each other.

A pang of envy had spiked through Percival at the scene. He wanted so much to have the same freedom of touch and emotion with Bertram. That was why they were undertaking this convoluted and strange scheme, wasn't it?

So their own adventure was settled. Armand convinced Laurent that he was not needed, as Armand would provide any necessary service to both Percival and Bertram. Cannes proved to be quite picturesque and an Arcadian diversion where Percival and Bertram unleashed pent-up desires in spirited romps.

After a couple of days, Percival, Bertram, and Armand headed for Marseilles. Berrick and François stayed in Cannes, sending prepared postcards to Bertram's mother and his cousin Nicholas.

In Marseilles, Percival and Bertram met with Lady Suffield, preparing more postcards for her to send later. All of the postcards were intended to not simply let family members know they were enjoying themselves, but to give them time to get away. Most importantly, Father needed to be pacified into complacency.

After a day with the countess in Marseilles, they headed to Spain. And here they were, the four of them, having luncheon at a tavern in Girona, relief at their successful escape creating an ebullient atmosphere.

There had been only a few hitches, most of which had been easily resolved. Laurent had an unpredictable temper and was a bit stubborn. Armand was always able to placate him, offering reasonable explanations for everything that was happening. The most chancy situation involved Viola. She was supposed to be pregnant for the ruse to work, but she knew she would start her courses during the time she remained in Nice. Apparently she kept a journal about such things. She feigned illness for a couple of nights and stayed at the countess' home, away from Mathilde, who might see her bloody rags

That women had to endure such ghastliness was unsettling.

The sharp, exuberant laughter of tavern patrons at the next table drew Percival back to the present—and Bertram's lips oh so close to his earlobe.

"You seem distracted, my lord."

He hated when Bertram called him that. Besides ruminating on all that had transpired over the last two weeks, he was impatient to be with his Bertie. He wanted a real honeymoon, one for the two of them.

But at the moment, they were staying at a small inn, the women in one room, the men, including Armand, in another. They had yet to find a permanent place of residence.

Percival turned his head, almost grazing Bertram's lips. "Let's spend today searching for a private house for our sojourn in Spain."

* * * * *

Girona, Spain, Early spring 1881

"CAN YOU PLEASE just kiss me now?"

Bertram grinned as he pecked his lips along the smooth skin of Percival's ribcage. "I *am* kissing you."

"I mean on my mouth." Percival pulled away. "You're tickling me, Bertie."

Drawing the tip of his tongue up the side of Percival's torso elicited more squirming. The reaction was all the more thrilling since Percival was grabbing the wrought iron arabesques and tendrils of the headboard in their bedroom, apparently in an attempt to gain purchase as he fended off Bertram's sensual assaults.

His struggles, of course, were futile. Bertram chuckled and pivoted to kiss down Percival's tensing abdominals to the line of muscles leading to his groin while his lover sighed in languid befuddlement. Bertram nipped and licked along the muscular ridge, stopping at the nest of light brown hair surrounding an excitingly rigid cock. He stretched out one hand to pinch Percival's nipples, then hovered his face over his lover's erection.

"Oh, God, yes, please, yes," Percival pleaded breathlessly.

Bertram drew the shaft into his mouth, wetting it, lingering with each lick along the length, the sound of sighs and the whispers of encouragement music to his ears. Giving his Percy pleasure, the pleasure he wanted, he needed, he deserved, was supremely rewarding.

He sucked slowly, deliberately, teasing the head with swirls of his tongue, eliciting oaths amidst the moans of satisfaction.

When he drew in Percy's cock all the way, there was a gasp, then silence. Bertram worked the tip of the shaft with steady strokes of his lips and tongue, gripping the base to work it with even slides of his fisted palm. Percival remained still for only a moment, then his hips rocked to the rhythm of Bertram's ministrations before quickening the pace—

And completely rotating his position on the bed until the two were topsy-turvy.

Percival grappled with Bertram until he found what he wanted, drawing Bertram's cock to the back of his throat, while Bertram still sucked Percival.

Christ almighty. He held firm, letting his mouth be used while Percy plunged inside. After the sensual fog cleared, Bertram thrust his own hips enthusiastically, his need for release as urgent as his lover's. Percival egged him on, his exhortations muffled while his own cock fucked Bertram's mouth.

They were both of them on the precipice, but who would fall first?

With one final jerk, Percival let loose his seed down Bertram's throat, the initial spurt almost choking him, distracting him from his own release. As he sucked and gulped, he renewed his momentum, working himself to the point of no return, jetting his emission in Percival's willing mouth.

They lay entangled, catching their breaths.

"Bertie darling, I want to hold you."

"Of course."

Moments later the two were face-to-face, entwined in each other's arms, the heat of their bodies mingling under a coverlet shielding them from the chill of early spring.

"This is what I've always wanted," said Percival. "You, in my arms, satisfied and safe."

Safe. An apt word, really. They were truly lucky to have gotten away with their scheme. At first, everything seemed fine, but after a couple of weeks living in Spain, missives from Nice reported otherwise. Laurent had confronted Berrick and François aggressively. The two had a difficult time convincing Laurent that Lord Norrington and Lord Ravensburgh went to Marseilles to visit their wives, but the two of them had wanted to return to Nice. Lady Suffield was also accosted by Laurent after she had returned alone. She'd explained that Fidela had learned of a family illness and went to Spain, and that the countess had only left Marseilles after

Lord Norrington and Lord Ravensburgh had arrived for their wives.

But after over a week of the lords and their wives supposedly being in Marseilles, Laurent had sent a telegram to the Duke of Amesbury with his suspicions regarding their escape. The countess wrote to the duke saying she was troubled by the supposed disappearances and would do everything in her power to help locate the foursome, but that she was certain there must have been some sort of misunderstanding.

Upon arrival in Girona, the foursome had decided to conceal the fact of their Englishness. They spoke French outside the house, although Penelope did not know much beyond the basics, so she never ventured out alone. The wives used their sewing skills to make alterations and simplify their clothing so they would not stand out as aristocrats. Bertram and Percival let their hair grow long. Bertram even tried growing a beard, but it was intolerably scratchy.

Fidela returned to Nice for a spell, feigning surprise when Laurent interrogated her. She claimed she knew nothing about what had happened to *les Anglais*. She'd only returned to pack the rest of her things and take her leave of Lady Suffield so she could help her elderly parents in Madrid. Fidela's family actually lived not far from Girona. She'd returned to deflect suspicion from herself, and to collect more funds from the countess.

Lady Suffield had insisted she pay for their "great adventure," and if Lord Norrington wished to pay her back, he could do so when it was all over.

Bertram nuzzled the crook of Percival's shoulder, breathing in his intoxicating scent. "I want to be with you as long as we can. It's been two months, and they haven't found us yet."

"Two months of bliss."

Indeed. Their house had only two master bedrooms. The wives slept in one, the husbands in another. Bertram missed Penelope's charms, but, as she was growing more concerned with her condition—and more fond of Viola—she was less interested in him. Percival filled the emotional and sensual gap deliciously.

"Love," Bertram began, "I've written to Nicholas to let him know of our scheme. I told him we have escaped for a spell for a real honeymoon. I did not say anything about the child. I only wanted him to let my mother know that we are very definitely fine. I would hate for her to worry. She'll need to know Orsa will be with her for a bit longer."

Percival lifted his head. "But what if my father finds the correspondence?"

"What?" Bertram shook his head in incredulity. "Percy, don't you start to worry. Armand sent the letter from over the border, in France. If your father happens upon the envelope, he won't know it was sent from Spain. Besides, how on earth would your father see a letter I sent to Nicholas in London?"

Percival deflated. "Yes, I see. I'm still so anxious."

"We'll all be fine until the child is born."

"And then what?" Percival arced his body against Bertram and tugged him close. "After the child is born, we'll have to once again repress our true selves. We won't be able to continue our intimacy. We won't be able to sleep together."

"And how is the child to know who is sleeping with whom?"

"Children are curious. They wander."

Bertram smiled. Some children apparently do. Young Percy did, which was how they met. "I suppose all we can do is raise our children to be accepting of all sorts of people, and tell them that men and women can show affection in private in various ways. Sometimes papa wants to spend the night with his friend, and mama wants to spend the night with her friend. If we make it seem normal, then the child won't question it."

"And if the child tells Grandpapa the duke?"

"Yes. Well." Bertram pecked Percival's cheek. "We can always leave the children at home and return to Nice."

* * * * *

Girona, Spain, Late spring 1881

ALONE ON THE DAY-BED against the window in her sun-drenched bedroom, Penelope put down her book and gazed out the window. Their flat overlooked the Onyar river with a view of the cathedral tower across the water.

It was a wonderful residence in a building that was perhaps a little shabby on the outside, but the elegance of the interior spoke of a grand family from an earlier time. Besides the two small servant bedrooms, there were two master bedrooms, adjoined in a style from one hundred years or so ago. Penelope and Viola shared one room, and Bertram and Percival shared the other.

She should feel a bit of jealousy, shouldn't she? Yet she did not. Bertram would always be there for her. And she adored spending time with Viola. Once their child was born and they returned to England, she had no idea what life would be like. Right now, she savored spending each night wrapped in the supple arms of a woman rather than the muscular arms of a man.

They'd been in hiding for about four months now. The town of Girona was very small, but luckily they had blended in as French academics wanting to spend time on a working holiday of sorts. Bertram, as Monsieur Barnabé, had become a familiar face in every bookshop and stationery store in town. Percival, as Monsieur Paulus, had perused every antique shop and museum, frequently with Viola at his side, who reported all the intrigue to Penelope.

The only lingering worry was for those back home in England. Bertram had sent a packet to his cousin Nicholas containing not only a missive to his mother Lady Ravensburgh, but also a letter from Penelope to Gertrude. With Nicholas as a conduit, Gertrude was able to write back and let Penelope know she understood her situation, she knew she was safe, and she would not tell a soul.

Penelope had not told Gertrude of her pregnancy, however. There could not ever be a hint that the child was not Viola and Percival's.

A light knock resounded on the door before Viola entered. Penelope could never subdue her happiness at her lover's presence. Viola's smile reflected that felicity.

She sat next to Penelope on the day-bed. "Fidela wants to know where you would like luncheon served, darling."

"I suppose in the dining room. It would give me a reason to get up off this bed and walk a few steps. It seems all the exercise I can manage these days."

Viola nuzzled against her neck. "We will walk along the river after luncheon." She tapped the book. "What are you reading?"

"A French novel. *Flamarande* by George Sand."

"I'm impressed," said Viola. "You've made incredible progress in only a few months." She gave Penelope a kiss on her cheek.

Penelope turned her head and kissed Viola's lips, lingering a while, the warm wetness ever so satisfying. Until the baby kicked.

"Oof," she groaned. "He's getting so strong."

"Can I feel him?"

Penelope nodded.

Viola lay her palm on Penelope's stomach and bent over to listen. As if he knew he had a visitor, he kicked again. Viola snatched her hand away.

"Oh lord, that was strong, Penny. I don't think I could handle that."

"Of course you could." Penelope laughed. "Well, you'd have to, at least."

Viola moved to the opposite end of the day-bed and lifted Penelope's stocking-clad legs into her lap. "Shall I give your feet a massage, my love?"

"I would very much enjoy that, thank you." She wiggled her toes.

Viola's hands worked their magic on Penelope's swollen feet and ankles. "I really hate seeing my once pretty legs getting puffy," she sighed. "All of me getting puffy, really."

Viola lifted a leg and kissed Penelope's toes. "I love what's happening to your body. All the changes." She kissed the arch of her foot. "Your cheeks have a rosy bloom." She kissed Penelope's ankle bone. "I love how your already full bosom is even fuller. So much more than a handful."

Penelope giggled.

Viola drew her index finger up Penelope's calf. "I love how your hips have filled out. And your belly." She caressed behind Penelope's knee. Penelope twitched at the ticklish touch, the movement betraying her arousal.

"And I love that you are carrying our child."

Penelope's eyes misted with happy tears. "Our child. It will be our child." She sighed. "I want him to understand about people like us without putting us in jeopardy."

"I know. I want so much to teach him acceptance of all people, no matter who they love."

"But he'll never know the truth of us," Penelope said wistfully.

"Unless he himself is like us."

She'd never considered that. "Do you think that may be true?"

"He is the son of two people who love and feel differently from the rest of society. I wonder if he will feel the same. I want to be able to teach him that it is not unnatural to feel that way. I'm scared that the Duke of Amesbury will have too much say in his upbringing." Viola stroked Penelope's legs. "But as his mother in name, I will insist the duke let Percival and me have a direct role in his moral guidance."

Penelope reached for Viola's hand. "Thank you." She pulled her lover to sit alongside her, then pecked her lips so tender and warm.

Viola's tongue swept along the seam of Penelope's mouth. Their lips melded as they embraced as closely as possible. Viola cupped a tender breast, then giggled.

"What?"

"Poor Fidela is waiting for us."

Penelope laughed. "Ah, yes. Luncheon." At least Fidela did not have to also wait for Percival—with his penchant to dawdle about—and Bertram. The husbands, along with Armand, had gone on holiday to the coast. "Help me up."

Viola took an arm to steady her. "What if we could make one surname from all of ours and give it to the child?"

"Hmm, what an interesting word game. All of the surnames?"

"Well, Athercastlewoodton might be a bit overmuch."

Penelope laughed. "What about something simple, like Ravenswood."

"Not the titles," Viola said with a grimace. "The proper surnames."

"Hardwood."

"Pemberley."

"Ravenscastle—no." Penelope grinned. "Castleton."

"Atherwood." Viola laughed as she took Penelope's arm. "Boy or girl. No matter what we name it, we will all raise this child." She touched her lips to Penelope's, her kiss delicate and emotion-filled. "I love you, Mrs. Castleton."

Penelope leaned her forehead against Viola's. "And I love you, too, Mrs. Atherwood."

CHAPTER FIFTEEN

Girona, Spain, July 1881

Bertram paced the corridor outside Penelope's bedroom, then sat on the ancient and overly ornate wood and leather throne chair shoved up against the wall. He focused on nothing, his mind too preoccupied for his eyes to do anything but glaze over as he drowned in obsessive worrying. The heat of summer added to his torpor.

He had to trust Fidela's judgment in choosing a midwife to birth the child. It was *her* Spain. While they'd all learned some of the language, they still stumbled over words and cultural differences.

Fidela had returned not only with a midwife but a nun for some inexplicable reason. The women, along with Viola, had surrounded a stunned Penelope, who quickly acquiesced under their obvious expert care and concern for her well-being. They had shooed Bertram out into the corridor while his child was being born, the sounds of Catalan instructions and Penelope's cries on the other side of the bedroom door tearing at his gut.

At least Viola's presence meant that his wife was not completely surrounded by strangers.

Bertram stood up and resumed his pacing.

Percival appeared from the shadows down the corridor and slumped against the wall.

"Stop pacing, Bertie. You're driving me out of my senses." His voice held a nervous edge. He plunked down on the empty throne chair and jiggled his knees.

They were both anxious. For Penelope, for the child, for whatever lay ahead in their lives.

Would they be able to pass off Bertram's son as the Amesbury heir?

If they unaffectedly told the duke this was his heir, he would accept it? What would happen when the child started to grow and develop facial features that did not seem quite right? What would the duke do then?

Boisterous yelling in Catalan and French, along with Penelope's anguished cries, drew their attention to the closed door cruelly separating them from their wives and child.

Bertram's gut clenched more, if that were possible. Distress heated his flesh to sweating, the sweat cooling to chills. He resumed pacing, his brain completely devoid of thoughts.

Suddenly there was silence.

He looked at the door.

My God. My Penelope. What the hell was going on? He struggled for breath.

The shriek of newborn life shattered the tension.

The door opened and the nun, grinning and perspiring, waved for the men to enter the room.

There she was, his wife, terrifically disheveled, dripping with sweat, but smiling like he had never seen before. In her arms she cradled a babe wrapped in a coarse, handwoven blanket.

His…child. Son or daughter, it did not matter. Penelope was radiant and alive, and so was their child.

His heart expanded with joy until it felt as if he were going to burst.

Penelope saw him amidst the chaos of the attendants. Her smile grew brighter.

"Penny, darling." He went to her tentatively, having absolutely no idea how one should act around a baby, and certainly not such a tiny one as was in her arms.

"Bertie, darling. Isn't she beautiful?"

She?

"You have a daughter, Lord Ravensburgh," said a smiling Fidela.

A daughter…a daughter.

Oh, God. A daughter.

Viola sat at Penelope's side, her countenance stoic beneath a crinkled brow. He flashed a glance at Percival whose pained, pallid expression made him look as if he had been kicked in the crotch. Percival met his gaze, shook his head, and offered a weak smile.

"It's a happy occasion, Bertram," he said. "Especially when mother and daughter look so healthy."

"Yes," he responded, knowing all too well the disappointment raging through Percival.

But for one moment he wanted to glory in the fact that his wife had just had a child, a daughter who would be as beautiful as Penelope, a daughter he could dote upon, buy pretty dresses for, mold with his values.

A daughter he could raise as his own, outwardly proud of his child, not hiding behind some pretense of merely being a close friend of the family that had a responsibility in helping raise the child, but no real say in the child's eventual future.

He would have given his son to Percival. Yes, he really would have. But something had greatly unsettled him about the whole scheme, something that he could never quite put a finger on. But now he knew, now he understood. There was a visceral attachment to the child that had swelled his wife's womb and had been a part of her for nine long months; months where they had all agreed to go into hiding so the four could construct a fantastical, noble deceit.

He lay a firm hand on Percival's shoulder. They would discuss the future later. Now was the time to celebrate Penelope and her daughter. Their daughter. The daughter of all four of them, a child they had promised to raise together.

They still needed to work out the details on that.

Bertram gave Percival's shoulder an empathetic squeeze, then sat on the bed at Penelope's side, gazing down at mother and daughter, the latter a tiny, chubby, pink creature that made him smile.

Out of the corner of his eye, he saw Percival wrap his arms around Viola. Bertram's gain was their loss. The couple remained childless, heirless, and something would have to be done.

What that something would be was anyone's guess.

Lying face up on the day-bed in the night-blackened parlor, Viola let her tears roll down the sides of her face. The last six months had been for naught. Well, she'd spent time with Penelope. Traveled to France and Spain. Had met some interesting people.

But she was still childless, the dukedom was without an heir, and that situation would have to be rectified now under the watchful eyes of the Duke and Duchess of Amesbury. Most likely, the Amesburys would not allow the two couples to travel so far away for so long ever again.

The plan to hide in Spain and return with an heir had seemed a brilliant one. But they'd had the one chance. And now that chance has passed.

A sob choked Viola's lungs. She panted, finding relief when she sat up.

The parlor was still, the furnishings shades of gray in the dull light. There had been no fire in the grate, given the heat of the summer days. Still, a chill lingered in the cool of the night.

A few hours before, she'd left the side of a slumbering Penelope. Fidela camped out on the bedroom's day-bed so she could be near the newborn. She would remain there every night until her own daughter arrived to act as nursemaid while Penelope recovered. By then, Viola was certain she would have the strength to once again sleep at Penelope's side. Just not tonight.

Her head pounded. She slowly drew in a long inhalation, releasing it with juddering spurts. Exhaustion dragged her back down to the day-bed, an exhaustion too overwhelming for sleep.

The door clicked open, then closed shut quietly. Someone stepped lightly on the carpet. Viola sat up. The shadow was familiar.

"Percival? Is that you?"

"Viola?" He walked toward her. "I couldn't sleep. I mean, I couldn't sleep next to Bertie. I thought I would try to sleep in the parlor."

"I know what you mean," she said. "I've already got the day-bed."

He chuckled. "I can take the sofa."

She sniffled, then wiped her face with the sleeve of her nightgown, her handkerchief long since drenched and useless.

"You're crying." He knelt down next to her.

"I can't stop. I'm surprised you're not."

He took her hand. "I'm too numb. It's been a terrible shock."

A wave of sorrow and despair once again overtook her. She shook with sobs.

Percival sat beside her and wrapped his arms around her. He drew her down to the bed and stretched out alongside her. He held her tightly. "We'll think of something."

"We have to."

Percival's silence and uneven breaths revealed he understood the magnitude of their situation.

Viola nestled in his arms. Knowing she was not alone in this predicament was a calming consolation.

CHAPTER SIXTEEN

Wood Hall, Hertfordshire, Late July 1881

Percival gazed out the window of the carriage at the all too familiar countryside as it passed by.

Home.

Well, his ancestral home anyway. Not the place that filled his heart with nostalgic notions. No. That was his home in London, which he shared with Bertram, and now their wives. That truly was home, because all the emotion, all the comfort, all the longing, all the love was there.

Certainly not here at Wood Hall.

He'd learned through letters from England that Father had been frantically looking for the four of them. Bertram's mother had revealed that Laurent had returned from Nice and met with the duke. Nicholas had urged Percival to send a letter to the duke and duchess assuring them he was having a grand time on his honeymoon and did not want to be disturbed, that he would join them at Wood Hall upon his return to England.

Except now he was returning from his honeymoon empty-handed. To say such a thing about not having a child was coarse. But that was the bald truth. A wife should return from a seven-month long honeymoon at the very least visibly pregnant.

He wrapped an arm around Viola at his side, she as sullen as he was. Across from them sat the happiest couple in England, cradling and cooing over their child.

Percival squeezed Viola against him. She held Orsa in her arms. She had insisted they stop at Ravensburgh Cottage and retrieve the dog from the dowager viscountess. Of course, Lady Ravensburgh had wanted to see her grandchild. The emotional reunion almost broke Viola, who now only had the lap dog to cling to.

The carriage pulled into the gravel drive before the entrance and came to a stop. The footman opened the door, and Percival stepped down to the ground that would one day be his own.

But would there be anyone to follow in his footsteps?

Viola approached to stand at his side.

He leaned over. "Are you ready to face the Duke and Duchess of Amesbury, Lady Norrington?" he murmured in her ear.

She straightened at his side. "I have been preparing for this moment for the last month, my lord marquess."

They strolled arm in arm through the entrance, servants at attention, then scurrying, taking coats, hats, and gloves. Mother was in the foyer, awaiting him with concern etched upon her face. Her gaze took in Viola, sliding from head to toe, then back up again. Concern contorted to disappointment. Percival took his wife's arm in support.

"Norrington," she said, "how wonderful to see you." She held out her arms.

He unhooked his arm from Viola's and approached Mother alone. Mother kissed his cheek, devoid of any emotion.

"I expect the Mediterranean coast was inspiring for you as newlyweds?"

At that very moment, Bertram and Penelope walked in, their daughter squirming and chirping in Penelope's arms.

"Oh," Mother said. "I see the honeymoon was inspiring for your friend Ravensburgh." She flashed Percival a withering look. "Has he found a new fascination, then? Will we be seeing him in your presence less?"

Percival fumed. "No, Your Grace. Lord Ravensburgh remains an important part of my life. Even more so now he has a wife and child. He is, and will continue to be, my true family."

Mother scowled, then turned away to greet Bertram.

"Viscount and Lady Ravensburgh, what a pleasure. And who is this child?"

"Georgiana, Your Grace. Named after my father, George."

Mother, Bertram, and Penelope cooed over the infant. Viola shifted Orsa in her arms.

"I see fatherhood suits you very well, Lord Ravensburgh."

"It does, Your Grace. Lady Ravensburgh and I are very happy."

"She looks like her mother," Mother said. "She has the same upturn to her nose."

Bertram gazed lovingly at Penelope, then at his daughter. "She does, doesn't she?"

"Perhaps you'll have one of your own one day, Norrington," Mother said over her shoulder. "And perhaps he'll look just like you."

Mother's words cut him to the bone. Percival glanced away, then once again took up Viola's arm. The sight of Father in the grand hall was chilling. Father caught his eye—his face devoid of emotion—before he turned and walked in the direction of his study without saying a word.

Viola squeezed Percival's arm.

He smiled at her.

"Lady Norrington," came Mother's voice behind them.

Viola turned. "Yes, Your Grace?"

"Would you please join me for tea in the morning parlor." The words held no lilt in the inflection, making it more of a command.

Viola stiffened at his side, then released a slow exhalation. "I would be honored to have tea with you, Your Grace."

Percival's heart sank as he watched his wife join his mother and stroll away.

"I'm certain Viola will be able to hold her own, Percy." Bertram's dulcet assurance was a balm to his frayed nerves.

"Let's hope so."

Father's personal secretary approached. "My lord marquess."

"Yes, Wilson?"

"His Grace has requested your immediate presence in the study."

Immediate presence. No moment to rest and rejuvenate after a long journey via rail and carriage. This was not going to be pleasant. "Lead the way, Wilson."

The slog to the study was like the march of a prisoner to the gallows, each step bringing more worry and fretting speculation about what would invariably happen.

Wilson opened the door. Every muscle in Percival's body tensed. He strode in. Wilson exited, closing the door behind him with a click of the latch.

Father stood with his back turned to the door, looking out the window. He would know Percival was there from the sound of the door opening and closing. And yet he did nothing.

"Your Grace, you requested my presence?"

Father slowly turned around. "You looked tanned." It was said with a modicum of derision.

Percival said nothing.

"I'll get to the point. I have been told Viscount and Viscountess Ravensburgh have a daughter."

"Yes, Your Grace."

Father scowled. "You need not stand on ceremony when we are alone, Norrington."

"Yes, Father."

"You've been gone on this honeymoon for how long?"

"Seven months."

"Lady Norrington looks unscathed."

Anger and humiliation spiked his gut. "What the hell is that supposed to mean?"

Father's gray-blue eyes flashed at him. "You had seven months to perform one task and you failed to do it."

Jesus. "Perform a task? Is that what it's called?"

"It seems, though, that Ravensburgh was able to perform such a task, and, as I understand it, before the honeymoon even. Does this mean he will no longer be a distraction for you?"

Percival fumed. "No, it does not. Lord Ravensburgh is my best friend and confidante. We have simply enlarged our sphere with our wives and Georgiana." He remained unmoving. "We will continue to live in our London house. You need not worry about anything untoward happening on any of your properties."

"I'm more worried about the lack of untoward activity." Father glared at him. "As long as there is the allurement of that man in your house, you will never produce an heir."

"Ravensburgh is not some sort of intrigue. How can I make that clear to you?"

"Ah, but now he has his wife and child, you can only be a trifling affair to him."

The cut burned deeply. But Percival was confident he would never be a mere dalliance to his lover. Bertram had said so himself.

"There is, perhaps, an added level of complexity to our relationship. But it only augments our lives with layers of interest."

"I don't think you understand marriage, Norrington."

"And I don't think you understand my relationship with Bertram, Father. It's not like I can become who I am not. And neither can he."

Father slammed his hand on his desk. "Damn it, Percival! Yes, you can."

Percival shrunk from the outburst. Father rarely called him by his Christian name.

Father let out a trembling exhale. "If I was able to do my duty, then you can as well."

"If you—" Percival stared wide-eyed at Father as disbelief and realization washed over him. Was it true? "My God, you're as I am." The thought had crossed his mind two years ago when he'd first learned of his parents having an arranged marriage, but Bertram had disabused him of the notion.

Father said nothing, his eyes bloodshot.

"That's why you never threatened me with prison."

Father snorted. "That and the fact that you are my only son. My only child. Thank God you were a son. I don't think I could have performed the act again."

Percival sank into an armchair opposite the desk. The idea of his own father with…with…other men. The notion had frankly never occurred to him. He gazed up at Father. "Does Mother know?"

"Your mother and I were good friends when we married. We still are. She knows my secret as she knows yours. And she has the patience of a saint. Well, she did, until you decided you wanted to rebel."

"It's not rebellion, Father. My generation is different than yours. We grew up with progress. Railways, telegrams, and steamships are part of our lives. We see possibilities. And we want to live as we are."

"Norrington, please understand, you cannot. The law still considers men who consort with other men as felons. And Society sees us as not…normal."

"Yes, you're right. Would that we could change minds as quickly as it takes to travel from Spain to London."

Father sighed. "Not in my lifetime. So, you see why I am so insistent. I, even the same as you, was able to father a child."

"I do see."

"And I would assume, much like my Eleanor, your Viola would like a child to care for."

Jesus. How to explain this to Father? Should he? Percival closed his eyes and drew in a bolstering breath. He looked Father in the eye but found no solace there. "Believe me, we have tried. It's been…difficult."

For one brief moment, empathy flitted over Father's countenance, only to be hardened by exasperation. "I trust you two will find a way."

"I will consider all that you have said to me. I swear to you, Viola and I will try more assiduously."

Father's revelation had changed everything. He had no excuses anymore.

DURING THE EXTRAVAGANZA that had been her wedding, Viola had not had the time to properly explore the grounds of Wood Hall. But now she very definitely had a reason to.

She needed to be very far away from the house, very far away from the Duchess of Amesbury and her effrontery.

Viola had just endured the most bizarre and angering tea in her life. Apparently, it was Viola's fault she did not yet have a child. Or at least that was how she felt when she excused herself as graciously as possible from the duchess.

The questions had been relentless.

Why couldn't she be more like her friend Lady Ravensburgh? She seemed so happy with her newborn. Even Lord Ravensburgh seemed happy. Surely Viola wanted to make her husband happy?

Didn't Viola want a child of her own to love and raise? Why, surely that was the uppermost aspiration of every woman, the very purpose of marriage. And children kept the bonds of husband and wife strong.

Perhaps Viola wasn't trying hard enough to encourage her husband in bed. At that point, the duchess had actually intimated that she would be happy to give advice based on her experience, as a mother might give a daughter.

Viola had felt the bile rise in her throat at that. She'd begged to be allowed to use the necessary, then made her escape to the impeccably manicured property, Orsa in her arms, the only source of comfort on the God-forsaken estate.

She wandered aimlessly, Orsa at her side. The pup's antics—stopping to sniff grass, then running to catch up—cheered her weary spirits.

How long had she been walking? Did it matter? Eventually, probably around dinner time, someone would discover her missing and send the servants looking for her.

With an excited yip, Orsa ran across the lawn toward a figure in the distance. A man. He was not quite walking toward her, more at an angle, but in her general direction.

Viola smiled. It appeared her husband also needed to be far away from the house and its occupants for a spell.

She changed her trajectory to meet him.

When Orsa reached her master, Percival greeted her with an equal amount of exuberance. He looked around and espied Viola. He walked in her direction, Orsa at his heels.

He beamed with outstretched hands. "You are a sight for sore eyes, my wife."

Not what she had expected to hear, but heartwarming nonetheless.

He wrapped her arm around his and walked with purpose in the direction she had originally been headed.

They walked in silence until they came upon a rustic bent-willow bench on a sloping hillside overlooking a small, picturesque lake.

"We'll stop there." Percival pointed to the bench.

They sat side by side. Orsa found a patch of grass to stretch out on.

"I suppose I should inquire as to why my wife is wandering my familial estate unescorted?"

"Perhaps you should, my lord," she said with a gibing air.

"Lady Norrington, I am all ears if you have something to say."

"The Duchess of Amesbury is somewhat presumptuous in her interactions with new members of her family, is she not?"

He faced her abruptly. "Good lord, Viola, what did she say to you?"

All pretense had been abandoned. "The duchess, your mother, inquired about my courses, my lord. About whether I had recently had my feminine time of the month. After the initial shock, I had responded that I would look in my diary for the precise date if she needed that information. She said no, and seemed to be satisfied that I kept such a diary."

Percival sighed heavily. "I apologize for my mother's bluntness." He draped his arm around her shoulder. "I've just had the most interesting conversation with my father," he said, his emphasis on the word *interesting* revealing it was perhaps also astonishing.

"Oh? And are you able to tell me anything about it? I mean, it could be something political given your father is a duke."

He chuckled at that. "It seems my father shares my predilection for men."

She turned to him with wide eyes. "Truly?"

"Yes. And despite his natural urges, as he emphasized, he was able to produce me as his heir." He huffed. "I suddenly feel so sorry for my mother not having a fulfilling, sensual life."

"And how do you know she did not?"

He laughed. "You're right. I don't know. Perhaps she did. God only knows with whom."

"I'm certain you would not want to know."

"Still," he said gravely, "I realize their purpose in separating us so quickly in the foyer was to keep us apart while each questioned one as to why you are not yet pregnant."

"It seems so." Viola leaned her head on his shoulder.

"Darling, we'll stay here for a while. I feel I have a bit of catching up to do with Father."

"With that revelation, I would expect you would."

"And then there is the christening of little Georgiana. We're to be godparents if you remember."

She laughed. "And yet, we are so ungodly in our actions."

"Well, I would say we are about as Christian in our actions as Bertram and Penelope are in theirs."

That set her to laughing again.

He kissed the crown of her head. "And then once we return to London, I feel we should make another attempt to provide the dukedom with an heir."

"I understand," she said with a sigh. If the Duke of Amesbury was like she and Percival, then perhaps a certain detachment from the act was in order.

Or they could attempt the unconventional arrangement he had proposed on their wedding night—the four of them in bed together.

CHAPTER SEVENTEEN

Atherley Keep, Hertfordshire, August 1881

Viola gulped the rest of her tea, then put down the empty porcelain cup and saucer. All around her in the magnificent drawing room were people she barely knew clucking and cooing over the newest member of the Atherley family. She avoided making eye contact with the cluckers and the cooers, but kept a smile on her face in the event anyone approached. She was, after all, the godmother and should deport herself as such.

The christening of the Honorable Georgiana Atherley at the cathedral that morning had been a solemn and joyous occasion. Standing before the Bishop of St. Albans, the godparents, the Marquess and Marchioness of Norrington, acted as if they were nothing less than an upstanding Christian married couple. Did the guests wonder why the marchioness had no charities in her name, no friends among the ton, and had returned from her overly long honeymoon childless?

Even if no one bothered to chat with her, she would be entirely entertained by the Earl of St. Albans's recently restored drawing room. Polished wood paneling reached up to a vivaciously painted and coffered ceiling. The massive fireplace was surrounded by intricately carved marble. Furnishings were upholstered in dark green velvet. Despite the opulence, the lavish room somehow felt homey. Yet Viola was still a stranger in their midst.

The butler, Mason, poured her a fresh cup of tea. All around treated him as if he were a member of the family. He had kind eyes and gray hair and for one moment made her feel like she belonged as well. Viola sipped her tea, letting the warmth soothe her rattled nerves.

She did recognize a few faces—from the Season, from her wedding. Penelope's former guardian Gertrude was there, as was Bertram's mother the dowager Viscountess Ravensburgh. The Earl of St. Albans—Bertram's cousin Nicholas—and his gorgeous wife were amongst those doting on the newborn. Lady St. Albans—Helena, as she insisted she be called—was visibly pregnant with her second child. She and Penelope seemed to be establishing something of a rapport.

Papa was in attendance, conversing in a lively manner with the Duke and Duchess of Amesbury. Papa and the duke had shared a room at Oxford. The duke's revelation to Percival left questions. Had Papa and the duke been more than mere classmates? That would make Papa like how Bertram was, partial to both sexes. Papa had loved Mama very openly, their affections, even in front of her as a young girl, physical, utterly natural. Not like how she and Percival had to pretend.

Although of late she and her husband were beginning to be more physical with each other, each believing it might help prepare them for the inevitable. Still, their touches were tentative and often prefaced with permission.

Movement off to her right drew her attention. Speak of the devil.

Percival came toward her and perched on the arm of the sofa. He placed a hand on her shoulder. "How is godmothering faring for you, my lady?"

She laughed. "I dare say the child has no concept of right or wrong at this moment."

He slipped into the space on the sofa at her side. "Do any of us?"

She glowered at him. "I do. I'm not sure you do."

The corner of his mouth curved in amusement. He leaned in, pressing his lips to her ear. "I'll have to ask Lady Ravensburgh about that."

A flush crept up her neck to burn her cheeks. She turned away in feigned insult.

And saw the most incredible expression on Papa's face. An expression she had not seen since Mama had been alive. An expression that spoke of love and happiness and attraction and, well, was probably the same look that had presaged some sensual scene in her parents' bedroom at night.

But Mama was dead, and Papa was directing that expression to the Duchess of Amesbury. And the duchess was taking it all in, a blush on her cheeks.

Viola lightly nudged her husband. "Percy," she hissed, "your mother and my father."

"What about them?"

"Look."

Percival looked. His eyes widened.

"I never noticed it before," she said quietly. "Now I think of it, I am certain they were acting in such a familiar manner at our wedding. But that whole day was such a blur and there were so many people I couldn't focus on any one of them."

Percival studied the pair. "What are you saying exactly, Viola?" he murmured.

"That my father and your mother are—were lovers."

"Jesus," Percival whispered. "I always wondered why you were chosen as one of the women I should marry." He looked sheepish. "Not that you are not a woman of inestimable qualities, but more like you're not a duke's daughter. Now I see my parents wanted you in our family for sentimental reasons."

A sudden thought disturbed her. "Oh God."

"What?"

"Do you think you and I are"—she glanced side to side and lowered her voice—"possibly related?"

He started at that, his spine straightening. "You mean your father and my mother?" he whispered. "Meaning I wouldn't be Amesbury's son?"

"It was simply a sudden suspicion. Look at the way they're acting."

"Hmm." He studied Papa, then the duchess, then the duke, then Papa again. "No. I think there would be more of a resemblance between your father and myself. Besides my light hair and eyes, I definitely have the Amesbury mouth and chin. Even my grandfather, when he was duke and I a small boy, used to rag me about it. Come to think of it, he would badger me in front of my father and say, "Neville, you did it, and you did it well'. This happened on more than one occasion." He shook his head slowly. "Good God, did my father endure from his father all the same chiding he's been giving me?" He looked at her. "Sorry, that was my own sudden suspicion. Not to detract from yours. Which is quite astonishing, really."

"How do you think it happened? And when?"

Percival knit his brow. "According to Lady Suffield, my father and mother married when he was thirty-one."

"My father married my mother before then, though. When he was still in his twenties."

"So maybe your father and my mother had an affair while our fathers were at university? Jesus," Percival sputtered. "I wonder if your father was my mother's first."

"Well, that's certainly a romantic speculation. It sounds quite plausible."

"Lady Suffield told me she arranged the betrothal of my parents at the behest of my grandfather," Percival said.

"And Lady Suffield told me my parents were truly in love." During their sojourn in Marseilles, Lady Suffield had regaled her with stories of Mama and Papa. "Perhaps my father went searching for a new love after your mother became engaged, and met my mother."

Suddenly, Viola felt all the pain and heartache that Papa must have felt when he had to give up one love for another. He truly loved Mama, there was no doubt about it. But one's first love left an indelible impression.

But Mama was dead. And now Papa would see his first love at family events for the rest of their lives.

Really, despite the notion being a little peculiar, it was rather touching.

CHAPTER EIGHTEEN

Wilton Crescent, Belgravia, London

Bertram drained his port, then poured himself another glass. Life was good and he wanted to celebrate.

The four of them—well, five with Georgiana, six including Orsa—were finally home. Their real home. The elegant terrace house on Wilton Crescent in Belgravia that Percival had chosen a couple of years ago. Bertram had needled Percival at the time about the surfeit of bedrooms, never thinking the house would contain more than just the two of them.

And now there was an entire family.

They were in the smaller drawing room, the one with a terrace that looked over the back garden. The open doors let in a slight summer evening breeze.

Penelope and Viola cuddled on one couch. Georgiana was upstairs in the nursery with her nursemaid. Helena had convinced Penelope that hiring a nursemaid was the best course for maintaining a happy home and robust marriage. She'd even helped procure one.

Orsa was asleep before the fireplace. She was no longer curled up, but in that curious, lazy, elongated position of sound canine slumber.

Bertram took his place at Percival's side on the couch. Percival stretched out and rested his head on Bertram's lap, a sly smile playing upon his lips.

"It is wonderful to be home." Percival toed off his shoes, letting them fall to the floor with a thud. "There's a sense of freedom, isn't there?"

"Especially with our own servants."

"God, yes." Percival let out an exasperated sigh. "We were so lucky to have Fidela in Spain. She and Armand did an exceptional job together. I gave Armand a raise. I do hope Lady Suffield did the same for Fidela."

Bertram chuckled. "I'm certain the countess knows Fidela's worth."

Opposite them, the wives giggled at some private amusement.

Percival sat up. He grabbed Bertram's glass and drank the remaining port, licking his lips provocatively. He set the glass down, then leaned forward to whisper in Bertram's ear. "I want to make love to you tonight. Spend the night with me."

A flush of desire mixed with a bristle of regret. "I would love to, Percy. I really would." Bertram placed a palm on his lover's cheek. "But I was hoping to sleep with my wife on our first night in our house. We haven't yet slept together in a bed we could properly call our own." Holiday villas and Wood Hall had their charms, but they certainly were not what Bertram would call home.

Percival reddened. "Yes, you're quite right. I hadn't even thought of that." He unfolded himself from the sofa and stood, his expression twisted as if in confusion. "I suppose we ought to sort out the sleeping arrangements."

The giggling across from them ceased. Viola and Penelope righted themselves and turned their attention to the marquess.

"Why so?" asked Viola.

"Bertie wants to be with Penny tonight." Percival focused his gaze on Viola. "And as there are only two beds, I suppose it means Viola and I will sleep together tonight."

Something like horror flitted over Viola's countenance.

"I can sleep here on a couch," said Viola.

"Absolutely not. I won't have it." A crinkle formed between Percival's brows. "My bed is massive. You won't even know I'm there."

Viola smiled thinly.

"I thought I saw a four-poster bed in one of the other bedrooms," said Penelope. "And there are so many bedrooms in this house, surely Viola has her choice of where to sleep?"

The four-poster bed had been sent from Marseilles on the advice of Lady Suffield. She thought sending such a large piece of furniture to London would be a brilliant distraction from any sort of fears the two couples had escaped. She was right. The shipment had indeed mollified the duke for a spell.

Percival thrust his hand through his hair. "I'm afraid there is no mattress for that bed yet. And the bed in the other suite is still in pieces."

He remained standing in the center of the drawing room staring at the carpet. Even Orsa's awakening and repositioning herself did not move him.

"Percy?"

"I'm all right, Bertie," Percival said. "However, I have a confession. Or, rather, I have an announcement."

Viola shifted in her seat. Bertram flashed Penelope a questioning look. She subtly shook her head and shrugged.

"When we returned to Wood Hall," Percival began, "my father made a stunning revelation. It seems he is like us." He glanced around the room. "Well, I mean he is like myself in that he is attracted to the male sex."

Astonishing. Penelope gasped. Viola looked worried.

"He told you this?" Bertram asked. "Directly?"

"Yes. He said that despite his predilections, he was able to father a son. Meaning me. He was able to bed my mother and create me."

"And is your mother like Viola," asked Bertram, "or does she prefer men?"

"She prefers men," said Percival.

That would have made one part of performing the act easier at least.

"She seemed to greatly enjoy the attentions of my widowed father at the christening celebration," added Viola.

Interesting.

"I have no more excuses," said Percival. "Viola and I must try to," he cleared his throat, "engage in intercourse and sire an heir."

Viola paled, recovering when Penelope put her arm around her shoulder.

Silence descended. Stupefaction immobilized Bertram until Percival sat beside him.

"Darling, Viola and I thought maybe you could help us?"

"Help you?" Bertram squawked. "I'm not bedding your wife if that's what you mean."

"No." Percival shook his head. "I mean the four of us. Together. In bed. You help me and Penelope helps Viola."

Bertram gaped.

"Don't look so stunned. Is it that horrid an idea?" Poignant disconsolation marred Percival's words.

"No." Bertram took Percival's trembling hands in his. "No, love. It is a creative but unusual idea." He kissed Percival's slender fingers. "Let's take tonight to think about it. All right?"

"Thank you."

Bertram pulled Percival against him. The marquess balked at first, then repositioned himself and relaxed, clinging to Bertram's waist and thigh.

With planning and choreography, such an act would work, even if it were awkward and stilted, like a ballet performed by amateurs. But if he and Penelope surprised the couple, passions might flare with some success.

Bertram grinned and kissed the top of Percival's head.

"I AM SO GLAD to finally be home."

Bertram's comforting baritone rumbled through Penelope's ear to her core. She nuzzled in the crook of his arm as they cuddled in bed, their nude bodies fitting together.

"I still feel like I'm traveling sometimes," she said.

Bertram kissed the top of her head. "I know. It has taken us a long time to get to this point. I hope you can call our humble abode home soon."

She laughed. The house on Wilton Crescent was anything but humble. "It is most definitely home. Especially with you and Georgiana." She shifted, finding a more comfortable position, sliding her hand across her husband's chest, the hair like silk against her palm, enticing her to move lower over his taut abdomen.

At the wiry hair of his groin, she raked her nails through the strands, avoiding his prick, provoking him.

He stroked her bare shoulder, slowly moving down her arm, curving his fingers around the contour of her upper arm, grazing the side of her breast, his touch igniting arousal all the way to her sex.

With her every pull of his pubic hair, he tauntingly scraped his nails against the sensitive flesh of her breast, making her squirm, until his grazing touch became too ticklish and she jerked away.

"Does my touch excite you so, Lady Ravensburgh, that you shy away from me?"

She giggled and fell on him, scratching his pectorals as she gripped the hair on his chest. "You besiege me, my lord, with sensual strokes, then tease me with tickles. So, which is it going to be?" She pulled his chest hair harder. "Make love to me or play with me?"

He grabbed her upper arms, lifted, turning until he was on top. He pushed open her legs with his knees and let his erection prod her pubic mound.

"I like the option of playing with you. Perhaps I shall start there."

She raised her head to kiss his lips, but he drew back.

"No. My rules," he said.

Which could only mean one thing. She braced herself.

He tickled.

She shrieked amid laughter with every tortuous touch, his fingers light but knowing, she twisting and turning, trying to evade every grope, he too quick, too strong, too determined.

Finally, she disentangled herself entirely from the bed, tumbling off to stand on the carpet, panting as she tried to catch her breath, a smile threatening to slash across her face.

Bertram leaned back against the headboard, his arms crossed behind his head. "Shall I assume I get the bed to myself tonight?"

Her jaw dropped. "If anything, I should send you away and garner the solace of the bed away from your grievous hectoring."

He grinned at her, a second later his expression taking on a mischievous air. "Or we could both find another bed to sleep in."

"Another bed?" She thought for only a moment before comprehension descended. "You mean you pawing your own lover while I make gentle love to mine?"

"Or we both do what we can to encourage the two of them to create a new life."

"Oh," she said thoughtfully. "Like what Percy asked earlier this evening."

"Exactly like that." Her husband quirked a brow mischievously.

"We might have to tie one of them up. Or both."

Bertram blushed, his eyes wide. "And what does my wife know of such things?"

A flush heated her. "A wife never tells. Except to remind my husband that it was Viola who blindfolded me during our first encounter."

"Yes, of course. So, she also knows about such things. However, I am reticent to restrain Percy in any way, given some abhorrent experiences in his past."

"But Percy loves and trusts you. He would know you don't mean him harm."

Bertram grinned. "He does. But we should try something a little more conventional our first time."

Penelope grabbed her dressing gown from the foot of the bed and slipped it on. She grabbed Bertram's robe and tossed it to him.

"What are you waiting for, my lord? Let's go make an heir."

PERCIVAL ROLLED OVER, trying to get comfortable, bunching the pillow under his head. He missed Bertram, the hair on his chest, the scratch of his unshaven cheeks, the subtle strength of his touch. His cock responded readily to his fantasies, goading him to frig himself. He pulled up the hem of his nightshirt—

But he shouldn't. At his side, Viola slept, her melodic wheezing not quite like Bertram's occasional snores, but offering the same comforting sound of the rhythm of sleep, the thought inspiring more visions of Bertram naked, kissing him, touching him, sucking him…

A bump in the corridor roused him from his sensual sleepiness. He unwrapped his fingers from around his cock, now slackening from distracted surprise.

The bedroom door creaked open, followed by giggling and another loud thump.

"Ouch," said a familiar masculine voice followed by more giggling in a feminine pitch.

Percival bolted upright. "Bertie? What the devil are you doing?"

"Shh, shh," came Penelope's not so very quiet admonishment. "You'll wake Viola."

"Percival," Viola said sleepily. "What's going on?"

Percival was fully awake. "I have no idea. But it appears we have midnight visitors."

The mattress sagged and jostled. And suddenly Bertie was on top of him, pulling off his nightshirt, his chest hair tickling him, his arms enveloping him, his hard prick dueling with his renewed cockstand.

Their mouths met, tongues and lips devouring each other with a hungering lust.

The mattress jostled again, followed by more giggles, the feminine tones in harmony. Penelope seducing Viola, no doubt.

Percival pushed Bertram back. "What are you up to, my lord?"

Bertram's chuckle reverberated deep in his core. "Lady Ravensburgh and I thought it a good idea to inspire the creation of an Amesbury heir."

"Ah." He smoothed his hands over Bertram's lower back, sliding his fingers up the ridges of his vertebrae to caress his shoulders, reveling in the hair-dappled flesh and well-built muscles, drinking in the masculine sensuality. He would need all the help he could get if he were to attempt what had time after time been impossible.

Bertram kissed his nose. "I know just the thing to prepare you."

Percival lifted his brows, the expression probably unnoticed in the dark. "Oh?"

Bertram leaned in and nibbled on his neck, sucking on a spot that drove Percival completely mad.

"Yes," he groaned. "That is a good start." It was definitely a distraction from the girlish moaning and bouncing to his right.

Bertram slowly slid down his body, licking his collar bone, cupping one pectoral while he rolled his tongue around the nipple of the other. The touch did not arouse so much as relax, allowing him to soften with the sensuality of the focused attention.

A sharp pinch and a nip simultaneously occurring on each nipple sent shards of lust to spike through him. He sucked air through his teeth. Bertram chuckled, his breath hot against his chest.

Percival was definitely awake now, his cock fully erect.

Bertram continued his slide down Percival's body, licking and nipping along the way. At his navel, he traced a wet spiral outwards around his abdomen. Percival's cock lay pressed between his thigh and Bertram's chest, nested in the downy hair, patiently awaiting stimulation.

But Bertram seemed perfectly content to arouse every other inch of Percival's flesh besides his cock.

After Percival's belly, Bertram moved his attention to his hip bones, his tongue meandering languidly along the ridge of muscles, along the edge of his pubic hair to the other hip. He continued, knowing full well there was a spot—

Percival jerked with a yelp at the tormenting touch on his most ticklish spot. Bertram simply chuckled, and moved his attention to a thigh.

Percival's cock was aching for attention. He restrained himself from grabbing the damned stiff stander by grabbing hanks of his lover's hair. Bertram had not touched his groin at all. Instead, he was kneading the top of his right thigh while running his tongue along the sensitive inner flesh. Percival's cock had sprung back and shifted to lay along his belly, about to burst from the too-close stimulation of flesh. Bertram shifted his attention to the other thigh, and now Percival's stones were yearning for his lover's touch.

Bertram slid his hands over Percival's buttocks, massaging as he sucked on the tender flesh right next to Percival's stones, the stubble of Bertram's jaw brushing his balls, the hair of his head tickling his groin. He licked the crease between Percival's groin and thigh, digging the pads of his fingers deeper into Percival's butt cheeks, lifting his hips to increase the reach of his tongue and mouth, still avoiding Percival's genitals.

His lover drew back. Then in one swift move, he flipped Percival over and grabbed his hips, pulling and lifting until Percival was positioned on his hands and knees on the mattress.

Percival's cock and balls throbbed for want of touch, for release. He reached for his erection only to have Bertram grip his wrist in a tight squeeze.

"Not yet, my lord."

Percival placed his hand back on the mattress.

His butt was exposed to Bertram, a thoroughly delicious position. Bertram drew his tongue along the seam of Percival's cleft, circling around the puckered hole. Percival groaned.

Jesus. He was so close to spontaneously spending.

Bertram blew on the wet trail, leaving coolness in its wake.

Every pore in Percival's body sparked with impatience. Bertram was up to something, and he had just realized what.

The split second of waiting was filled with the unsettling sighs of their wives on the bed next to them.

Percival's agonizingly hard cock twitched as the cool wetness of cold cream was slathered on his puckered hole.

Bertram slid a finger inside, then two, separating, making space, increasing Percival's excitement. His balls tightened as Bertram stroked the sensitive spot within. He twisted his eyes shut and tried to calm his libidinous body.

Bertram cupped his stones before petting them ever so nimbly, rolling them between his fingers.

He needed to spend. He was going to spend if Bertram didn't stop.

Unfortunately, Bertram stopped, now taunting Percival's anus with the head of his cock. Bertram pushed in gently, each tiny shove simultaneously thrilling and painful. Percival loved getting fucked. Bertram had not done so in a very long time, now that he had elsewhere to dip his cock.

Percival concentrated on the pain melting into pleasure, regulating his breathing to help him relax. Bertram's heavy, labored huffs were music to his ears, lulling him into a sensual ecstasy. And when he thought he could bear the pain no longer, it turned into exquisite pleasure as Bertram's pubic hair tickled against his arse.

Only then did Bertram grab Percival's erection, the feeling jolting him to push back into Bertram allowing his lover to plow deeper inside.

Bertram gripped Percival's yearning cock and rubbed his thumb over the eye, smearing the wetness over the head. Slowly, he began to pump. Too slowly, as if the act were an absentminded stroke on the velvet of a sofa.

Every muscle in Percival's abdomen tightened in anticipation. He had been too long on the edge. He could relax now and let go.

Bertram increased the tempo of his strokes, the rhythm between each upstroke and down stroke increasing. Percival's balls tightened. He let out a husky moan.

"Now!"

Bertram's command filled the air over the moans of the foursome on the bed. He let go of Percival's cock and wrapped his arm around Percival's waist, lifting, maneuvering the two of them, still joined intimately, to the middle of the bed.

"Penny? What are you doing?" came Viola's plea, her voice under him.

Feet knocked against his knees, pushing him forward, causing him to continue to right himself, finding their way until the feet and the legs they belonged to were between his knees. A waft of Penelope's perfume signaled she was the one arranging the legs, one of which was being placed, not without more knocking about, on the outside of his knee.

Annoyance began to displace languid sensuality as Bertram had not only stopped his stroking of Percival's cock, he had stilled his own movements in Percival's arsehole, as if waiting for a command.

This is not going to work...

The thought killed his erection. At the first sign of slackening, Bertram began his pumping anew, the vigorous action exciting Percival once again to hardness.

Percival decided he'd let go, let it happen, whatever it was, now he was at the verge of spending. Bertram adjusted himself, changing the angle of his attack, rubbing along a sensual spot inside—

"Bertie," he pleaded, his voice hoarse.

Bertram pushed Percival's hips toward the mattress, toward the female body between his legs, as he slammed inside Percival's arse and pumped his cock furiously.

Percival came with a clipped cry and a shudder. Bertram's grip on his cock slipped with the wet seed, but he persisted in aiming Percival's ejaculating cock to its intended orifice.

A sticky wetness engulfed the tip of Percival's prick.

Viola screamed from beneath him, clawing and pushing away frantically.

Percival and Bertram tumbled to the side. Bertram slipped off the mattress, his abrupt slide out of Percival's arse a shock of pain, then fell to the floor with a thud.

"Fuck." Bertram's oath was muffled by the carpet.

To Percival's left, Viola panted and whimpered while Penelope soothed her with pretty words.

Jesus. The whole thing had been a horrible disaster.

He and Viola couldn't do it on their own, and they couldn't do it with their lovers helping them.

Bertram climbed back onto the bed and pulled Percival into his arms.

"We'll try again, Percy. We thought making it a surprise would be fun and exciting. We won't make it a surprise next time."

Despondent, Percival nestled into Bertram's chest. "I don't think we'll make any more progress if there is a next time."

How was he ever going to create an heir?

CHAPTER NINETEEN

Cousin Nicholas looked a bit worn and beleaguered as he stood in Bertram's entryway. Helena was at his side, holding their sleeping son. The perambulator sat at the ready on the pavement with the nanny.

Helena's demeanor was the opposite of her husband's. She appeared composed and refreshed, smiling and cooing over baby Robert in her arms, unwearied despite being pregnant with her second child. And when Penelope joined her holding Georgiana, the two acted like old friends, kissing cheeks and fussing over the children. Penelope made sure her own perambulator and nanny were ready, and the two women and their children left for an outing in the nearby park.

The outing had been Helena's idea, a chance for the cousins-in-law to get to know each other better. Privately, Penelope had been astonished and honored, and had fretted about what to talk about and what to wear.

"If you're nervous, let Helena direct the course of conversation, love," Bertram had counseled the night before.

As he'd expected, Penelope had found the perfect dress. The two women looked like they had leapt from the pages of a French fashion magazine.

After the wives had left, Bertram called for tea, then ushered Nicholas into the morning room.

Nicholas milled about as if his mind were elsewhere, picking up objects and perusing the artwork hanging on the walls until the tea arrived. After the footman had closed the door behind him, Nicholas promptly plopped onto the couch and surveyed his surroundings.

"Who's got the good taste, you or Percy?"

Bertram chuckled as he poured tea. "Both of us." He handed a cup to Nicholas.

Nicholas took a sip of tea, letting out a long sigh. He placed his teacup on the side table, toed off his shoes, and stretched out on the couch, his heels propped up on the armrest. "Sometimes I miss my bachelor rooms in London. I cannot do this at the Phillips' house. It's too uncouth."

"You forget Percy and I are both married. Our house is no longer a bachelor domain. At any moment a wife could saunter in and be appalled."

"But will either of your wives care if they find your cousin stretched out on your couch?"

"No." Bertram chuckled again. "Although Viola might make a snide comment. And Penelope might be surprised to find you feel so comfortable in this house."

Nicholas closed his eyes. "Why is that? Your house is a refuge from politics and my father-in-law's formidable presence." He opened his eyes with a start. "Damn, I should have brought my medical journals," he muttered.

"So, it's not at all strange for you, is it?"

Nicholas lifted his head. "What would be strange?"

"That I'm married to Penelope Hardcastle?"

Nicholas paled briefly, then covered his face with his hands as he laid his head back against the armrest. "Oh, God. She doesn't talk to you about it, does she? I'm positively mortified."

Bertram chuckled. "Perhaps I shouldn't have told you."

Nicholas propped himself up on his elbows. "Oh, no, Bertie, you can't do that. Not now. What did she say?"

"That you were one of the best she's ever had."

Nicholas turned beet red.

"Until me, of course."

Nicholas laughed.

"She was beside herself fretting about spending an afternoon with your wife, however."

"Bollocks." Nicholas groaned. "I hope they don't start gossiping about my legendary prowess in bed."

Now it was Bertram's turn to laugh.

The door swung open, and Percival strode in, the door closing with a determined click behind him.

Nicholas scrambled to sit up. "Oh, it's only you. Good afternoon, Percy."

"When were you going to tell me the brother of my dead lover was visiting us, Bertie, dear?" He took Bertram's hand, lifted it to his lips, and kissed the palm.

Nicholas gaped. "I thought you two had, well, changed."

"Just me," said Bertram, smirking behind his cup after taking a sip of tea.

Percival sat on the sofa next to Nicholas. "I'm still inverted. Bertie's discovered he's merely half-inverted."

Bertram scowled. He despised that word.

Percival motioned for Nicholas to resume his relaxed pose. Nicholas stretched his legs out, his feet in Percival's lap.

"You're not going to try to seduce me, are you?" Nicholas grinned.

"Sorry, Nicky," Percival patted Nicholas's ankles. "As devastatingly handsome as you are, you're just not as handsome as your late brother. But if you wanted to…" Percival sighed. "Too bad the love of other men doesn't run in your family."

Nicholas winked with a glance at Bertram. "Oh, I think it does."

"Don't you think it odd, Nicky, that you've never been with a man?" Bertram baited.

"What? No!"

"Not even in the desolate hills of Asia Minor?" Percival continued the game. "Bundled up with your servant boy for warmth during the long cold winter nights in your yurt?"

Nicholas shook his head with a grin. "You should write erotic stories, Percy. My father-in-law reads that sort of thing."

"The same father-in-law you're trying to escape from?" asked Bertram.

"Him, and the stack of legislation on my desk. Something about newspapers printing libelous statements, I think. Terrifically riveting stuff," Nicholas scoffed. He eyed Bertram. "You're a writer, perhaps you can advise me?"

Bertram rolled his eyes. "I want nothing to do with Parliament, thank you very much."

Nicholas laughed. "You don't know what you're missing, Percy. You'll love Parliament once you become duke. Or you'll be smart and take your duke's prerogative and simply decide not to show up."

Percival snorted. "Luckily, my father hasn't bothered me about that yet."

Nicholas studied him. He wiggled his toes. "But he is bothering you about something. I can tell."

Percival sighed. "An heir. He wants an heir as quickly as possible."

"Why as quickly as possible?" Nicholas sat up a bit. "Is Amesbury dying?" His tone held a touch of alarm.

"No. But he wants me to have an heir in his lifetime. He's worried I won't make any effort at all."

Nicholas glanced between the two men. "Because you two are still carrying on?"

Percival remained silent.

"We are," said Bertram. "However, the issue is because Percy and Viola haven't, well, been carrying on."

"Ah." Nicholas sat up to drink his tea. "So, tell me about Lady Norrington, Percy."

Percival sighed. "I'm fond of Viola. We've become close, just not in the traditional way a husband and wife are expected to be."

"Meaning you're not sharing a bed."

"Believe it or not, we do sometimes. We decided that we should get used to each other and get to know each other's bodies. She has a nice form, and I admire her as one might a sculpture in a museum. But so far, she's about as arousing to me as, well," Percival smirked at Nicholas, "as I am to you."

Nicholas chuckled.

"We've tried," Percival continued. "Trust me, we've tried." He raised a knowing eyebrow at Bertram.

Which set Bertram to laughing, eliciting guffaws from Percival.

Nicholas regarded them with a confused mien. "What's so funny?"

"I really don't think we should tell you, Nicky," said Percival. "Let's just say four people in a bed gets tricky. Too many legs and knees and such."

Nicholas blushed crimson. "Well, that's an image I will have to contemplate later." He winked at Bertram. "Especially if Penelope was in the mix."

"She was focused on Viola's needs," said Percival.

Bertram raised a brow at his lover. Percival shrugged.

Nicholas looked between the two men. "What? Or perhaps I don't want to know?"

"It's relevant to the topic," said Bertram. "Although it's a secret, Nicky. Only the four of us know."

Nicholas nodded. "I understand. I'm used to keeping family secrets, as Percy can attest. And as a doctor."

"Of course," Bertram nodded, then drew in a long inhale. "Viola is a woman who only loves other women—"

Nicholas emitted a choking sound.

"So, she also cannot, or rather does not want to perform with her husband. Still, there is the urgency to create an heir. And the duke is quite beside himself that the four of us returned to England with only Penny and I having a child."

How much more of the story should he reveal? Bertram glanced at Percival, who nodded.

As a doctor, his cousin might be able to offer advice. "There is an even darker secret, though."

Nicholas stared wide-eyed between the two men. "You have my word I will keep anything you say to me confidential."

Bertram breathed out slowly. "Had Georgiana been a boy, we had planned to pass the child off as Percy and Viola's son. That's why we stayed away for so many months. Except, well, then she turned out to be a girl."

Nicholas regarded him sympathetically. "So, you kept her as your own daughter."

"Had she been a boy, we were determined to go through with the deception. Penny and I would still have had a hand in raising the boy, since we all live together."

"We would have presented the child to my father as my heir," said Percival.

"Good God," Nicholas muttered. "I wonder how often such a thing has happened in the past. I suspect you are not the first to come up with such an idea."

"We thought it rather clever," Percival pouted.

"Yes," Nicholas agreed. "Definitely. I do suspect you are the first 'inverted' married couple to attempt such a deception with a 'half-inverted' couple."

Bertram chortled darkly. Nicholas's perspicaciousness was one reason the three of them got along so well.

"I would imagine a conventional woman in the same situation would attempt seduction of her husband with no success," Nicholas continued. "Then she would probably end up sleeping with a footman with beneficial results." He slumped against the couch, pursing his lips thoughtfully. "This is all quite fascinating from my perspective. Frustrating from yours, I can well imagine. What other strategies have been considered?"

"Besides fraudulently passing off an infant as a duke's heir and a four-way seduction?" quipped Percival. "Nothing else."

Bertram flushed. "Well, we really haven't given the four-way erotic entanglement enough of a chance, Percy."

Percival groaned. "It was a fucking disaster, Bertie, and you know it."

"I don't know. It was too much of a surprise. We'll have to plan it better next time."

"And my prick will stay flaccid knowing it's supposed to perform."

"Not if I can help it, Percy, love."

From the depths of the sofa Nicholas convulsed in delight. Having friends who understood much of their bickering was in jest was such a relief.

"Well," Bertram said. "If you ask me, the four-way is still under consideration. The problem will be one of us getting the courage to instigate the act."

Nicholas sat up and leaned his elbows on his knees. "What if I told you there might be a medical procedure that could offer a solution?"

CHAPTER TWENTY

Percival gaped at Nicholas. "A procedure? How do you mean?"

He glanced at Bertram, whose eyes were wide in hopeful surprise. "Oh, please, Dr. Atherley, do tell."

"I was, rather, Dr. Ramsay, and I may have to bring him back," Nicholas said with a grunt. "Anyway, I have read studies of something called mechanical impregnation, whereby the sperm is placed inside the female via a syringe."

Bertram's jaw dropped. "Are you serious?"

"Yes, it has been successfully performed on animals."

Jesus. Percival's heart pounded. "What about people?"

"A Scottish doctor performed the procedure successfully on a woman about a century ago—"

"A century ago?" Percival's hopefulness turned to disappointment. "A century ago? Why hasn't anyone continued, what seems to my mind, this brilliant method of procreation?"

Nicholas pursed his lips as if suppressing a grin. "There have been a few more attempts during our century. An American doctor, whose overall scientific methods were not altogether ethical in my opinion, continued with experimentation. He was able to achieve a pregnancy about fifteen years ago."

Hope once again ignited in Percival's heart. "Why haven't we heard about this before? Surely such a miracle should be taking place far more often."

"Well, it is rather radical," said Nicholas. "The procedure necessitates a thorough comprehension of the functions of the female body, and not all doctors have such an education. Then, there are moral implications of a man who is a doctor and not the woman's husband touching her in an intimate way in order to produce a child. The procedure might be considered emasculating to some men. Then there are the issues of a doctor playing God, in a way."

"I don't care what my vicar thinks," Percival spat excitedly. "I only care what my father thinks."

"Which brings up a point," Bertram began. "Will the duke somehow know the child was conceived in this manner?"

One corner of Nicholas's mouth turned upward. "It will probably be less suspicious than presenting the duke with Bertie's child." He patted Percival's knee. "I cannot imagine there will be anything unusual about the child except for the manner of its conception."

Percival rose and began to pace. "How on earth do you know about such things?"

"Despite my responsibilities as Earl of St. Albans, I keep up with my former profession by reading family practice publications and other research journals. More importantly, I keep my mind open not only to new discoveries but also to reconsidering past practices. During my sojourn to Asia Minor, instead of sleeping with servant boys"—Nicholas winked at Percival—"I was busy learning about intriguing remedies and treatments. When I returned to England, I practiced with a doctor who has very radical notions about women's sexuality."

Bertram beamed revealing his keenness for the outrageous idea. "How do we do this, Nicky? Can you perform the procedure?"

"The best equipment would be in a doctor's office. But that would be too public, I fear. There might be gossip or speculation as to why Lady Norrington kept going to a doctor."

"Kept going?" Percival stopped his pacing.

"Fertilization might not happen on the first try, Percy," Nicholas explained. "Pregnancy can result following one encounter or take one hundred encounters."

He stared, dumbfounded by the pronouncement. "Is there anything Viola or I could do to better ensure immediate success?"

"If a woman keeps track of her menses—"

Percival gasped, perhaps a little too loudly.

"I mean her courses," Nicholas explained.

"Yes, yes." Percival nodded. "I do know what all of that means, Nicky. Go on."

"If she keeps a record of her menses, then with my help, we should be able to determine her more fertile days. Those would be the best days to perform the procedure."

"Could we do it here?" Percy tried to contain his excitement. "In our bedroom? That would help mitigate any scandal about why Viola might be seeing a doctor. After all, you are family. And you really should visit us more often."

Nicholas snorted. "Yes, I can do the procedure here. I will have to acquire the necessary equipment to collect and, er, distribute your sperm, Percy."

"Yes, of course." *God*, this was going to be spectacular.

"Can you get the equipment without yourself alerting suspicion?" Bertram's query was placid yet earnest. "You are no longer practicing."

Nicholas thought a moment. "I do still have a connection with that radical family practice doctor. A meeting between us should not raise questions. I know he will be discreet."

"Good, good." The day Father discovered Viola was finally pregnant could not come soon enough.

"Is the sex of the child somehow determined with this modern method?" asked Bertram.

Nicholas scrunched up his face. "Ah, no. It is very much like the conventional approach to fertilization in that way. Unfortunately, you get what you get."

"So, the procedure might have to be performed again if the child is a girl?" Bertram inquired.

"Yes. Especially in your situation, since you require a male child eventually."

Damn and blast. Percival sighed. "I want to discuss all of this with Viola first. She needs to approve of the procedure."

Nicholas nodded. "I agree."

"How will this work, exactly? I want to tell her what to expect."

"She can be in her own bed, her legs separated. I'll have to spread some oil on her," he gestured to his own crotch. "It will facilitate the insertion of the instrument containing the sperm." Nicholas cleared his throat. "So, Lady Norrington will be prepared and waiting while Percy is, er, well, providing the donation."

"Oh, so you want me to be there."

"You *have* to be present, Percy." Nicholas laughed. "I guess you don't have to be in the very same room—"

"I can easily be here at home if you need me."

Nicholas shook his head. "Percy, I don't think you quite understand. I need you at home on the day, in a place that is very near where your wife will be splayed out waiting, because I need you to masturbate and spend your seed into a receptacle."

Percival flushed. "What?"

Bertram chuckled. "I can help with that, Percy dear."

Nicholas offered a bemused smile. "You asked what your wife could expect. She can expect to be on her bed, her legs spread open, while her husband, located very nearby, frigs and spends into the barrel of a syringe I hope to obtain from a colleague. Then, as swiftly as possible, I will inject Lady Norrington's privates with your sperm using the syringe."

Percival blinked. "Oh. I see." He shook his head, letting it fall back as he looked up blankly. "Jesus." He plopped down next to Bertram. "I guess I wasn't picturing how this would actually transpire. I don't have to frig myself in front of you Nicky, do I?"

Nicholas laughed. "God, no. And I prefer you do not. Bertie can be with you, that is not a problem. I presume your bedroom has some sort of room attached to it. A dressing area or a bath?"

Bertram wrapped an arm around Percival's shoulders. "Yes. We'll manage." He grinned at Nicholas. "Thank you, Nicky, for consenting to help us with such a complicated and unusual scheme."

"I have no doubt that it will work. And thank you both. It will be wonderful to be a scientist again."

Percival shrugged Bertram off. "I'll go get Viola. Nicky, will you explain all of this to her?"

"Of course. I'm here until my wife returns." Nicholas stretched his legs along the couch again.

Percival rushed out the door. There was hope at last.

Viola stared blankly out the window of the bedroom reading nook, her book forgotten in her lap. It wasn't a bad book. Mrs. Gaskell's novel was quite good, but something she read reminded her of Penelope. As her mind wandered, she began daydreaming about her Penny, musings that filled her with a sense of yearning.

One day it would be she and Penelope strolling with their respective children in the park. And it would be they who would invite the pretty Countess of St. Albans and her son to join them.

This was a surprising daydream to have. Viola had never wanted children, partly because once she realized she desired women, she'd assumed she would never have the opportunity to have children. Plus, Edwin had been a wretched older brother—so why would any person want to have children like that? But seeing Penelope with her daughter, knowing Georgiana would be raised in a loving household with four parents, made her want to give the little girl a sibling. A brother, eventually. But until the brother arrived, perhaps a sister would do.

A knock on the bedroom door stirred her from her reverie.

"Come."

Percival entered, his cheeks flushed, eyes wide, grinning ear-to-ear. "Viola, darling. I just heard about a wonderful discovery. A medical treatment that can help us."

She turned on the bench, letting her legs dangle above the carpet. "Oh? What do you mean by a treatment?"

"Nicky's downstairs—"

"Nicholas? The Earl of St. Albans?" The use of boyish sobriquets by the long-time friends was so endearing.

"Yes." Percival's brow scrunched. "You do know Nicky used to be a doctor?"

"Oh, I've heard that. I think Penny mentioned it."

"Well, it seems he continues to keep abreast of his former profession out of sheer enjoyment. He has come up with a solution to our predicament."

Her heart thumped. "About having a son?"

"About having any children at all." Percival sighed. "It's rather brilliant, I must say. But he can explain it all to you. He's downstairs visiting while he waits for Helena."

The beautiful countess was undoubtedly having a wonderful time with Penelope.

"He wants to ask you some questions of a medical nature."

Viola put her book aside. "All right." She slipped on her shoes, then held out her hand. "Take me downstairs to Doctor St. Albans."

In the morning room, the earl was pacing the carpet, talking and gesturing, while Bertram watched and laughed at whatever story was being told. The merriment subsided as soon as Percival and Viola entered.

"Nicky, I've brought the Marchioness of Norrington." Her husband gazed at her as if in admiration. "Viola."

The earl approached, his smile wide and genuine. He took her hands in his. "Lady Norrington, it is good to see you."

His brown eyes held kindness. His respectful demeanor inspired trust.

"My husband says you have a remedy for our situation?"

"I hope so." He indicated she should sit, then he continued his pacing anew.

Percival sat on the armrest of the couch next to her, his hand on her shoulder. They were both eager for a resolution.

St. Albans stopped and looked at her. "Did Percy explain anything to you yet?"

"No. He just said you wanted to ask me some questions."

"Right." St. Albans pursed his lips as he resumed his slow strides. "I understand the two of you cannot engage in marital relations, yet still need to procreate. The method I'm considering involves introducing the sperm of the male into the female via a syringe. It is a procedure that has been used successfully on animals—"

"Animals?" Viola squawked.

"Yes," continued the earl, as if that were not so strange a notion. "Dogs, as a point of fact."

"Do you see me as a dog, doctor?" Shock riffled through Viola. Was that how he saw people like her and Percival?

St. Albans paled. "I apologize, my lady. I mean no insult whatsoever. I was simply trying to explain that this unconventional technique has mostly been tested on animals. It has been tried on human subjects as well."

"Human subjects?"

"Yes. I mean women."

"You make it sound so…so scientific."

"It is, rather," said the earl with a nervous laugh. "I apologize if I seem a bit scientific myself. I'm curious whether the process will work. The experiments using women and men are few and far between."

"You could write a paper," offered Viola.

St. Albans chuckled.

"I don't want my private life in some medical journal," Percival protested.

"If it helps others like us, dear husband, then perhaps it will be necessary. The doctor does not have to use our names." Viola turned her attention to the earl. "Please, continue."

St. Albans steepled his fingers and tapped the formation on his chin. "The sperm must be fresh"—he glanced at Percival—"so we will have to arrange for Percy to be in a nearby room, as I understand the two of you are not intimate in that way."

Viola snickered. "I daresay my husband does not find me provocative enough to spend in my presence."

St. Albans blushed briefly, then smiled. "Well, I see I can be as explicit as I need to be, Lady Norrington. Thank you for that."

She nodded with a sly smile.

"Once we have Percy's sperm, I will inject it inside you, emulating the act of procreation as if the two of you had engaged in sexual intercourse."

"Oh." Viola hadn't expected St. Albans to be quite so explicit.

St. Albans stopped before her. "However, in order for this to be successful, I need to have a calendar of your feminine cycles." The pacing resumed. "See, women are only fertile at certain times of the month, or more precisely, are more fertile during these times. So, I would need to know when you have your courses over a length of time. Perhaps several months."

"Ah. And how would you need me to keep this information and provide it to you?"

"Perhaps a calendar, or a diary."

Viola smiled. "Lord St. Albans, what if I told you I kept such a journal?"

The earl stared wide-eyed, brows raised in astonishment. "A diary with information about your courses?"

"Yes."

St. Albans knelt before her. "I would be most grateful if you would supply this information to me as soon as possible. I can attempt to track when you are most fertile—" He studied her. "When were your courses last?"

"Monday was my last day."

"Excellent." The earl had a very charismatic smile. "Do you have information about your courses for the last, er, perhaps six months?"

"I do indeed."

"Oh, marvelous." There was that trust-inducing glimmer again. St. Albans stood and resumed his pacing, albeit far more slowly.

"Darling," Percival asked, "you've mentioned this journal before. What on earth ever inspired you to make note of such information?"

"I began keeping a journal once I realized I was...I was..." Viola looked sidelong at Percival.

"Nicky knows, dear. About me, about Bertie, about you."

"And Penelope?"

St. Albans abruptly stopped his pacing. He blushed in her direction, then coughed.

Bertram grinned. "Ah, yes, Nicky does know a little about you and Penelope."

A deep crinkle formed between St. Albans's eyes as he shook his head slowly. "And I thought my in-laws had a complicated arrangement."

Viola glanced between Percival and Bertram. "I wouldn't call it complicated. Especially since we all live together."

"There is that," St. Albans chuckled.

"Well," Viola began, "I started keeping a diary when I first had my courses because I had no idea what they were, really. I did not want to pester my father, especially since the bleeding stopped after a day or two. Later, one of the maids told me that bleeding monthly is what made me weak and a woman."

St. Albans thinned his lips and shook his head in silence.

"As I matured, I kept the journal out of habit. And then one day, because it really did seem to be one particular day, I realized I preferred the company of women. That I desired women. And I certainly did not desire the boys I was forced to dance with at assemblies and balls.

"I decided to continue the journal because I thought my courses might go away since I realized I didn't fancy men. I feared I would become like a man. But no such thing ever happened. I understand better now that some women simply love other women."

St. Albans smiled at her. "And some men simply love other men."

"But you are not of that mind?"

He chuckled. "No. Far from it. But my late brother was." He flicked a somber glance at Percival.

Of course. She had almost forgotten the connection. The man who had abused Percival in his youth was the earl's deceased elder brother.

"I would love to see that journal, Lady Norrington, or if you could copy down the information. Then I can best schedule when the procedure should be done for greatest effect."

"By all means, my lord. I will retrieve it now. You will have the information in your hands before your beautiful wife returns from her outing with my beloved." She winked.

He blushed and glanced away sheepishly before meeting her gaze. "I thank you, my lady, for your willing complicity in this innovative scheme."

Viola stood, bowed to the men, and left the morning room. Her step along the stairs was light and full of hope.

CHAPTER TWENTY-ONE

Notes had been taken, cycles had been determined, a plan put in place. And finally, the day had arrived. Percival was as nervous as Bertram had been the day his daughter was born.

Except today was the day Percival hoped his son would be conceived.

He stared at his useless cock in his hand as he sat on the bed.

Nicholas had once again assured him the procedure would—well, *should* work. When Viola was in a fertile period, Nicky had explained, it would be time to perform the procedure. All Percival had to do was spend in a metal receptacle. The procedure would be repeated once a day over five days.

It all sounded very simple.

Percival really shouldn't be nervous.

Except now that the day had actually arrived, he was incredibly nervous.

So nervous he didn't think he could spend.

Bollocks.

He generally gloried in masturbating, but now, every time he tried, unwanted images flashed in his brain. Sometimes an image of Viola naked, or a memory of Father berating him. Or an image of the large metal cylinder in which he was meant to spew his seed. Whatever the thought, his cock would shrivel.

In the adjoining room, Viola was waiting for him. More specifically, she was waiting for his contribution to their cause. Penelope was with her, presumably offering emotional and physical succor. Nicholas was somewhere, having arrived early. Probably not with the wives. Possibly in the library or the breakfast room—

Ugh. Percival fell back onto the mattress. Why on earth did he care?

All these people counting on him to perform was positively distressing. How could he endure five days of this?

What he needed was something to distract him from his distractions.

He sighed. Eventually, Viola would need his contribution, and someone would send Bertie looking for him. Percival stared at the bedroom door, willing Bertie to wander through.

He'd better arrive soon, or there would be no heir for the dukedom.

BERTRAM FIGURED HE'D lingered over his coffee and the *Morning Post* long enough. Percival had left the breakfast table about an hour before, assuring him that he would be able to "take care of it himself". Except Percival's hands had been shaking as he'd poured his coffee, and Bertram knew his lover would be far too distracted to perform his aristocratic duty.

He chuckled as he bounded up the stairs to Percival's bedroom.

Nicholas paced in the corridor, occasionally stopping to peruse a painting or some *objet d'art* that cluttered the hall.

"Nicky? Is everything all right? Shouldn't you be with Viola?"

"Lady Ravensburgh—"

"Penelope," Bertram interrupted. "She wants you to call her Penelope."

A faint blush colored Nicholas's cheeks, then dissipated quickly. "I am waiting for Penelope to let me know when Lady Norrington is ready for me to enter. I suspect she's very nervous. I hope Penelope is able to calm her. Nervousness can be a hindrance to conception."

Bertram chuckled. "I do believe Percy is having the same bout of nerves. You'd think we were asking them to copulate."

Nicholas grinned. "But I completely understand. Modern medical techniques can be daunting to the layman."

"In Percy's case, I fear it is more his father's expectations that are daunting."

"Yes. Pressure to produce an heir could be much more worrisome."

Bertram patted Nicholas on the shoulder. "I am about to encourage the marquess, Nicky."

"Yes, of course. Ah, but don't encourage him, er, too much, Bertie."

Bertram shot Nicholas a querying look.

"This is a very time-sensitive operation. I need Percy's contribution to be extremely fresh."

Bertram chuckled. "Don't worry. We will be ready to provide his sample at a moment's notice. Just knock on the adjoining door."

Nicholas grinned. "All right."

"Should I send tea up while you wait in the corridor?"

"Thank you, but that won't be necessary. I think I'll continue my own nervous pacing. I've never done such a thing, you know."

Bertram gave Nicholas's shoulder a squeeze, then slowly opened the door to the bedroom where his lover waited.

Percival sat on the bed, wearing his drawers and shirt, his hand holding his flaccid cock, a pitiful expression marring his handsome visage.

"Tut, tut, Percy. You didn't already spend, did you?"

Percival fell back against the mattress with a groan. "I'm useless. It's hopeless. I'm never going to have a bloody son."

Bertram grabbed Percival's drawers at the knees and yanked them to his ankles. He climbed on the bed, straddling him. "You are going to have a bloody son, and I am going to help you do it." He grabbed Percival's cock.

Percival flailed in an attempt to wriggle out from under him, cursing as he tried to kick off his drawers, only succeeding in having Bertram release his grip on his manhood. Bertram instead held him down by his shoulders.

"Stop struggling," he growled.

Percival scowled. "Stop mocking me."

"I am not mocking you, I'm trying to help. My understanding, my lord, is that there is a very delicate balance to this plan. You need to be ready, but not overly ready."

Percival calmed. "How do you mean?"

"We can't have you spending until your sperm is needed."

"Jesus, Bertie, I can't even get a stiff stander. How the hell am I going to spend?"

Bertram leaned in, brushing his lips along Percival's cheekbone. "Darling, have I ever failed in my duty as your lover?"

A sigh escaped Percival's lips. "No."

He swept his tongue over the seam of Percival's mouth. "Then have confidence in my strategy. Give in, love."

Percival's regular rhythm of inhalation and exhalation faltered, a sign he was beginning to be aroused. "What are you going to do to me?" A touch of fear inhabited the question.

Bertram offered a half-grin, not sure if his mischievousness was discernible. "I can assure you that you will enjoy it."

He scrambled off the bed to the nightstand where he kept the leather strips he sometimes used to tie Penelope's wrists. He untangled and straightened the strips, shielding himself from Percival's view as he did so.

"What's that?" Percival said over his shoulder.

Bertram turned sharply. "I've wanted to do this for a long while. I think it's time."

He grabbed Percival's arm and hauled him off the bed. His lover had kicked off his drawers while Bertram was searching for the leather strips. Percival wore only his shirt.

Perfect.

Bertram held the leather strips between his teeth and pushed Percival back against the bedpost. He wrapped his arms around the post and held him secure with one hand. With the other, he took a leather strip.

Percival's eyes widened. "You're not going to do what I think you're going to do, are you?"

Bertram merely chuckled, a mouthful of leather keeping him from responding with words.

He molded his body against Percival's as he tied each wrist to the bedpost. When he was finished, he patted Percival's cheek, a gesture the marquess greatly disliked. "How's that, love?"

Percival tried to free himself to no avail. He scowled.

Bertram grinned. "Looks as if that will do just fine." He grabbed the hem of Percival's shirt and tied it in a knot at his waist, revealing a prick now half-hard in its dark blond nest.

"I see my efforts have had the intended effect." Bertram slid a hand under Percival's prick to cradle it in his palm. He licked his lips. Torturing Percival was going to be sweet.

He dropped to his knees and drew Percival's semi-aroused cock into his mouth, sucking, willing him to full hardness. Success was achieved in mere seconds.

Bertram drew back with suction, releasing Percival's prick with a pop. The gorgeous rod bobbed before him. He pecked the head before flicking the tip of his tongue at the eye, then swirled circles around the glans.

Percival's breathing became ragged. He slumped against the bedpost with a groan.

Bertram slid his tongue down the shaft, then dragged the upstroke at a languid pace. He knew Percival's face would have that sumptuous, dreamy look, his lids half closed, his lips dry from heaving air through his open mouth.

He continued his leisurely strokes with his tongue, feeling thigh muscles melt under his hands. Percival's eyes would be closed now, his lips curved in a faraway smile.

Such a wondrous thing to see a lover under one's control. Bertram stood, palming Percival's cock, now stiff as stone, and gazed at his lover's face.

Percival was as he imagined, except with a slight awkwardness given he was bound and probably a bit uncomfortable.

"I know you prefer to be sucked," Bertram murmured in his ear. "But I want to watch you, want to see your face as you descend into erotic oblivion, want to see you give in to my touch."

Want to see the moment you create our son. He wouldn't say that aloud. It would be a distraction. Bertram wanted this child as much as Percival. Possibly more. He wanted them to experience fatherhood together.

He gripped Percival's cock and rubbed the soft skin over the iron-hard core, pulled the foreskin over the glans, all the while watching Percival's expression dissolve into rapturous insensibility.

Bertram maintained a steady rhythm, letting Percival acclimate himself to the slow pace of arousal, watching him succumb drowsily. Very subtly, he increased the pace of his strokes, a change the mind might find imperceptible, until the cock began demanding even more.

Percival's eyes flickered open, his pupils large, their depths filled with lust. He smiled and let out a whimpering moan. He had just connected cock to mind and began that glorious climb to lubriciousness.

Precisely where Bertram intended to keep him. Perhaps taunt him even further by taking him to the edge.

Bertram regularized his strokes, maintaining the rhythm the cock found delicious. Percival's jaw slackened.

"Please." He licked his lips. "Please, Bertie."

Bertram tucked his lower lip between his teeth and raised a brow. He did not deviate from his steady pace.

Percival's breath fell in rhythmic pants. His eyes closed tightly. "Damn you, Bertie," he hissed. "Damn you."

That was better. Percival was on the edge now, being held there, his desire utterly in Bertram's control.

Bertram released him. Percival slumped forward, his forehead on Bertram's shoulder.

"What are you doing to me?" He lifted his head, his lashes damp from the agony of forced restraint.

"Making sure you are ready when needed, my lord."

Percival exhaled loudly. "Just this once. I'll allow this once. But damn you, Bertie. You are the worst fiend."

Bertram kissed his dry lips, moistening them. "And your best friend."

From under the covers in her bed, Viola clung to Penelope, searching for comfort against the fears and worries deluging her.

"Penny, I'm scared. What if it doesn't work?"

"Then we'll try again."

Oh God. Not the foursome. "The same way?"

Penelope laughed. "Unless you want to make love to your husband."

Viola turned onto her back. "No, I really don't. I suppose this new way to make a baby is good for women like me."

"And men like your husband."

"At least the doctor instills confidence that the procedure will work."

Penelope propped herself on her elbow and brushed the edges of Viola's face. "It will work, and you'll be fine." She pressed her lips to Viola's, her kiss sensuous and warming.

Viola arched her back, wanting more of her lover's touch.

Penelope slid her hand under the covers to fondle Viola's breasts. Viola, as she had been directed, wore only her chemise. Penelope was fully clothed, as was proper given the circumstance, but unfortunate at that very moment.

"Bertie always makes sure I am ready for him before we make love." Penelope pulled up Viola's chemise slowly. "He pleasures me with his mouth and fingers, ensuring I desire him thoroughly." The chemise was up around her waist now. "I'm certain a bit of pleasure will help you relax." She kissed Viola's cheek.

Viola moaned her approval. Already Penelope's questing fingers tickling her belly were stirring a spark of warmth inside.

Her fingers moved further, sliding through the strands of her mons. "Close your eyes, love," Penelope purred. "Shut out the world. Just think of your pleasure." Her lips tickled Viola's ear. "Think of you and me."

Viola closed her eyes. Suddenly before her was the glorious golden sun of southern France, warming the sand between her toes.

And a promise of a fantasy she always wished could have been true.

She and Penelope naked on the beach, kissing and caressing, the rays of the sun browning their bodies, the rhythm of the ocean and the song of the birds the accompaniment to their moans and giggles.

They would kiss, their tongues teasingly twining, tempting each other with what was to come when tongues sought pleasure elsewhere.

Viola would roll on top of her lover, their breasts pressing together, nipples exciting under the crush of yielding flesh. She would kiss Penelope's perfumed neck, then nip her pale shoulder, brushing off the sand sparkling on her upper arm as she moved to a succulent breast.

Penelope's bounteous bosom would fill her mouth as she twirled her tongue around a puckering peak. Penelope would arch her back, wanting more, the fullness of her breast pressing into Viola's nose, almost smothering her.

Viola would know the sensual movement meant Penelope desired a fulfillment beyond the mini-orgasm that burst with attention to her nipples. As if in agreement, Penelope would undulate her hips, pressing her mount against Viola's.

Viola would move further, kissing and sucking the soft flesh of Penelope's belly.

"Yes," her lover would moan as she slid even further.

Viola would study the lovely mount and its thatch of light brown hair. She would part the wiry curls, separate the plump lips, and once uncovered, blow on the erect pearl.

Penelope would sigh at that.

And then Viola would delve in, kissing the nether lips as if they were the petals of Penelope's smile, sucking the hardened nub before plumbing her depths.

Penelope would thrash under her with each lick, pushing her sex against Viola's mouth, wanting more, but not wanting the finality.

Viola understood. She wished the two of them could remain suspended in that space between elation and climax. There they would know pure joy.

As she pleasured her lover, Viola would seek her own sex, touching herself, her sticky wetness facilitating her own satisfaction. She would rub as hard as her tongue licked and her lips sucked, taking them both to the precipice of rapture, holding Penelope there for a moment before releasing her to ecstasy, her lover's sweet wail being her own downfall into the abyss of concupiscence.

Viola opened her eyes. The sight of the bedroom ceiling reminded her that she was not on a beach in France. She was, however, in her lover's arms, satiated and serene.

Penelope kissed her nose as she removed her hand from between Viola's legs.

"I'll alert Doctor St. Albans that you are ready, love," she said. Penelope got off the bed and went out the door.

Viola drew in a deep breath and exhaled any lingering trepidation. She was ready, she was excited even. She would give Percival a son. Then perhaps there would be a daughter in a year or two.

The Earl of St. Albans entered with Penelope in tow. He approached Viola.

"Good morning, my lady. How are you feeling?"

"Very well, doctor."

He smiled at the honorific. "Now, my lady, I apologize, but I must request you draw down the bed covers and lie in a most unladylike manner."

"How shall I position myself?" she asked as she folded the covers back.

St. Albans cleared his throat. "I need you to put a pillow under your backside, then bend your knees and separate your legs."

As she did so, he muttered approbations and smiled politely.

She held her unladylike position. "Like this?"

He nodded. "I'll fetch Percy, or his contribution, rather."

Viola giggled as Penelope took her hand.

"Let's make a son, doctor."

A KNOCK ON THE ADJOINING DOOR between the bedrooms roused Percival from his fog of unrequited lust. He had been on edge so long, he was exhausted. His body had slumped until the leather bindings were cutting into his wrists.

Bertram kissed his cheek, then left to check on the door.

"Lady Norrington is ready when you are," said Nicholas at the threshold. He handed something to Bertram.

Something that glinted in the sunlight filtering through the bedroom windows. Something metal and shiny that looked very much like a large syringe.

The fog dissipated to be partially replaced by those pesky nerves again.

"If I have to start all over again, Percy, I will."

The sonorous sensuality of Bertram's baritone made his cock twitch to full stand. Well, mostly anyway.

Bertram grabbed his cock and pulled, sparking every pleasure center back to life.

"Good," he chuckled. "I see you are ready." He tugged on Percival's prick cruelly, eliciting an unwanted yelp. "You will spend for me, my lord. And you will spend now."

The forceful tone sparked a desire long buried. Playing the dominant was a role Bertram clearly relished. That he was as enthusiastic for what was happening was thrilling.

Percival moved his hips in meek encouragement. "Please, my lord. Make me spend."

Bertram smiled a half-smile as he began his strokes, gentle and slow, letting lust rise languidly. Percival released a moan and thrust his hips forward.

"You want more, my lord?" Bertram's breath fell hot and damp on his cheek as his efforts quickened. "Beg for it."

"God, yes. Please, please." Each tug brought him closer to the edge, until he hovered at the precipice.

Until Bertram slowed once again. "I can't hear you, my lord. How badly do you want to spend?"

Percival sighed.

The strokes quickened a little more.

"Please, I've been on edge for too long. I need to spend. I want to spend." Percival swallowed, although his mouth was dry. "I wish I could spend in your arse."

Bertram's whimper filled his ears. His hand pumped furiously, taking Percival to the edge. He held himself there, knowing so much was at stake this time.

"Bertie, now. I'm going to spend now."

The cool tube encased his cock, the shock momentarily halting his emission. He jerked forward, but Bertram urged him back.

A finger sought its way into his arsehole, bending inside to rub that spot, encouraging his sac to empty itself, the sheer excitement making him spend quantities like he never had before.

Moments later, he was bereft of Bertram's presence. His lover was doing something with the syringe. He glanced at Percival, then reached around and loosened the leather strips from his wrists.

"Join us when you're decent," he said, then left through the adjoining door.

T HE ADJOINING DOOR to the bedroom clicked open. Penelope looked up from gazing into Viola's brown eyes to see Bertram with a smug, almost triumphant expression. He strode forward carrying a silver tube—the syringe containing Percival's contribution. He handed the syringe to Nicholas.

Nicholas scowled. "This is Percy's, right?"

Bertram chuckled. "Without a doubt." Triumph turned to sheepishness once he saw Viola.

The four of them had decided they would all be in the room together for the event. Not one of them truly knew what to expect. Penelope held out her hand for her husband. Bertram stood at her side, keeping his gaze away from the inelegantly splayed Viola.

Nicholas checked the tube and returned to his position between Viola's legs.

With a slight stumble, Percival entered the bedroom, half-dressed, his face flushed, his hair disheveled, rubbing his wrists. Viola smiled at her husband's obvious state of post-orgasm. He looked so vulnerable at that moment, like all men do after they had released their essence.

"Lady Norrington," said Nicholas, "it's time." He urged her legs further apart, then opened her feminine folds, spreading oil on the area. He paled briefly and paused.

"My lady," he began gently. "Viola, you may feel some discomfort, like a pinch. I apologize for my hesitation. I hadn't expected you to be intact."

Of course. Viola was a virgin. From a man's perspective, anyway.

"There may also be some blood—"

"Blood?" Percival asked, dismayed.

"It's natural and normal, Percy." Nicholas rubbed oil on the syringe. "I am merely saying this as an observation for what to expect. The hymen will recover quickly."

Percival came round to stand at Nicholas's side, pale and perhaps a little terrified. Suddenly witness to his wife on display, he gawked, then quickly moved to join her on the bed, placing a hand on her shoulder.

Nicholas met Viola's gaze, she wide-eyed and dazed. "Are you ready?"

"Yes, doctor."

Penelope squeezed her hand, watching Nicholas perform his duty, seriousness and wonder etched on his face.

Viola inhaled with a shudder. With crinkled brow, she flicked her gaze at Penelope and squeezed her hand hard.

"Let out your breath, Viola," Penelope counseled. "Try to relax. It will be over soon." It had been years since Penelope had lost her virginity, but she still remembered her first time. Unfortunately for Viola, the pinch would not be followed by pleasure.

Viola exhaled. Nicholas moved the plunger of the syringe.

"Thank you, Lady Norrington," said Nicholas. "Now I need to remove the implement. There may be a brief feeling of discomfort."

Percival exhaled loudly. A tear coursed down Viola's cheek.

Nicholas waved to Bertram. "Another pillow."

Bertram pulled one from behind Penelope and handed it to him. Nicholas carefully raised Viola's hips and placed the pillow underneath.

"I'd like you to stay in that position for half an hour, my lady. Just as a precaution. With conventional intercourse, this would not be necessary. But this is new to me, to all of us, and I want success."

"As do we all, doctor." Viola smiled, relief and gratitude softening her countenance.

Penelope sighed. Four more days of this, and they would be done with that month's procedures. She just wished there was more she could do to help Viola become with child.

CHAPTER TWENTY-TWO

Wilton Crescent, Belgravia, London, October 1881

Viola turned over drowsily in bed, waking from the morning's second doze. She reached out along the mattress, stroking the fading warmth of the sheet beside her. A rustling at the other end of the room meant her companion was returning from the bathroom.

It was nice to have a bathroom attached to the bedroom, especially one with a water closet. She certainly did not grow up with such modern amenities. Luxury was one aspect of being a marquess's wife she did not mind so much.

Penelope stood at the edge of the mattress. "You're awake."

"I am." Viola patted the sheets. "Come back to bed."

Penelope shrugged out of her dressing gown, revealing her glorious nudity. Ivory breasts tipped by hardening pink nipples. She slid in beside Viola, who embraced her against her own nakedness.

Their warmths merged, sending another wave of drowsiness to engulf Viola, this time tinged with sensuality and desire.

"Vi, darling," began Penelope, "do you think you're pregnant?"

Her courses were late, but Nicholas—she called him by his Christian name now that they had been "intimate", as they had joked—had said sometimes anxiety could disrupt a woman's cycle. "Could I be? We've only done the procedure one month so far." They would be doing this month's procedure later that day. "I wish it were over, really, and poor Percy and I didn't have to go through this" *almost shameful* "performance." She sighed a little too loudly. "And how would I know?"

"Hmm, well, are you overly tired? Hungry?"

Viola laughed. "I do like to eat. Cakes with afternoon tea are heavenly."

"Oh, yes, I quite agree." Penelope giggled. "But do you feel more hungry than usual?"

"I don't think so."

"Or the opposite, I suppose. Like when I was sick in Nice. Then we realized I was pregnant."

"Ugh." Viola groaned. "I'm not looking forward to that part of being with child."

Penelope stroked Viola's arms. "You might have a different experience."

Viola kissed Penelope's shoulder, relishing the perfume that lingered on her skin. "Do you remember how we were together in Spain? I adored being with you, sleeping with you every night, as if we were two wives."

"Wives, yes." Penelope turned, the tips of their noses touching. "But we *are* two wives, silly. Just not to each other." She pecked Viola's lips.

Viola caught her kiss, deepening the union. "I miss our playfulness. The beach in Nice with the sand between our toes. Our bedroom in Girona, where we spent lazy mornings."

A blush rose on Penelope's cheeks. "I think about those days too." She bent her head and teased Viola's neck with tiny nibbles. Viola relaxed into the pillow.

Penelope continued the tickling nibbles along her left shoulder, down to her breast. Nibbles became kisses as she slowly trailed over the sensitive flesh while Viola thrust out her chest in encouragement. Penelope's puff of amusement warmed her now-puckering nipple.

"Please, Penny, please."

Warm wetness engulfed her needy peak. Viola exhaled satisfaction, her body sinking into the mattress. She threaded her hands in Penelope's silky tresses, the strands sliding through her fingers as Penelope moved lower, kissing her waist, her belly, her mons, her—

Viola yelped. "No, no, Penny."

Penelope raised her head from between Viola's legs, worry crinkling her forehead. "Vi? Is something wrong?"

God, the sadness in her voice struck a nerve within. "No, no, Penny, darling." She urged her lover up until they were once again side by side. "I know later today you'll have to pleasure me—"

"You make it sound like a chore." Penelope kissed her cheek.

"The part with the doctor and the syringe certainly is." She sought and found her lips, pressing hers against them in reassurance. "So, let me pleasure you right now instead."

Penelope's smile was the answer she needed.

Viola climbed on top, straddling and propping herself up to get a view of her luscious lover. Blond hair tousled against the pillow framed a face filled with expectation and enticement. Viola palmed the plump breasts, kneading them before bending over to take an excited nipple in her mouth. She sucked and swirled her tongue, the motions a promise of what she would do elsewhere.

She stroked Penelope's curves, the nip of the waist, the swell of the hips, eliciting giggles and sighs. Viola pecked a trail of kisses to the soft belly, nibbling the delicate skin while Penelope squirmed and flinched. Viola smiled, then proceeded further until her head was between two fleshy thighs.

Before her was a thatch of light brown hair concealing a treat both would delight in. Should she delay pleasure? Just like wanting orgiastic rapture to last forever, she wanted her Penny to be with her forever. But bliss eventually dissipated, and Penelope had another lover.

Viola delved in, taking, tasting what was hers at that very moment. She clutched Penelope's hips, restraining herself from holding on too tightly. Under her, Penelope writhed, her breathy moans an auditory accompaniment to the rise and fall of her body.

Deep in her throes of ecstasy, Penelope groped around Viola's head, stroking then gripping her unbound hair. Viola stretched out her arms, fumbling over Penelope's breasts until she felt the hardened nipples, gently pinching, eliciting more gasps of appreciation.

She rocked her own hips against the mattress, finding no release there. She would have to be patient. Her time would come later that day, and when that time arrived, she would be more than ready.

"Vi, Vi, Vi." Penelope's panted exhortations revealed she was on the verge of release. Viola restrained her enthusiasm, wanting her love to remain poised on that precipice for as long as she could.

"Please."

As commanded, Viola sent her over the edge. Penelope let out a yowl, then promptly clapped her hands over her mouth. Viola slid up alongside her, grinning.

"I suppose everyone in the house knows." Penelope giggled, setting Viola off on her own mirthful fit.

She snuggled against Penelope, who wrapped her arms around her.

Despair descended despite the comforting embrace. "Penny, I want you to be with me during my confinement. As I was with you."

"Of course. I'm not going anywhere."

"I mean in my bed. Every night. Like we were in Girona."

"Oh." She sounded almost despondent. "But what about my husband? I very much like sleeping with him."

"I won't stop you. I'm not possessive. Well, perhaps during my confinement I will be covetous of your attention. I know I won't find comfort and empathy elsewhere."

Penelope remained silent.

"I'm afraid."

"Oh, darling. Don't be." Penelope hugged her more closely.

"I've never been in love before. Until now, until you. I want to explore that connection." She propped herself up on her elbows. "And I know you love Bertram. I know you and he share a different sort of sensuality than you and I." The viscount, from what Penelope had told her, was developing a taste for more vigorous sexual acts. "But right now, I need you like I've never needed another. I'm sick and tired of being thought of as a mere vessel to provide an heir to the dukedom. I want a true emotional connection, and I want it to be with you."

Penelope kissed her cheek. "I will be here for you, Viola. I will not leave your side."

"I love you, Penelope. I love you so very much."

"I love you, too, Viola." Penelope grinned. "I cannot imagine life without you."

Viola nuzzled against Penelope with a sigh. Funny, wasn't it, how one could be so profoundly attached to another person when one had, only a few years earlier, felt so alone.

PERCIVAL STOOD NEXT to the bed because Bertram had told him he should stand. That standing while he frigged himself was the best aspect for producing and acquiring the contribution.

Ugh. Contribution. His purpose in life was now reduced to a spoonful of fluid.

Of course, over the last two hundred years, every damned Duke of Amesbury had likewise been reduced.

After spending his contribution once a day for five days last month, he'd needed a respite. He and Bertram had barely had a chance to resume their usual sensual escapades before he was called to duty once again.

It was only the second month and he was already annoyed with the whole procedure.

"Percy? Need I remind you Nicholas is in the next room waiting?" Bertram said from his perch on the mattress.

No, he needn't be reminded of that fact. What he needed, or rather what his prick needed, was to be reminded of a time when frigging himself in the presence of his lover was an enjoyable act.

"Darling." Bertram stood at his side, a hand cupping his cheek. He pressed a kiss to Percival's lips. Percival kissed back. Why couldn't they just do that for a spell?

"Percy, what's wrong?"

"I can't." His flaccid prick was evidence of that fact.

Bertram pecked his cheek. "Yes, you can." He lifted Percival's chin to meet his gaze. "Remember the other night?"

Percival's cock revived at the memory. In a rare concession, Bertram had let Percival act the dominant, tie him up and torment him sensually before Percival fucked his arse.

"Ah," Bertram said with a chuckle. "I see that you do."

"I feel conspicuous, like we have an audience. It's shameful."

Bertram's embrace was comforting. "I understand." He sighed, his breath hot on Percival's neck. "Darling, there will be an end to all of this, but first we must slog through."

An apt expression. "I need a distraction. Please, Bertie." Having to plead was yet another humiliation.

"All right." Bertram kissed him again. "Give me a moment." He left Percival standing alone and went into the adjoining bedroom where Viola, Penelope, and Nicholas waited for Percival's contribution.

He slumped against the mattress.

A moment later, Bertram returned, probably having assured the others that Percival was being rather dull at the moment. He grabbed the pillows off the bed and tossed them onto the carpet, then wrapped his arms around Percival and kissed him once again.

But this kiss was possessive, a little aggressive even. Percival tried to pull away, but Bertram held strong, thrusting his tongue deep into his mouth, tickling his throat, until Percival relented. Bertram chuckled darkly as he drew back, then grabbed Percival's now-hard cock.

Bertram knelt and took Percival's cock in his mouth, the humid warmth exciting him even more. As he sucked, Bertram fumbled with his own clothing, unbuttoning and shrugging off garments as well as he could in his position. With a *pop*, he released Percival, then stood, his braces hanging limp at his sides, his fly unbuttoned.

He pulled off his shirt, revealing his glorious masculine torso, then took off his trousers revealing an eager stiff stander. "On your knees, my lord marquess." He spun Percival half a rotation until the pillows were before him and the bedroom door behind, then pushed him down to all fours.

Bertram went to the nightstand, lingering restlessly. He tossed the metal cylinder on the pillows, then rounded Percival, taking his place at his backside.

The scrape of the lid of a jar of cold cream sent a frisson of anticipation to shimmy down Percival's spine and land in his stones. He knew what was going to happen, and the fingers lubricating his arsehole signaled it was imminent.

The head of Bertram's prick prodded the cleft before finding the sought-for orifice and delving inside. Bertram's nails dug into Percival's hips as he let out a groan. Agonizing pleasure weakened Percival to the point of collapse.

"Percy." Bertram's voice held a gravelly quaver. "Up." He encircled Percival's waist and hauled him to all fours. "Frig yourself. Now."

He grabbed his utterly hard cock and stroked, matching the rhythm of Bertram's increasingly rapid thrusts. Urgency reverberated in his lover's panting huffs, an urgency that goaded him toward his culmination.

His mind knew what was expected of him, but his body had stopped caring about all that. Merged as he was with Bertram, he craved release now, craved his lover's release, craved the life they once shared where an act such as this was an ordinary occurrence.

"Fuck!" Bertram stilled as he came, his fingers tightening on Percival's hips. A moment later he sagged, his breath hot on Percival's back.

Percival grabbed the cylinder, emptying his seed.

"Penny!"

The bedroom door clicked open.

Bertram grabbed the cylinder, then twisted his torso, keeping their bodies joined.

The bedroom door clicked shut.

Tears spiked Percival's eyes as the slump of post-orgasm descended. Yes, the sex had been pleasurable, interesting even, as they almost never did it on the floor. But he just wanted it to be over.

There had to be something more in his life. He needed something more in his life.

He needed his Bertie back. Like how they used to be. Just the two of them.

CHAPTER TWENTY-THREE

Wilton Crescent, Belgravia, London, November 1881

Two months and no courses.

Viola stared at her diary open to the entry from August, the writing on the page slowly blurring as her eyes lost focus with disbelief. She really, really had not menstruated since then.

She stared out the window next to her writing desk. She felt fine. Perhaps a little hungrier than normal. But she certainly did not feel the nausea that had plagued Penelope.

Perhaps she *had* been feeling a bit bloated of late, and maybe a little more tired than usual…

She huffed an exhalation, her heart suddenly pounding with realization.

She was pregnant. At least she was pretty sure she was.

Well, there was only one way to be sure of it. She needed a visit from the doctor. Her wondrous Doctor St. Albans with his miraculous modern procedures. And if she were pregnant, then they need not proceed with November's experiment.

Diary in hand, she ran to fetch Penelope in the library.

Viola opened the door slowly. Her darling was sitting in the window seat, a book open in her lap, her face turned to the dim autumn sunlight filtering through the panes of glass.

"Penny?" Viola remained standing near the door.

"Oh, Viola. I didn't hear you enter." Penelope's smile waned. "Is something the matter? You look troubled."

"I do?" She touched her fingers to her cheeks in a vain attempt to check her emotions. "I suppose I am."

Penelope put her book aside and stood, her countenance now ashen. "What's wrong?"

"I…" She couldn't say the words out loud. She couldn't. She had to. "I think I'm pregnant."

Penelope clapped her hands and strode toward her. "How wonderful!" She studied her face. "You do not look pleased."

"I think I'm mostly confused. And we need to make sure it is true."

"We'll send Nicholas an invitation to please come visit his cousins."

They had been relying on coded communications with Nicholas in the event a curious associate read any of their missives and had a mind to gossip.

While Viola sunk into the depths of the sofa, Penelope went to the writing desk. She busied herself with the correspondence, then handed the letter to a servant. After ascertaining that their husbands were out, she called for tea for two, then joined Viola on the sofa.

She took Viola's hand and sat silently at her side, probably comprehending Viola's brain was overwhelmed by a cacophony of thoughts.

Two months without her courses. Did that mean she had become pregnant during the first procedure two months ago?

Had last month's procedure been unnecessary? Had she endured the indignity of spreading her legs—and Percival the indignity of spending into a syringe—for naught?

Or perhaps she was being too hopeful. She had been far more irregular than usual since her wedding day. The stress of uxorial obligations, plus all the running about escaping spies, had not been good for her feminine functions. Plus, she quite possibly had undergone a sort of sympathetic pregnancy during the first few months when Penelope was pregnant. Nicholas had suggested all these theories during his rather enthusiastic consultations with Viola, his mind obviously churning, seeking hypotheses, as she conveyed all the details of her menses.

Her tea sat on the tea table, untouched and probably cold, while Penelope held her in her arms as she leaned against the corner of the sofa.

The door to the library banged open and Percival strode in. "Viola?" His voice croaked with concern. "I saw Nicky at our front door. He said he was summoned."

Nicholas and Bertram followed, both with severe expressions.

Well, the truth would soon be revealed. Viola drew in a long inhalation, letting it out slowly, trying to stymie the lightheadedness that threatened to make her faint.

"Good afternoon, ladies," said Nicholas with a measure of cheer. "I came as soon as I could. Since no bones appear to be broken, I suspect there is some good news?"

"Well, doctor," Viola said, steadying the shake in her voice. "I do believe you have been successful with your radical scientific scheme to get me with child."

Nicholas beamed. Percival gaped.

"But, Nicholas, we need to be absolutely certain—"

"Of course, Viola," he said, kindness in his tone.

"Because the duke will need assurances." She flashed a pained glance at Percival.

Nicholas nodded. "Yes, and Amesbury will most likely hire his own doctor, despite what my findings are today." He patted his jacket pockets. "I brought my equipment in anticipation of doing just this." He became serious. "But I will need to perform my assessment of your condition while you are undressed. I mean to your chemise. And lying down. You know, how we've been doing these last few months."

Penelope placed a hand on Viola's shoulder, her touch soothing. "Give us a quarter hour, then join us upstairs."

For every step of the way, Penelope was there. Up the staircase, into the bedroom, undressing, wrapping a shawl around Viola's shoulders when she shivered because of a chill or perhaps nerves, settling her on the bed, and sitting at Viola's side. They were physically ready when Nicholas walked through the door, but Viola's mind was still clouded by the fog of anxiety and disbelief.

Nicholas was genial in his instructions, a calming quality to his voice, and efficient in his examination, all the while nodding and grunting. He placed his hands on her stomach, applying pressure with a light touch. He listened to her belly with his stethoscope. After Viola's consent, he inserted the end of a different stethoscope inside her vagina and listened, then removed the instrument and inserted his finger. He prodded, then removed his finger and wiped it on his handkerchief.

"I dare say, Lady Norrington, you are with child."

Penelope squealed.

Relief mixed with despair flooded over Viola. She was going to be a mother.

"Viola," Nicholas began in his kindly way, "you will need the services of a real doctor. Your well-being is out of my hands now. You're carrying the Amesbury heir and there will be expectations about your treatment."

"Yes, Doctor St. Albans. I mean, Nicholas."

"Well, I will take my leave. My own wife is about to give birth, and I don't want to be apart from her for too long." Nicholas smiled. "Congratulations to you and Percy. You can trust I will not utter a word about your condition."

"Thank you, Nicholas. And, please, tell our husbands the good news."

The moment he left, Penelope wrapped her arms around Viola.

"Oh, Viola, why so glum? This is wonderful news."

"I don't know what I feel. I guess relief that it's over, but worry that it won't be a boy. I am not looking forward to all those aches and pains you suffered. And I still don't feel that…zest for motherhood."

"It will come, love," Penelope soothed. "Especially since we are to be mothers together. We will have so much fun ordering new dresses during your confinement and gossiping with other mothers in the park. We'll have teas, and invite everyone who is anyone. You're carrying a duke's heir. There will be spiteful envy and heartfelt felicity."

All those things Penelope never got to experience while she was hidden away in Spain.

The blood drained from Viola's head. *Christ.* How horrid she was being. She should embrace her condition, even if only for Penelope's sake. She loved Penelope and she should let Penelope have her fun.

She might even let Penelope convince her that motherhood was going to be wonderful.

"Thank you, Penny." She snuggled against Penelope, the joy of their friendship burbling deep within as despondency melted and gratitude took hold. "I love you." She wiped a tear. "I love you so much."

Penelope kissed her lips, tenderly. "I love you so much. I love that we will be mothers together."

I hope to God it's a son.

Wood Hall, Hertfordshire, January 1882

PERCIVAL HAD WANTED to wait until Viola was visibly pregnant before they made their announcement to his parents. He needed physical evidence to back up his news, otherwise—he was entirely certain—Father, at least, would not be convinced.

He also wanted desperately to not have to have Viola undergo examination by one of Father's callous doctors. Viola had of late, and with the help of Penelope, taken to the idea of motherhood, but she was reticent to have any man but Nicholas touch her in so intimate a way. She had convinced Percival that "Doctor St. Albans" should oversee her medical care.

Nicholas was certainly the best doctor he knew. Probably the best doctor ever. The problem was, he was no longer a practicing doctor. Eventually, Viola would have to be seen by the Amesbury family doctor.

The carriage wheels crunched on the gravel drive and the entrance to Wood Hall came into view. Orsa stirred, sensing her mistress's distress. Percival squeezed Viola's hand.

She put on a smile before alighting from the carriage.

The moment Viola walked through the front door, Mother was at her side, exuding an ebullience he had never before witnessed.

She took Viola by the arm as she led her to the front parlor. "Oh, my dear Viola—"

Mother had never called her that. Perhaps "Viola dear" with a hint of derision.

"You are positively glowing. And that gown suits you ever so well. Oh, you must tell me who your seamstress is."

Viola flashed him a helpless look before answering Mother's questions one by one, their conversation continuing as Mother assisted her onto an armchair. Mother even fussed over the usually disregarded Orsa, remarking how endearing it was that the pup wanted to be in Viola's lap.

Father had stayed at Percival's side while they walked to the parlor, muttering approbations with an underlying current of disbelief.

Percival sighed as he sat on the chair next to Viola, her expression now rather beleaguered. Where were Bertram and Penelope to bolster them, to fend off the usual attacks? Sadly, he and Viola were going it alone. Percival wanted this to be a civil affair, with no accusations of Bertram being a distraction.

Mother poured tea from a service Percival had not seen in years. His great-grandfather's gilded blue-and-white porcelain, which had been a gift from Tsar Alexander.

Well, this *was* a special occasion, indeed.

Father paced while Mother served the tea. Percival tried not to watch Father, but it was difficult. Did he approve? Was he satisfied?

"And Rochdale," Mother was saying to Viola, "how has he taken the news? About you giving him a grandchild?"

Viola glanced down at her teacup. She had written her father, and he had responded with indifferent congratulations. His restraint had upset her. She had expected him to show up on their doorstep unbidden with open arms and boisterous well-wishes.

"My father sent his compliments and felicitations," she said.

"I'm certain Rochdale is being coy, my dear. It is one thing to celebrate the birth of one's child, but one's grandchild may be a reminder of one's age." Mother sipped her tea. "He will be ecstatic when you next see him."

"Yes, thank you, Your Grace," Viola said with clearly feigned accord.

All the while, Percival surreptitiously kept watch over Father's reactions. Percival snorted to himself. Was Father feeling the effects of age at his sudden advancement to being a grandfather?

Or was that a look of suspicion?

As he sipped his tea, Percival caught Father's eye. That's when the vague look of suspicion turned to horror.

It was almost imperceptible, and it was gone in a flash. But Percival would swear that Father looked horrified. A stabbing chill cramped Percival's chest.

Bloody hell. Was it really true? He and Viola half-siblings? Was that also why Rochdale was so restrained in his congratulations?

His vision clouded. *Christ*. Had his life really just become a Byronesque nightmare?

Father cleared his throat. "It gratifies me, son, that you and Lady Norrington have found an affinity in the state of marriage."

Affinity? Is that what one called it?

"I'm glad you have paid us a visit," Father continued. "If you had merely sent a letter, I would not have believed it."

Believed what, exactly? That one who was inverted could create a child? Or that he could create a child with his half-sister?

Bollocks.

"My dear Viola," Mother said congenially. "Perhaps if you called upon your father. You know, so he can see for himself."

Percival stared into his tea. He had to get out of there.

No. He couldn't run away. Somehow, he had to ascertain the truth. But a family tea celebrating joyous news was not the time to do that.

He'd wait until his child was born to confront Father. Wait to see if his son or daughter resembled a little monster. And if so, he would throw it in Father's face.

CHAPTER TWENTY-FOUR

Wilton Crescent, Belgravia, London, February 1882

"I've missed you, Bertie."

From his cozy corner of the sofa in the library, Bertram looked up from *The Evening Standard*. Percival stood at the hearth, leaning on the mantel, staring at the fire.

"I'm right here, Percy. How can you miss me?"

"You know what I mean. I miss being alone with you. Being lovers. Going on adventures where we can be alone and in bed. Like how we would be in France. How we were in Spain."

"Nothing's changed between us."

Percival snorted. "Everything's changed."

Bertram folded the paper and tossed it on the tea table. "Percy, we have obligations now."

"So, because we have wives and children, we have to stop being lovers?" Percival's hiss was filled with anguish.

"No." Bertram stared at his empty hands. He loved Penelope and little Georgiana, but something was definitely missing in his life. A hole that had grown larger of late. "I think we should start sleeping together again. Go back to the way things were. Well, except we should permanently share a bedroom."

"What about Penelope?"

"Penny and I are allowed more freedom with our affections in public. Some of the physical need is satisfied that way." Bertram stood and slowly approached Percival. He placed a hand on his shoulder.

Percival's warm hand enveloped his. "That feels good. Even a small touch like that feels good, Bertie."

Standing behind, Bertram wrapped his arms around Percival's waist. "There has been so much stress of late. And so much preoccupation with duty." He hugged harder, resting his head in the crook of Percival's neck. "I've missed you as well."

Percival leaned into his embrace.

"But we both know it's more than just the two of us now. Who would have thought we'd have wives and children?"

Percival laughed. "Certainly not I."

"Nor I. My attraction to Penelope came as a complete surprise. You know that. And I suppose I've been selfish, taking the time to wallow in that new feeling and explore a new sensuality."

Percival's chest expanded as he drew in a deep inhalation. He emitted a low whimper on the exhale.

"I've been selfish, and you've been jealous."

"Jealousy is an ugly emotion." Percival shuddered. "I swore after Jack's jealous rages I would never be that way."

"But you aren't that way. And, no, you're not actually jealous of me having another lover. You're aggrieved because I haven't been spending time with you."

"I suppose it might be different if Viola and I were lovers. Or if Viola were a man."

Bertram chuckled.

"Because then I'd have someone to fill my days and nights as you used to do."

"Percy, darling, despite all that's happened with our marriages and children, I love you. I know you might think having Penny in my life would be a distraction for my heart. But having her and Georgiana in my life has expanded my heart. I've encompassed all of you. And, yes, Viola as well. Love is not a finite emotion, but infinite. However, I admit I have not shown that love properly to you."

Silence descended, intermittently broken by the crackle of the fire.

"I love you, too. But it's not just love I want, Bertie."

A frisson of understanding slithered over Bertram. He had been very neglectful of their physical connection of late. He, too, had missed their playful caresses, their furtive kisses. Their mind-numbing sex.

"And I think you have a new letch you want to explore."

"Percy, love, I don't need to—"

Percival turned in his arms to face him, their noses almost touching. "But I think I want to. Well, try at least. I know you won't hurt me. I need to conquer the fears Jack instilled in me. Bury them."

Bertram couldn't stop a smile. Because he was holding his lover? Because his lover had said he'd be willing to try something new? Because his prick had a mind of its own and was thinking about sex?

All of those things.

Percival rested his forehead against Bertram's. "Let's explore that new letch of yours, shall we?"

"But it's only four in the afternoon."

"That didn't used to bother you before." His words fanned over Bertram's mouth. Percival angled his chin and pressed a tender kiss to his lips.

Bertram unwrapped his arms. "No, it didn't. You're right." He grabbed Percival's hand. "Let's go upstairs."

* * * * *

Percival followed Bertram's lead and took the stairs two at a time. With a glance down both sides of the bedroom corridor, Bertram urged Percival through the door to his bedroom, then locked it behind him.

Then he locked the adjoining door to Percival's bedroom and the servants' backstairs door.

"I don't want you to worry that someone might walk in."

Percival's pulse picked up its pace. "What the devil are you going to do to me?"

Bertram took his hands, rubbing the backs with circles of his thumb pads. "Percy, love, sometimes pleasure comes from not knowing, from expectation and anticipation." He licked his lips. "Do you trust me?"

"I do."

"Implicitly?"

Percival hesitated. Did he lack confidence in Bertram or himself? "I trust you with my life," he murmured. "You know that."

A blush tinted Bertram's cheeks. "And you know I am humbled by your trust."

"But now you'd like to do God only knows what to me. I'm reticent, not because I don't trust you, but because I'm not certain I will enjoy it."

Bertram raised an eyebrow. "But you are willing to try."

"Blast it." Frustration burbled at a moment when sensuality should have been paramount. "I *am* willing to try because I love you. If you find enjoyment in"—he gestured randomly—"whatever, then I'll be satisfied." His heart banged too forcefully. "I'm just a tad apprehensive."

Bertram smiled and pressed his forehead to Percival's. "I completely understand. I promise it will be merely a taste of what could be." He drew back. "Percy, remember the first time you had to provide a contribution for Viola? You were nervous, and I helped you."

"Yes." Percival narrowed his eyes. "And you did it most unconventionally." He threw a glance at the nightstand in which Bertram had fumbled that afternoon, eventually retrieving strips of leather. "Is that what you mean to do to me now?"

One corner of Bertram's mouth quirked upward. "Perhaps."

His sultry utterance was enough for Percival's cock to thicken.

At the time, the experience had been frustrating. Bertram had taken him to the edge of release over and over again, the multiple climbs to the peak exhausting and thrilling at the same time. He had continued to relive the memory, letting it arouse him before self-pleasuring.

Percival's qualms eased, possibly reflected in his countenance. Bertram's sly smile broadened. A flush crept up the back of Percival's neck, as anticipation spiked his groin.

"All right. Do with me what you will, my lord viscount."

A sigh escaped Bertram's throat. He brushed his lips against Percival's. "You won't regret it, love." He pulled back, fire in his eyes, then went to the nightstand. When he returned, he held the strips of leather he had used before. And something else.

A length of black silk.

Alarm shuddered through him.

Bertram dropped the lot onto the bed, then shrugged out of his short *robe de chambre*. He stripped off his cravat and waistcoat and rolled up his shirtsleeves. As if he were going to do a strenuous task.

Alarm burgeoned into fear.

Percival should just stop the whole theatrical right then and there, but curiosity was beginning to eclipse the fear.

Bertram slid his fingers along the shawl collar of Percival's jacket until he reached the neck. He yanked the jacket off.

Percival's heart skipped a beat as a frisson of lust coursed through him.

Next, his tie was unwrapped and slithered off his throat. Bertram unbuttoned Percival's waistcoat with trembling fingers. Eagerness? Impatience?

Nervousness that their sensual journey would be a failure?

No, that was not Bertram's fear, but his own.

And yet, nothing they had done together before had been so disastrous as to cause a rift in their relationship.

Percival willed himself to remain calm, even while Bertram unbuttoned the flies of his trousers and drawers.

"To afford you a bit of room for your engorged state."

He grabbed the strip of black silk, pulling it taut between his fists. He placed it over Percival's eyes.

Percival recoiled before regret stabbed through him. A glimmer of self-reproach marred Bertram's expression.

"I apologize, Bertie." Percival stepped forward. "I am unused to such things being used in an agreeable manner."

"I understand." Bertram held up the silk. "Will you trust me?" His gaze held genuine concern.

"Yes."

Bertram wound the cloth around Percival's head, covering his eyes, and tied it at the back. He encircled his fingers around Percival's wrists and lifted his arms above his head.

"Hold onto the bedpost."

Percival did so, and Bertram wrapped the leather strips around him, securing him to the wooden post.

The heat of Bertram's body seared his back. Bertram unfastened Percival's braces, sliding them over his shoulders, down his torso, then tugged his trousers and drawers to his ankles. The garments bound him where he stood.

Next, Percival's shirt was lifted and knotted around his waist.

Cool air on his bottom signaled he had been left to stand alone, vulnerable. What was Bertram doing? Percival concentrated on the senses left to him.

Water pouring from the pitcher into the basin. More water, or perhaps a towel being wrung out.

The slap of a cold wet cloth on his right butt cheek sent him lurching forward. Bertram steadied him with a strong arm around his waist as he began to swab the cloth over his bum.

Was Bertram washing him? Washing his—

The cloth ran down the furrow of his buttocks, then back again, stopping to circle his hole.

Every muscle in Percival's body tensed.

"Relax, love. We've done this before many a time."

No, that was not true. Bertram had never washed him before. He had always performed such ablutions himself.

One hand bathed while the other taunted with teasing strokes along his inner thigh, tickling the sensitive flesh, never touching his yearning stones.

Bertram's breath puffed in his ear as fingertips danced on his abdomen. "The beauty of the blindfold is that you can imagine any lover—"

No, just you. Just my Bertie.

"Or any location."

The south of France, unfettered by wives and the weight of duty.

Bertram gripped his butt cheeks, drawing them apart. The delicate touch of the tip of his tongue tasting the puckered rim, circling insistently, circling hypnotically…

Lulling Percival into a fantasy of crisp white linen sheets under naked flesh, the Mediterranean sun spilling through opened windows, the sea-scented air filling his nostrils, while indescribable delight created sensual chaos within.

The tongue continued its wanton laving as Bertram inserted a finger, its aim precise, seeking, then massaging the secret spot within. An enlivening twitch of his cock brought Percival back to the present, back to the leather bindings, back to the blindfold. Back to the need that ached in his untouched stones, back to his cock agonizingly awaiting release, while his puckered hole flexed, welcoming invasion.

But satisfaction did not come. Instead, the ceaseless ministrations of the sensual spot within brought him to the edge of rapture, holding him at the peak, momentarily stopping to let him slide back to frustration.

Percival focused his mind on the climb to orgasm, grasping at the sensation, straining toward release, reaching, reaching, hoping by sheer force of will he could spend.

Bertram's mouth encircled his cock, warm, wet, wonderful. Percival heaved an exhale, exhausted from his struggle, welcoming the opportunity to let his lover finish him off. Bertram continued his probing torment, now compounded by skillful squeezes of Percival's stones. All sensation merged into one lubricious muddle, surging Percival forward, this time letting him climb to the peak unfaltering, letting him hover for a moment, savoring the sweet air of rapture, before sending him falling into the abyss of pleasure.

All too suddenly, he was left bereft, afterglow only a tingle that signaled the enervation of his spent sex.

Bertram caught his sigh with a deep kiss, the taste of his tongue acrid and tangy. The ache in Percival's arms was not from bondage, but from want of holding his lover. His lover who had shown him a new way to experience their deep connection.

The blindfold was stripped off first, Percival's eyes adjusting as he watched Bertram untie his wrists. Upon his release, he slumped forward into Bertram's welcoming arms.

Bertram kissed his temple. "So, what do you think, my love?"

"Bertie, I want you to sleep with me from here forward. I want us to be, what does one call it? The principal pairing. I don't care if you sleep with Penny. I don't. But I need you in my life. I am willing to explore this letch with you if you are willing to share my bed most every night."

"I can share your bed every night. Penny and I can have sex at four in the afternoon."

Percival chuckled. "All right. But you should talk to Penny about it. And I'll talk to Viola. I think she would rejoice at the opportunity to sleep with your wife."

PENELOPE FRETTED AS SHE STARED into the dressing mirror, her hair perfectly coiffed, the diamonds of her necklace glittering in the lamplight. She had dismissed her lady's maid after she'd clasped and positioned the necklace. Bertram would be in soon to dress for dinner, and she needed to talk to him without distraction.

She had news and a proposition.

He entered and looked around. "Where's Reynolds?"

"I've dismissed your valet. I told him to have a glass of sherry and that I would attend to my husband this evening."

He grinned. "All right. I suppose it doesn't matter who inserts my links and studs." He began to disrobe his day clothes. With each garment he shed, lust grew in her core.

No, no, no. She was there to negotiate, not seduce. She'd have to assume Reynolds' usual demeanor—disinterested and dignified—concentrating on the art of dressing, not the sculptural qualities of the body beneath the attire.

She was tested when Bertram stripped off his shirt, revealing his glorious torso. She swallowed her desire along with a pool of saliva.

Reynolds had left all the required garments neatly folded or draped on the bed. Penelope shook out the shirt, beautifully tailored with vertical tucks. Bertram stood before her, his mien quizzical, as if dubious she could perform her job.

Because she was hesitating. And staring. All she really wanted to do was thread her fingers through the fine hair on his chest and palm the well-muscled physique.

He took the shirt from her and pulled it over his head. She handed him his trousers.

Bertram chuckled.

"What, my lord? Did I do something wrong?"

"I might as well be dressing myself while you watch."

She sucked in her lower lip.

"Ah, I see that is agreeable to you." He stepped toward her. "Well then—"

Penelope held up her hand. "You still need someone to button your braces and secure your studs and links, remember."

His quivering smile was a façade for squelched laughter.

Bertram continued dressing, Penelope helping, their closeness a profound distraction. She loved him desperately. Wanted him frequently. She just needed to be with Viola, to explore the possibilities of that relationship.

But now with Bertram before her and the prospect of their separation hanging over her, she simply craved him. Especially him dressed to the nines for dinner. She loved seeing him in dinner dress, or, even better, evening dress at a ball.

She picked up the whisk Reynolds had placed on the dressing table and brushed the lapels and shoulders of Bertram's jacket.

He grabbed her around the waist with such force she dropped the little broom.

"You look delectable, Lady Ravensburgh. It is a shame we must go down to dinner."

His kiss was fleeting, a peck so brief the memory of it was stronger.

He let her go, his countenance suddenly grave.

"Penny—"

"Bertie—"

Their voices rang at the same time.

"You go first," she blurted, wanting to put off the inevitable.

"No, darling, after you."

Penelope sighed and plopped down on the day-bed. "Bertie, this is so difficult for me to say." She couldn't look at him, so she looked at her hands in her lap. "I suppose I should explain that I love you very much. I am very happy to be your wife, to be mother to our children." She twisted the wedding band on her fourth finger. "But I need to, no, I *want* to take some time to explore and deepen a relationship I've neglected." Tears smarted in her eyes.

Bertram knelt before her and took her hands in his. "You wish to spend more time with Viola, don't you?" He said it so kindly.

She looked at him then, the creases on his forehead betraying the emotion within. But not sorrow. No. Something akin to hopefulness.

"Yes. Viola and I would like to renew the friendship we began so long ago. We want to be lovers again, but in such a way that I am hers."

"She would be your primary lover. And I would be your secondary lover."

"No! Not secondary—"

"Penny, Penny, darling, this term is not meant to be deprecatory, merely descriptive." He sat next to her with a long exhalation, still clinging to her hand. "Percy and I were discussing the very same thing. I mean with the two of us. We've grown apart because of you and me growing together. Plus, the children. This whole situation is so…complex."

"But we're secure in our love, aren't we Bertie? We can handle this."

He draped an arm around her shoulders and squeezed. "Yes. I love you so very much. And I know you love me. We'll just have to find time for physical love."

"And sort out the bedroom situation."

Bertram laughed. "Yes, absolutely. Something to talk about over dinner."

"There will be something else to talk about, love."

"Oh?" He raised an eyebrow.

"Yes." She couldn't contain a smile. "I'm pregnant again."

His smile was as wide as hers. "Oh, Penny." He enfolded her in his arms. "Such wonderful news. I'm going to be a father again."

She shook him off before something more than an embrace might happen.

Arm-in-arm, and each sporting a grin, Bertram led her out of the bedroom and down the stairs to the drawing room.

VIOLA CAUGHT PENELOPE'S EYE as she and Bertram sauntered into the drawing room, their arms linked. Bertram was grinning, while a lovely blush colored Penelope's cheeks.

Her dress fit her so perfectly. Ice-blue was such a fetching color for her ivory complexion and blond hair. It highlighted her lovely eyes.

Penelope nodded demurely in Viola's direction while she let Bertram lead her to an armchair opposite. She sat, while Bertram stood behind her.

As if he were going to give a speech.

Viola ran her fingers over the etched crystal decoration of her sherry glass, then rested her palm on her increasing belly. Next to her on the sofa, Percival stiffened.

Bertram glanced at his beautiful wife who looked up at him, beaming. With a sweeping gaze, he took in Viola and Percival. "We have news."

Viola downed the contents of her glass.

"Lady Ravensburgh is with child."

Percival made a choking sound.

Viola stifled a gasp. She remained unmoved on the sofa. "Congratulations, Lord and Lady Ravensburgh. This is wonderful news."

Percival coughed. "Yes, yes, it is."

Bertram appeared possessed, his eyes wide in rapturous wonder. "I am overwhelmed," he said. "I never thought I would have even one child, and now I am to be blessed with two."

A shiver furred Viola's shoulders. *Blessed.* What an interesting way to conceive of such a notion when the act itself was so mechanical, really. A sudden wave of boldness inspired her. "Isn't it all of us who are blessed, my lord?"

Bertram appeared stunned. "Why, yes, Viola, I suppose you're right."

"Oh, absolutely!" Penelope clapped. "We agreed to raise our children collectively, did we not?"

"We did," Percival admitted with a grumble.

Bertram's countenance sobered as he flicked his gaze to Percival. "We did," he said, now subdued. He drew in an inhalation as he looked at all in attendance. "There is something else we all must discuss."

He moved away from Penelope to the hearth, where he began pacing. He stopped and bent his arm to lean against the mantle in a contemplative fashion.

Silence weighed heavy in the room. Each knew what needed to be discussed. Presumably, Bertram and Penelope had just had a little chat like she and Percival. But who was going to speak first?

Viola handed her empty glass to Percival. His brow lifted in understanding. He got up and poured her another. As he handed the glass back to her, she looked up at him expectantly. He held her gaze but addressed the room.

"Remember how we were in Spain? Penelope with Viola, Bertram and I together. We were so happy then. I want to return to that arrangement."

Viola offered a congratulatory smile at her husband, then dared to glance at Penelope.

She was beaming and blushing. Heat rose in Viola's face in flustered exhilaration.

Penelope hurriedly joined her on the sofa, relieving her of the glass so she could take Viola's hands in hers. "We had a sense of freedom there. No one was watching us."

Percival chuckled. "Not like in France."

"And no one will be watching us here," said Bertram. "The servants are scrutinized and investigated before we hire them."

"They are quite used to Bertie and I sleeping together. I can't see why they would think it unusual for our wives to do the same."

Percival refreshed his now empty glass. "As far as the practicalities, Bertie will sleep with me in my bedroom."

Viola's heartbeat quickened. Did this mean—

"And, well, Penelope and Viola, you can sleep wherever you wish, just not in my bed."

Bertram chuckled.

How long had Viola waited for this moment? Sharing her life with Penelope meant not having the lingering trace of any man. She turned to Penelope. "Oh, Penny. We'll make a proper love nest for the two of us."

Penelope's beautiful blue eyes widened.

"I will spend my husband's money to redecorate in any fashion that suits you."

Penelope giggled, then nestled against Viola, placing her hand on Viola's stomach.

Bertram plopped into the chair Penelope had vacated. "Well, then, Penny. Looks like my old bedroom will be available as our own private haven."

Percival exhaled loudly. "I'm glad that's all settled then."

"Not quite, Percy," Penelope said. "What do we tell the children?"

"Ah, yes. The children." Percival returned his attention to his sherry. "Now there will be three. At least."

"Do they have to know?" said Viola. "Or, rather, why would they know? They will be in bed before we retire. We'll request the nursemaids and governesses imply nothing is unusual about their parents." Viola turned to Percival. "Your own father is like us, and yet you never knew."

"I suppose," Percival said quietly. He glanced at Bertram. "I believe it was you who said we should tell the children that sometimes papa wants to spend the night with his friend and mama wants to spend the night with her friend. Such a situation would be our children's normality."

Penelope relaxed against the cushions. "Then don't be so glum Percy. That sounds quite reasonable. Besides, it will be ages before the children are old enough to understand. In the meantime, we'll figure out how to live our new life. I daresay, you and Bertie have put up a fine show all these years."

Both men chuckled.

A knock on the door presaged the announcement for dinner.

Percival took Viola's hand, helped her to stand. He offered his arm.

"I think, husband, I would rather go in to dinner on Lady Ravensburgh's arm."

He stepped aside as a beaming Penelope held out her elbow. "If you please, Lady Norrington."

Viola wrapped her arm around Penelope's and together they strolled to the dining room and their newly settled life.

CHAPTER TWENTY-FIVE

Wilton Crescent, Belgravia, London, June 1882

Viola stared at the babe in her arms, a tear rolling down her cheek, catching a strand of sweat-drenched hair stuck to her jaw.

Now she understood why childbirth was called labor. Exhaustion enervated her, as if she had built a railway line in four hours rather than pushing out a living being from her body.

It was all rather unexpected, really. She had been in the morning room with Penelope, waiting for her father to arrive for tea, when a spasm of pain had shot through her low back all the way to her knees. Penelope suggested they send a message to Nicholas. But the pain went away, and Viola dismissed the idea.

Then, in a bizarre twist of fate, the St. Albanses rang the doorbell. They were in the neighborhood and thought to check on Viola, knowing her child was due very soon. As Viola stood at the bell pull to call for more tea, the most violent of cramps felled her. She landed on the carpet with a sensation that her petticoats had been drenched.

The day became a blur after that, punctuated with panicked shouting. Bertram and Percival helped her to her bedroom but left soon afterwards. Nicholas took charge while maidservants milled about doing his bidding. Penelope and Helena held her hands and encouraged her every step of the way.

There was pain, to be sure. But mostly there was exertion. And when the babe was born, a grin had spread over Nicholas's face. He'd busied about out of her view, then minutes later, after a sharp cry from the infant, handed her the freshly cleaned child, naked so she could see for herself.

"You have a son, Viola."

She'd burst into sobs as she'd clutched the tiny, wrinkled, perfect boy to her breast, Penelope hugging her, calming and soothing her.

Little by little, realization dawned. A son. She and Percival had successfully created a son. And in the most remarkable way.

Her tears subsided. She looked up at Nicholas. "Thank you, doctor."

He beamed. "I think we should tell your husband. Percy is probably beside himself with worry right about now."

She laughed. "Yes, please. Send him in. And Bertram, too."

As soon as Nicholas opened the door, Percival rushed inside. Helena left Viola's side, gesturing for him to sit.

He stretched out on the bed next to Viola, wrapping an arm around her shoulder.

"My God, a son." He sniffled. "We have a son."

"We do."

"I never thought I would have a child." His voice was hoarse. "I never thought I would have a wife, for that matter. But here you both are, so perfect. I would have it no other way."

His body shook as emotion overtook him. He kissed her cheek, warming her wet skin. She turned and gave him a smile, then pecked his lips, tasting the salt of his tears. She'd never wanted to kiss a man before, but this seemed so natural, so right, so perfect for that moment. Two people who had become parents in the most unconventional way.

He drew back, his face crinkled in grateful disbelief.

"It's over, Percy. We have a son."

"And a miracle." He pressed his forehead against hers. "*O brave new world, that has such people in it.*"

She chuckled at his Shakespeare.

Penelope touched her shoulder. She looked up to meet her sympathetic gaze. Bertram sat on the other side, wrapping his arms around Percival.

One big happy family.

"My lords and ladies," Helena said, "shall I call the nursery maid to fetch Georgiana to meet her new brother?"

"Oh, please do, Helena," said Viola. "And your little ones as well. I'm sure Robert and Josephine would like to meet their new cousin." Such a splendid idea to have loving family surrounding her son.

Helena's exit was followed by a knock on the door.

Percival extracted himself from the pile on the bed. "Yes?"

"My lord?" Sturgis the butler called from the corridor. "The Earl of Rochdale has arrived, apologizing for his tardiness. What shall I tell him?"

Papa. Viola's heart skipped a beat. She had asked him to tea and now...*this* instead. "Please send him in."

Through correspondence, Papa had admitted his reticence with having a grandchild. Due to lack of funds, he had to be frugal. That his grandchild would be a duke's heir weighed upon him, and he shouldered the burden of shame. Viola had reassured him that he did not need to shower his grandchild with gifts he could not afford. "A boy does not need silver spoons and gilded teacups from his grandfather," she had told him over tea one day. "But he will want you to show him how to float a toy sailboat on a pond or identify birds by their songs."

And when Papa walked through the door, excited and overjoyed, that was all the gift she needed.

He kissed her cheek. "Viola, darling, I am so pleased."

The force of emotion underlying his words reminded her that he understood what she had gone through, understood what effort had been involved in bringing the boy into the world, even if he did not quite know the precise nature of that effort.

With a sweeping gaze she took in Penelope, Bertram, Percival, and their son. "Welcome to our family, Papa."

Amesbury House, Mayfair, London

DESPITE VIOLA DELIVERING the long hoped-for son, Percival was not looking forward to his meeting with Father. Once word had been delivered to his parents about the birth of Benedict, Father had insisted he congratulate Viola and Percival in person and meet the child.

Which was really subterfuge to see that the child actually existed.

The meeting a few days ago had gone more smoothly than Percival had expected. Father had even been present while Benedict was washed.

Which was subterfuge to see that the child was a boy.

After the overt inspections and rote felicitations, Father had withdrawn to his London abode.

A few days later, Nicholas had sent Percival a brief missive that the duke was requesting he meet with the duke's doctor to give a report of Lady Norrington's experience.

Percival had fumed at that. It was as if Father somehow did not accept the reality that Viola had indeed been pregnant and had indeed delivered a son.

And now here he was, sitting in a not-too-comfortable armchair in the office of the Amesbury London house waiting for his father.

At least he wasn't forced to wait outside the office.

Percival eyed a shelf with tambour doors tucked away in the corner. The slatted sliding hatchway hid Father's liquor from polite company. Brandy was kept there, sometimes port, sometimes something stronger.

He rose with the intention of exploring the shelf when the door to the office clicked open.

"Norrington," Father greeted. "A pleasure to see you."

"Good day, Your Grace."

Father crossed the room and sat in the padded leather chair behind his desk. "I suppose you want to know why I called you here."

"I do."

"So," he said coolly. "You have a son."

"I do."

"Which indicates you found a way to bow to fate and enjoy your wife's favors."

Percival's cheeks burned. "Something like that."

Father eyed him. "Please tell me Benedict is your son."

Percival snorted. "I absolutely, positively assure you Benedict is my son."

Father eyed him more closely. "But you did not conceive him in a natural way."

A chill stabbed up Percival's spine. "Natural?" Had Nicholas exposed their secret to Father's appointed doctor? *No.* Nicky would never betray him—them—like that. "You saw Viola pregnant. Your doctor examined her. We did not sculpt the child out of clay."

"Ah, I mean, how shall I put this? You did not get your wife pregnant in the traditional manner."

Percival flushed. "I do not think I need to explain to my father, even if he is the Duke of Amesbury, in what manner or position I got my wife pregnant."

Father turned beet red. "No. I apologize." He cleared his throat. "After all we've been through, I had my scruples about your, er, abilities, as it were. I should only concern myself with the outcome."

"Scruples?"

"That you would have a child in the conventional way."

"As opposed to…what, exactly?"

"Garnering one from an unwed street urchin."

"Once again, may I remind you that you, Mother, and your doctor saw Viola pregnant."

Father glowered. "Or allowing your wife to have an affair."

Holy Christ. Was it true? Is that what Father did for Mother? "Tell me, Father, did *you* have a child in the conventional way?"

Anger flashed in his eyes. "What the devil is that supposed to mean?"

He should just out with it. Now. "Rochdale. I always wondered why the penniless daughter of an insignificant earl was chosen to be my bride. It was because Rochdale and Mother were lovers, weren't they?"

Father paled.

"Tell me plainly, Father. Is Viola my half-sister?"

The pallor turned a ghostly shade of gray. "Good God. Is that what you think?"

He really could use that brandy right about now. "Until I have been told otherwise, yes. I have suspected exactly that since Georgiana's christening."

"Christ, that was almost a year ago." Father heaved a breath, like a man who'd reached the top of a hill. "No. No. It's not like that. You wouldn't understand." Father eyed him, as if searching for some answer. A full minute later, Father's countenance melted in defeat.

He closed his eyes as his lungs deflated. He raised his gaze to Percival, the lines on his face suddenly etched more deeply. "Eleanor and Cedric were sweethearts. When he was viscount. Before he became earl. But Rochdale is not your father. I am."

Pain crinkled Father's forehead and limned his eyes. "Rochdale was happily married with two children when you were born."

Ah, yes. Viola and her brother were both older than Percival.

"Cedric and your mother began their affair while he and I were at Oxford. They were smitten." A smile curled Father's lips before he sobered. "They were incautious, and she became pregnant. But money and property were the reasons one married in those days. The Rochdale earldom has always been saddled with debts. And your mother's father, an earl, had expected Eleanor to marry higher than her station."

Father drew in a long inhalation before letting it out slowly. "Eleanor was whisked away to some relative on the continent. She miscarried the child not long after. She returned to England and made her debut quietly, with her scandal kept snug, but soon found herself on the shelf, as the saying goes. Later, Cedric fell in love with Viola's mother. Theirs was a true love match. But I do know that before he met Violet, Cedric pined for Eleanor."

A twinge of sadness pierced Percival's heart.

"It was only after the death of the Countess of Rochdale that Eleanor resumed a correspondence." Father offered a weak smile. "Your mother's well-being is important to me. If she is carrying on with Rochdale now, far be it from me to complain or put a stop to it."

Percival's heart sunk at the tragedy of lost love.

"I did my duty, Norrington, know that I did. But I will admit, I thought of all manner of schemes to not bed your mother and still produce a child. My conscience did me in. I could not disavow two hundred years of the Amesbury dukedom because of my qualms." Father stared blankly at his desk. "I feared that since you were like me, you would feel the same and seek to do the same."

"Hence the spies," Percival said blandly.

"I apologize. But, yes, I hired spies. I had no confidence in you at the time." Father snorted a dark chuckle. "You thwarted me on that measure."

"I did."

Father looked at him, his face suddenly not that of a duke, but a man seeking solace. "How did you do it? You are so fond of Ravensburgh. And you two continue to be together despite wives and children."

There was a touch of melancholy in his voice, perhaps wistfulness.

Was father envious?

Had Father once had a lover, a love of his life like Percival had with Bertram? Like Mother had with Rochdale? Perhaps a young man when at university? A great love of his life that he still dreamed about?

How utterly inconsolable that Father had chosen to live a lie and forsake this man.

But now that Mother was carrying on with Rochdale, could Father dream of reconnecting with this paramour from his past?

And then it dawned on him who this man was.

"Berrick."

Father closed his eyes, his lashes damp. "He wasn't earl yet. He was merely Basil Goring."

"At Harrow?"

"Yes. We were friends from the start. We became lovers during our final years."

The plural implied their relationship was deep and devoted. Suddenly his father, the powerful duke, became a mere man. "What happened?"

"What happened?" Father let out a dark chuckle. "Duty happened. I was heir to a dukedom. I could not, in good conscience, continue such conduct. At Oxford, I distanced myself from Basil. I became involved in Cedric's intrigues instead. I just told you how that story ended."

Sympathy overwhelmed Percival while confusion niggled in his gut. "You knew Mother when you were at Oxford, but that was years before you married her."

"Clever boy." Father nodded. "My father, your grandfather, did not know about my—how should I say this?—disinterest in women. I kept it well hidden until I happened to see Basil at some event years after leaving university. We renewed our affair." Father blinked as his eyes reddened. "My father discovered us and threatened to expose Basil if he and I did not end our liaison. Basil fled to France soon after. Lady Suffield was retained to arrange my marriage as swiftly as possible. Eleanor was deemed perfect as she was a fallen woman and, as such, it was assumed, would tolerate my abnormal predilections, or at least was in no position to put up a fuss. She was already in her mid-twenties."

Pity turned to empathy tinged with chagrin. "You've not seen Berrick since."

"No." A tear fell on Father's cheek, and he brushed it away. "It was Lady Suffield who went to France to console Basil. She was disgusted by my father's despicable actions."

"And she stayed there?"

"Basil remained in France while your grandfather was alive. I suspect he grew to prefer it there. As for Cora, after frequent sojourns visiting Basil, she set up residence in Nice."

An absolute tragedy for his father and his first love. "I admit, I don't know what to say. Perhaps gratitude for finally telling me the truth of our family."

Father lifted his head as if to say a prayer to the heavens, then lowered his gaze to Percival with a wan smile. "And now there is an heir to continue that family."

Defiance seized Percival. "Be assured, Benedict is mine. And I am fond of my wife. Viola and I are friends. I also love Bertram and will do so until the end of my days. The two of us, along with our wives, plan to raise Benedict and Georgiana and Penny's next child in a household of love, respect, and understanding. If our children become like us, we will protect and guide them. It's what families do."

Father looked askance, his lips pursed, his brow deeply furrowed. "I am glad you have found a way to live the life you want to live. I hope this will be the normality in our modern age."

Percival exhaled. "I hope so too, Father."

Father brightened. "Would you like a whiskey, Percival?"

Finally. "I would love one, Father."

CHAPTER TWENTY-SIX

Wood Hall, Hertfordshire, July 1882

The Duke of Amesbury had invited Bertram and Percival to a pre-christening symposium in his library, a room steeped with the scents of leather, cigars, and whiskey. As Bertram sipped his liquor, a sense of comfort settled within.

One day, of course, Wood Hall would be his and Percival's country home for their intermingled family. For now, they were happy in London with the occasional holiday elsewhere. France, Italy, Spain, or Hertfordshire—it did not matter, as long as they were together.

The Duke raised his tumbler. "To Benedict."

Percival and Bertram raised their glasses.

"May Bertram guide my son in all matters spiritual."

Bertram almost spilled the liquor in his crystal tumbler. Good thing he hadn't taken a drink as whiskey would have been sprayed across the room.

Percival winked at him. Of course he would be a proper godfather to Benedict. As Percival was a proper godfather to Georgiana.

"Boys," began the duke, "I am proud of you both. You have grown into men worthy of your fathers' esteem."

A blush dusted Percival's cheeks. He gulped his whiskey and set down his glass.

"Father." He paused. "Papa, I've invited someone to Benedict's christening. A few people, actually."

The duke raised a brow. "Oh?" He set down his glass.

"Lady Suffield."

"Cora?" The duke said in happy surprise.

"She was most supportive of us in evading your spies in Nice."

Bertram chuckled. "She is also an admirable and engaging woman."

"Yes, she is," Percival agreed. "There's someone else." He went to the door and rapped once.

The door to the library opened, and in walked the Earl of Berrick.

Silence weighed heavily as the duke and earl stared at each other.

"Basil." Amesbury paled. "My God." He exhaled with a labored huff. "It's been almost thirty years."

Berrick, exquisitely dressed and looking every inch the debonair man he was, smiled. "I suppose it has been, Neville. Or shall I say, 'Your Grace'?"

"You of all people have leave to call me whatever the hell you like."

With a wide grin, the earl held out his arms in invitation.

The years slipped from the duke's countenance, the lines of his face softening, his eyes regaining a sparkle of youth. He fell into an embrace with his former lover, his body shaking as the sorrowful regret of a lost life descended.

Both Bertram and Percival had to dab their eyes.

After a beat too long, the duke pulled back, patting Berrick's shoulder as if reluctant to end their embrace. "Thank you for coming."

"I would not miss this occasion, Neville. A grandson. How joyous."

"Yes." The duke's gaze darted to the handsome man who entered the library with trepidation.

Bertram smiled. Of course they'd had to invite Berrick's beloved François.

Berrick extended his arm to the younger man. "Neville, I would like to make an introduction." François grasped Berrick's hand. "This is François Bisset, my life companion."

The duke gaped in astonishment, then smiled and nodded. "Life companion. My goodness, that is a fine turn of phrase."

"I finally discovered happiness," said Berrick. "I daresay it took a long time. One never forgets one's first love."

The duke thinned his lips and squeezed his eyes shut for a moment, his lashes damp.

"Did you ever find contentment Neville?"

"No." Amesbury snorted. "I became a duke as was my duty."

"I hope you will allow young Percival his happiness."

"It appears he has found a way to be happy and perform his obligations."

Berrick grinned. "The younger generation always astounds, does it not?"

Amesbury enlivened at that. "Where are you staying? You must stay with us at Wood Hall."

"The dowager Viscountess Ravensburgh is our hostess at her cottage."

The duke seemed disappointed. "We must keep in touch after the christening."

"Yes, we must. And you must visit us in Nice. Life is different in France. More tolerant of"—Berrick paused thoughtfully—"an unconventional way of life."

"I hear the weather in Nice is quite pleasant in the winter."

"Yes." Berrick beamed brightly. "You have an open invitation." He bowed. "We will see you at the church."

Berrick and François offered well wishes and shook Percival's hand before exiting the library.

"I fear I must also take my leave, Father," said Percival. "The bishop wants to talk to Viola and me as well as the godparents before the christening." He turned to Bertram. "Bertie? Shall we?"

"Yes." He finished his whiskey.

Amesbury reached for Bertram's glass. "If I may have a word?"

Bertram nodded. "I'll see you in a moment, Percy," he called.

The duke cleared his throat as he placed the tumbler on his desk. "I know you and Percival are also life companions." He glanced at Bertram's right hand.

Bertram twisted the gold ring on his little finger, the mate of the band Percival wore, the two rings symbolizing their commitment to each other. "We are."

"I am glad Percival is happy. He has chosen a fine partner in life."

"There are four of us in the partnership, Your Grace."

The duke's eyebrows quirked upwards. "Oh, yes, I suppose there are. Then you are doubly lucky."

"But Percival and I do have a very special bond."

"One that you will share to the end of your days." Amesbury's smile revealed the father behind the duke. "I admire you and my son for being so daring with your love and your lives. I envy you and hope for a better future for men like us."

Bertram took Amesbury's hand between his own. "We will do what we can, Your Grace, to make a better future. I hope, one day, you will take that holiday to Nice and reconcile with your past."

The duke stood still and stared as Bertram left to join his life companion.

* * * * *

St. Albans Cathedral, Hertfordshire

PERCIVAL GAZED DOWN at Benedict cradled in his arms, the hushed restlessness of the occupants of the cathedral echoing around him.

The Saxon founders of the church dedicated to a Roman martyr would most likely not believe the story of the child they were christening today.

Or maybe they would. Viola was still a virgin, which made Benedict the result of a virgin birth. The stuff of mythology and belief.

Percival tugged back the grin threatening to break out from his distasteful joke. He was supposed to convey the very serious demeanor of an upstanding Christian father promising to raise his child in the traditions of the Church of England.

"Percival," Viola hissed at his side on the pew. "The gospel has been read."

Which meant they had to proceed to the baptismal font.

The congregation quieted as he and Viola stood. Bertram and Penelope followed as they glided up the aisle. They met the bishop at the font, his intricately embroidered vestments as ancient as the dukedom of Amesbury. He bowed his head and cleared his throat.

"Dearly beloved—"

Beloved indeed. That's what Benedict was, what Viola was. Even Penelope. And especially Bertram.

Bertram was definitely his most dearly beloved, as Percival was his. Their love-making the night before had been truly transporting, an affirmation that they would be together forever. Percival did not try to contain his smile. He was expected to be jubilant. No one would know why he was really smiling.

A gentle nudge at his waist brought him back to the present, back to the Saxon and Gothic edifice. The bishop was speaking. "…do you acknowledge the obligation…"

"We do," he and Viola responded in unison.

The bishop called for the godparents. Bertram and Penelope stepped forward. Percival passed his son to Bertram, their hands briefly touching, sparking a tingle of excitement. He looked into the depths of Bertram's brown eyes, beyond the lashes damp with restrained tears. Emotion welled within him as well.

Because Benedict was *their* son.

The speech was repeated, and Bertram and Penelope also responded with "we do".

"Name this child," said the bishop.

Percival and Bertram had together decided upon a name that would honor the past and the future.

"Benedict Basil Wood."

A fleeting gasp, then a murmur echoed through the cathedral. Percival hoped Father recognized the honor paid to his first and only love.

With the four of them before the font and the bishop in the middle, it was as if another type of ceremony were taking place this Sunday morning. Their family and friends were witness to not merely a ritual assigning Bertram and Penelope the responsibility to raise the child on the path of Christian virtue, but a revolutionary acknowledgment that the four of them were promising to raise Benedict as a family.

And their family would grow. Penelope and Bertram's enthusiasm for her impending birth was affecting Viola. She had intimated she would consider having a second child, but only by modern methods. They could do it themselves without Nicholas.

Percival scanned the pews crowded with family and friends and people he did not even know. Father and Mother were in the front, as was the Earl of Rochdale. Even Viola's brother had deigned to attend. Bertram's mother sat with her good friend Margaretta and Penelope's former guardian Lady Gertrude. Nicholas and Helena sat just beyond, their two children between them. Helena's family was there. Mr. and Mrs. Phillips, the Earl and Countess of Petersham, the Marquess and Marchioness of Richmond sat together with their friends. On the other side of the aisle sat a beaming Berrick flanked by François and Lady Suffield. Armand and the Atherley family butler Mason sat solemnly in the back pew. The two servants had been stalwart supports during Percival's formative years.

Most everyone knew about the special relationship Percival shared with Bertram, and a few knew about Viola and Penelope. And there they all were, supporting them, filling the momentous ceremony with joy.

Life's adventures had given Percival a family he never thought he wanted, and affirmed the devotion of the family he already had.

The Harwell Heirs

Victorian aristocracy has very strict rules concerning marital connections and familial obligations. But the Harwell heirs—Helena, Sophia, and Arthur—discover love doesn't always follow the rules. Scandalous affairs force these scions of society to choose between duty and desire, deference and destiny.

Book 1: *The Pleasure Device*
Helena and Nicholas's story

Book 2: *Disobedience By Design*
Sophia and Joseph's – and Arthur and Joseph's – story

Book 3: *Where Destiny Plays*
Arthur and Lavinia's story

Book 4: *A Delicate Seduction*
Percival and Bertram's story

Book 5: *Discovering Her Delight*
William and Beatrice's story

Book 6: *Their Noble Deceit*
Percival, Bertram, Penelope, and Viola's story

More historical romance by Regina

Victorian
The Westerman Affair (*Art & Discipline* Book 1)
The Invitation (*Art & Discipline* Book 1.5)
Disputed Boundaries (*Stories from the San Juan Islands*)

American Revolution
The General's Wife: An American Revolutionary Tale
Winter Interlude: An American Revolutionary Novelette

About the Author

Regina Kammer is a librarian, an art historian, and a multi-published writer of provocative historical romance and contemporary romance with a touch of history. Her short stories and novels make history sexier, whether the era is Roman, Byzantine, Viking, American Revolution, or Victorian. She's even sexed up contemporary settings, Steampunk, and Greco-Roman mythology. She has been published by Cleis Press, Go Deeper Press, Ellora's Cave, House of Erotica, Story Ink, Loose Id, The Naughty Literati, and her own imprint, Viridium Press. She began writing historical fiction with romantic elements during National Novel Writing Month 2006, switching to erotica when all her characters suddenly demanded to have sex.

Keep up with Regina
Check out her website: https://reginakammer.com/
Never miss a new release! Subscribe to *Kammerotica News*:
   https://reginakammer.com/newsletter/

9 781953 496058